D1146179

ONE OF
OUR
MINISTERS
IS
MISSING

By Alan Johnson and available from Headline

The Late Train to Gipsy Hill

One of Our Ministers is Missing

ALAN JOHNSON

ONE OF OUR MINISTERS IS MISSING

WILDFIRE

Copyright © 2022 Alan Johnson

The right of Alan Johnson to be identified as the Author of
the Work has been asserted by him in accordance with the
Copyright, Designs and Patents Act 1988.

First published in 2022 by
WILDFIRE
an imprint of HEADLINE PUBLISHING GROUP

1

Apart from any use permitted under UK copyright law, this publication may
only be reproduced, stored, or transmitted, in any form, or by any means,
with prior permission in writing of the publishers or, in the case of
reprographic production, in accordance with the terms of licences
issued by the Copyright Licensing Agency.

All characters in this publication are fictitious and any resemblance
to real persons, living or dead, is purely coincidental.

Cataloguing in Publication Data is available from the British Library

Hardback ISBN 978 1 4722 8621 5
Trade paperback ISBN 978 1 4722 8622 2

Typeset in Sabon LT Pro by EM&EN
Printed and bound in Great Britain by Clays Ltd, Elcograf S.p.A.

Headline's policy is to use papers that are natural, renewable and recyclable
products and made from wood grown in well-managed forests and other
controlled sources. The logging and manufacturing processes are expected
to conform to the environmental regulations of the country of origin.

HEADLINE PUBLISHING GROUP
An Hachette UK Company
Carmelite House
50 Victoria Embankment
London EC4Y 0DZ

www.headline.co.uk
www.hachette.co.uk

For Carolyn,

whose idea this was.

1

A COUPLE OF JOBS A YEAR

Brady walked with the swagger of a man who considered himself invincible. Over six feet tall, with strong features and a full head of dark hair flecked with grey, his weight was the same in middle age as it had been when he was twenty. On this lovely spring day, the first good weather of the year, he cut an impressive figure sauntering along Stoke Newington High Street towards Stamford Hill, on his way to confirm a business transaction – one of only two he'd need to make in 2017.

At a hundred grand a time, Brady could live comfortably on a couple of jobs a year. It helped that his earnings were untaxed, and that he operated at the expensive end of the market – because he was good, very good, at what he did. In a sector filled with novices, blowhards and psychopaths, Brady was the supreme professional.

Raised in west Belfast during the Troubles, he'd been recruited by republican paramilitaries as a sixteen-year-old. They'd trained him well, soon discovering that Brady had all the qualities required of an expert sniper: discipline, concentration, sound judgement and an inexhaustible reserve of patience.

He and his wife had been living in this opulent part of north London for fifteen years. Cathleen had no idea how her husband earned his money. She thought he was an international trader in gilts and bonds, who worked from home except when he had to attend meetings or conferences – a couple of times a year.

Discipline, concentration, sound judgement and an inexhaustible reserve of patience; characteristics essential to the success of a contract killer.

The swagger was a mannerism that Brady had never quite managed to eliminate. While his profession demanded that he attract as little attention as possible, his height made that difficult. The way he walked was a product of his physique, enhanced by the need to look menacing in the tough district in which he'd been raised. He'd acquired a gum-chewing habit in his youth, finding that it aided concentration, but had never taken to smoking or drinking. Chewing was his only vice – apart from killing.

His destination on this fine spring morning was Clissold Park. He always finalised business deals there, in the open air, immune to any covert listening devices. His services were advertised on the dark web, along with those of hundreds of self-styled hitmen, enforcers and eliminators. He knew that all but a handful of the ads were put up by fantasists. Of that handful, most were likely to have been posted by criminal gangs with dubious credentials – Serbian knuckleheads, as he thought of them – or by the police posing as hitmen in entrapment operations.

In almost twenty years, most of that time in London, Brady had never come close to getting caught. In the early days, his engagements would come by word-of-mouth, through former colleagues in Northern Ireland decommissioned from the paramilitary struggle by the peace process. As Brady's skills were honed and his reputation grew in Northern Ireland, he realised he couldn't risk staying in the vicinity of his former activities. He needed a bigger stage. That was when he'd moved from Belfast to London. The only thing that came with him was the false identity his former comrades had provided; the birth certificate of an infant who'd died in a car crash in Enniskillen forty years ago. Once in London, he'd met Cathleen, and used his new identity to get married, buy a house and acquire a passport. Having an alter ego didn't completely separate Brady's peaceful domestic existence from his far from peaceful professional life, but it helped.

He knew that his crimes evaded detection because of the absence of motive, and because he was careful. As for the morality of it (and Brady considered himself to be a moral person), he had his rules. He only killed adults, never children, would have nothing to do with torture, and avoided killing priests and peace activists. Any job that involved the Middle East was refused (Mossad was too ruthless; Palestinian terrorists too fanatical), and while he occasionally contracted with organised crime, he insisted on remaining completely independent. Brady was an elite maestro, not a mob hitman.

As for method, he preferred the bullet to the blade, marksmanship being his particular area of expertise. But he wasn't averse to other means of disposal – explosives, strangulation, falls from a great height. Once, he'd even slipped a lethal poison into a hospital meal to fulfil a contract against a man who'd survived a near-fatal shooting – near-fatal was not good enough for Brady. He'd also used poison when a contractor stipulated that no violence was to be used against the victim – a curious consideration, but it was not for him to question why. On that occasion, he'd hijacked a pizza outlet's scooter to deliver a Hawaiian with extra pineapple and added strychnine.

His most recent job had been late last year – on Christmas Day, in fact. He'd been contracted to kill a married couple, Mr and Mrs Furnell, who ran a boarding house in Lincoln. Brady had no idea why he'd been paid to eliminate the Furnells. His customers had no requirement to provide a motive. Neither was it necessary for him to dislike the people he was about to kill. He'd grown fond of Mrs Furnell in particular, having lived beneath her roof for a week planning the operation.

She was a small, plump woman in her forties who laughed easily and seemed to take a maternal interest in the welfare of her guests. Brady had told her he was a stonemason hired to advise on the restoration of the stone carvings in the roof of Lincoln Cathedral, and that for some unspecified reason, this necessitated him being in the city over Christmas.

On Christmas morning, he was the only guest, and Mrs Furnell had put a little wrapped present on the dining table when he came in for breakfast.

He never did unwrap that gift. He killed the husband first, the Glock 19 pistol with silencer attached placed against Mr Furnell's right temple as the man tucked into his sausages and bacon, having wished Brady a Happy Christmas. When Mrs Furnell bustled in with Brady's poached egg on toast, she let out a little cry of what seemed more like exasperation than horror as she saw her husband's body slumped sideways off the chair. She hardly noticed Brady until he placed the gun nozzle against her forehead.

Knowing that the murders were unlikely to be discovered for a couple of days, he departed at a leisurely pace, with a double fee secured as a Christmas bonus.

As he walked past the cafés and patisseries, the trendy trinket shops, hipster pubs and avant-garde clothing stores of Stoke Newington, Brady felt the familiar tingle of excitement; the thrill he always felt at the prospect of a new assignment.

He carried a satellite phone in a bag loosely draped across his shoulder. An encrypted algorithm allowed him to talk to clients with no fear of eavesdropping and, because the phone bypassed local telecoms systems, no risk of wiretapping. There was a spot in Clissold Park where reception was consistently good. He already had one job in hand this year for which he would receive a substantial amount, his usual six-figure charge doubled to reflect the status of his prey. The one he was on his way to discuss now would be even more lucrative, and the two together would allow him to retire undefeated with enough money to live on for the rest of his life. All he needed now was the victim's name. Most of the necessary information had already been conveyed over the dark web. He knew, for instance, where this job was to be carried out. Brady's parameters were international, although most of his work took place in the UK. There would be further details to be sorted out, but this most crucial piece of information, the name, needed to be delivered verbally, via the satellite phone. The call was timed for twelve noon.

As he entered the park, Brady saw a crowd of young men playing football – big lads in their street clothes, representatives of the ethnic diversity of the neighbourhood. There didn't seem to be any touchline, with the pitch extending to cover whatever area the ball was kicked into. If there were proxy goalposts, Brady couldn't see them. As he walked to the spot near the tennis courts where satellite connection worked best, the ball, kicked with venomous ferocity, thudded against the back of his head. Brady felt a tide of anger rise within him. The blow was painful and, he suspected, deliberate. Having ricocheted between his head and a park bench, the football landed at Brady's feet. He picked it up and held it defiantly as a muscular young man with razor lines cut through his hair in several directions confronted him. The young man wore a red T-shirt, was almost as tall as Brady and seemed, from the way his fellow footballers fanned out behind him, to be the leader. The gang stared at the man who'd picked up their ball as if he'd defiled some sacred object.

'Give me the ball, man,' Razor Parting said softly, his accent confirming Brady's initial assessment that he was part of the Turkish community prominent in this area of London.

'Aren't you going to say sorry?' Brady asked, chewing hard on his gum and looking directly into the young man's eyes.

'Just give me the ball.' The order was repeated.

The park seemed stilled by the sudden inactivity of this twenty-strong crowd gathered around Brady. A couple of dog walkers ambled along in the distance; a few mothers were taking advantage of the spring weather to push their toddlers on swings by the park entrance. But essentially, it was just Brady and this bunch of teenagers. The situation reminded him of how he'd felt as a twelve-year-old, straying into a loyalist neighbourhood of Belfast and finding himself confronted by boys of a similar age but a different religion. On that occasion, two women on their way to the shops had intervened. Nobody was going to intervene now.

Still smarting from the smack of the football against his skull, Brady's anger was exacerbated by the cocksure attitude of his antagonist, who was possibly one of the Stokey Mob or the Hoxton Boys, gangs who were notorious in the area but were usually a danger only to others in their age group. Brady was old enough to be their father, but they now posed a real and present danger to him. However, he was disinclined to hand over the ball without some sign of contrition from those responsible for the blow to his head – and his dignity.

As usual, he carried no weapons. Brady always left the tools of his trade securely hidden from the world and (literally) his wife. If he'd had his long-bladed dagger, he'd have been tempted to use it to destroy the ball, right there in front of this arrogant punk, and then fling the tattered remains back in his face. If he'd had his Barrett M82 rifle with him, just the sight of it would have sent this rabble running. If he'd produced his Glock 19 and fired in the air, it would have loosened their bowels. But he had nothing, just his fists, which he'd never been that good with, and his demeanour, with which he tried to convey how dangerous he could be.

The stand-off was about to enter its second minute when one of the lads behind Razor Parting stepped forward. 'Sorry we hit you, dude, that was my bad – kickin' wild as usual. Can we have our ball back, please?'

The tension snapped. Brady threw the ball to this peacemaker while continuing to lock eyes with Razor Parting, who stared back for several seconds before turning to join his friends, who were running off to continue their match.

Brady walked on, relieved to have avoided a more serious confrontation, but concerned about how close he'd come to one. Everything he'd achieved depended on anonymity, and anonymity depended on passivity. He'd thought he was programmed to avoid the kind of rush of anger he'd just experienced. The images of revenge disturbed him. Nothing must jeopardise the inconsequential life he led. Looking across at the chaotic game of football that had resumed, the players moving en masse towards the other side of the park, he could see the bright red T-shirt of Razor Parting. It may have been his imagination, but he had the distinct impression that the guy's air of resentful malevolence was being directed towards him.

A few moments later, Brady reached the spot where reception was optimal, just inside the eastern perimeter of the park. At twelve noon precisely, his satellite phone rang. The client gave a name and waited for Brady to confirm. The phone had a voice distortion device fitted so that his real voice was never heard, although in truth he never said much anyway. On this occasion, Brady paused, realising how significant this killing would be. After a momentary hesitation, all he said was 'Yes,' before finishing the call.

2

LORD AND LADY BELLINGHAM

The best time to visit Crete, according to most of those who know the island well, is in May, before the intense heat of summer tightens its grip. The temperate spring air carries a scent of herbaceous wildflowers – peonies, crocus and chamomile. Although sea temperature is a comfortable twenty-one degrees Centigrade, the beaches, rarely full even at the height of the season, are almost empty.

The Bellinghams certainly preferred Crete in spring rather than summer. They'd purchased a holiday home on the island in 2012, when villas were going cheap in the wake of the Greek financial crash, and had plumped for one on the south coast, where the hot, North African winds blow in across the Libyan Sea.

Edward Bellingham had just been ennobled when they'd made the purchase. Now, Lord Bellingham of South Ormsby (the place in Lincolnshire where he'd been born into wealth and privilege) was a junior minister at the Foreign and Commonwealth Office and felt an increasing need for this Cretan sanctuary away from the pressures of Whitehall. In his early fifties, he was one of the youngest members of the House of Lords, where the average age was seventy-four. His fortune had been made in property development, but his passion had always been for politics. Indeed, Bellingham's ambition had been to achieve ministerial office as a Conservative Member of Parliament, but he'd become so immersed in business that the opportunities for constituency nominations had passed him by. However, he had served as a Wandsworth councillor and this, together with his charitable donations, had earned him a peerage, accepted as a sort of political consolation prize. At least it provided the status he'd always craved without the botheration of having to represent a constituency.

Sitting on the terrace of his villa in the hills above Agia Galini, he could feel the stresses and tensions of London drain from his system. His wife, Miranda, and the twins lived out here from April to September every year, and Bellingham had been able to join them for this spring break a couple of days ago. If he'd been an MP, taking a break like this would have been unthinkable. The Prime Minister had called a snap election for 8 June, and Bellingham would have been immersed in the campaign to keep his seat. As a lord, with no constituency to retain, the Foreign Secretary had allowed him to slip away for a week, as long as he kept in close touch with the department, where his ministerial duties included responsibility for Britain's overseas territories.

His workload was hardly overwhelming. While this wasn't the political pinnacle Edward Bellingham had set out to reach, it was a less demanding and very comfortable alternative. As he mused on this and other aspects of his fortunate existence, he was joined on the terrace by his wife, who was carrying two stubby glasses of gin and tonic, the ice cubes clunking like dice in a cup.

'Here you are, darling,' she said sweetly. 'Something to remind you of home.'

'I don't wish to be reminded of home, thanks very much.'

'If you're not careful, I'll replace it with a glass of warm retsina.'

Lady Miranda Bellingham wore a loose blouse over a swimming costume. Ten years younger than her husband, she had a good figure and an abundance of dark auburn hair swept back into a ponytail, which swayed from side to side in rhythm with her hips as she stepped gracefully across the wide terrace to where her husband was sitting. The contrast between them was stark, and wasn't confined to age. Against her cool sophistication, he seemed drab and awkward. Of average height and with thick grey hair, his belly extended across the waistband of the unflattering khaki shorts he wore below an unbuttoned white shirt. His most distinctive feature was the thin moustache, of which he was inordinately proud, and which he insisted on maintaining despite his wife's objections.

They'd met in circumstances that could hardly have been less conducive to a sustained relationship. For a start, the as-yet un-ennobled Edward Bellingham was already married. As for Miranda, she was a lawyer on the legal team that was trying to stop his company, Bellingham Developments, from demolishing several attractive old buildings in Norwich in order to construct a block of expensive apartments. Edward, seeing her across the courtroom, had been immediately smitten by her pellucid beauty. A couple of months after winning the court case, he'd been at a party organised by Bellingham Development's legal representatives, and was delighted to see Miranda there. One of the partners at Chesterton, Kane and Palfrey, his friend Quentin Kane, wanted to poach her for the practice, hence the party invitation. Edward, while transfixed, felt awkward in Miranda's presence, but persevered in trying to tempt her out for dinner. By the end of the evening, both Bellingham and Kane had achieved their objectives. Chesterton, Kane and Palfrey had a new solicitor, and Edward Bellingham had a date.

Bellingham's divorce had been messy and expensive, but within two years Miranda had become the second Mrs Bellingham. A year later, the twins were born, and now, four years after that, Lord and Lady Bellingham sat on the terrace of their Cretan home contemplating the evening ahead.

It was five o'clock and the sun cast its angled light across the cypress grove that stretched for half a mile behind the villa.

'Where are the kids?' Bellingham asked.

'Nanny is winding them down towards bedtime,' his wife said, nonchalantly swirling her glass to redistribute the melting ice.

Bellingham's first marriage had been childless, and in truth he would have been perfectly happy for things to remain that way in his second. But Miranda had wanted children – two, to be precise, and both, rather conveniently, had arrived together. She'd given birth to twins at the age of thirty-nine. 'Nanny' had been recruited three years ago, when Tyrone and Tess were a year old. Sharron Fuller, an energetic eighteen-year-old Geordie with a BTEC in childcare, wasn't paid much, but had full board with the Bellinghams, and considered the five months spent in Crete every year as a considerable perk of the job. Miranda was determined to ensure that she and the twins spent as much time together on the island as possible before the restrictions of formal education descended.

'Shall we go to Dimitri's tonight?' Miranda asked.

'Of course. He'll have only just reopened for the season, so it may be best to give him a call.'

'Oh, I'm sure there'll be a table for Lord and Lady Bellingham,' Miranda said, tucking her legs up beneath her on the wicker chair. 'We can hear all the local gossip and you can get Dimitri's suggestions for your next hike.'

Edward loved walking on the island and was always keen to find new routes. He favoured ones that weren't in the guidebooks or online: the ones only locals knew about. It was his favourite form of exercise. Indeed, it was practically the only one, save for an occasional slow jog round Putney Heath, near where they lived in London.

He longed to find a more adventurous challenge on Crete, to go higher into the mountains in pursuit of peace and solitude, although he fully understood the perils of simply wandering off unprepared into the unknown. There were ditches and ravines even on the shorter walks (which were all he could manage). His great ambition was to get up into the Lefka Ori – the White Mountains – and Dimitri, a walker himself, had promised to map out a route that would be as safe as possible and well within Bellingham's limited range.

'I don't think I can risk a hike on this visit,' Edward said. 'Being incommunicado while my ministerial colleagues are engaged in the mucky business of democracy wouldn't be good form. But Dimitri can give me a route for when we're back in August.'

By eight-thirty, the Bellinghams had showered, dressed (casually), kissed the twins goodnight and were in Miranda's Mercedes convertible, ready to drive away. 'Nanny' came outside to wave them off.

'Be back around eleven-thirty,' Miranda shouted as she reversed the car noisily down the drive.

'Farewell, Nanny,' Edward called as they drove away.

Sharron waved cheerfully before reaching for her phone to send a text. Being called 'Nanny' was just one of the many things she disliked about the Bellinghams. Now, for a few hours, the villa would belong to her – and her lover, who she knew would soon be tapping gently on the kitchen window, even as the Bellinghams' car disappeared down the road to Agia Galini.

3

A BENCH IN HYDE PARK

When Brady had left Belfast, he didn't leave much behind. Both his parents were dead. His father had been killed on the Shankill Road by a bullet that could have been fired by a British soldier or by a member of the Ulster Volunteer Force (UVF), the notorious loyalist paramilitary group. As the eldest child, Brady remembered that, along with the sorrow, there came a sense of something being expected of him. Not yet thirteen years of age, he'd assumed a responsibility that nobody articulated but everyone – neighbours, uncles, aunts, cousins, the boys at his school – silently conveyed.

His mother had collapsed under the weight of her grief. Brady could still hear her awful cry of anguish after she'd gone to answer the knock at the door. It was said by relatives that the cancer that killed her two years later began then, on her doorstep, as two RUC officers, part of a heavily armed convoy, broke the terrible news. It was claimed by the aunts and uncles and cousins that the Shankill bullet had killed both his parents, one immediately, the other eventually. The military denied any involvement and the UVF never claimed responsibility. The only thing anyone knew for sure was that Brady's father was the victim of an unknown sniper.

His four younger siblings were all girls. Nothing was expected of them. The obligation to avenge fell on his shoulders alone. His sisters married and moved away, one by one – to the South, mainly, with one going to Montreal having wed a Canadian.

In a sense, his own life had ended with the death of his father. It was as if a different person had emerged when the ice entered his soul, a man insensitive to the suffering of others, immune to feelings of guilt and regret. Just as some boys enter their teens wanting to be footballers or rock stars or airline pilots, Brady knew he only had one purpose in life: to avenge his father's death. By the time he'd arrived in north London after ten years of avenging, he had become a different person. He was Brady, who continued to seek revenge with each lucrative agreement made to end the life of someone who had no connection whatsoever to the death of his father.

The easiest jobs were those where he'd simply be given the victim's name and allowed to complete the task in his own way and at a time of his choosing. On this occasion, though, there were stipulations and he needed to meet the person the deal had been made with – the one who Brady always thought of as the actual murderer. In his distorted logic, he was merely a weapon, an unthinking, inanimate object. Expecting him to feel guilt at the death of a victim was like expecting the iceberg to feel bad about the sinking of the *Titanic*.

Sometimes, meetings like this would be arranged at Brady's own insistence, so he could be doubly sure he wasn't being led into a trap devised by a rival or even the police; although with the boys in blue, the methods of entrapment were so obvious that only the most inexperienced amateur would be fooled. This job was too elaborate and well-thought-out to be a hoax.

When contact was necessary, Brady always dictated the venue, usually a specific park bench in a remote corner of Hyde Park, which he could keep under observation from the high terrace of a hotel on Kensington Gore. On this day in early June, he was finalising the details for one of his two jobs this year. Combined with the one he'd accepted in Clissold Park last month, Brady hoped to be able to retire on the proceeds. The rendezvous had been arranged for 8am. Brady was sipping a latte, for which he'd paid an exorbitant amount simply to be able to watch the park bench from the terrace as he waited for the right person to come along, sit down and send the agreed signal, which was removing a jacket to reveal a pink shirt or blouse. Brady would then saunter across to the park. The isolated location of this particular park bench wasn't its only advantage. It was one of very few 'doubles': two three-seater benches positioned back to back. The person he was meeting had been instructed to sit on the side facing into the park so that Brady could occupy the one facing out towards the road. If by chance there was someone already in situ, Brady would wait for them to move on. He'd never had to wait long, although he had once needed to threaten a vagrant who looked as if he was settling in for an extended occupation. The other main advantage of the location was the lack of any cover from which an ambush could be organised.

Brady watched and waited. A young woman jogger stopped to use the bench for a few minutes of stretching exercises; an elderly man wearing an overcoat against the early summer chill sat down, but moved on again without removing his coat. At 8am precisely, the person Brady was waiting for came along – a heavily set man in his sixties wearing a dark zipped up jacket over a pink shirt. Ten minutes later, a back-to-back conversation took place, after which Brady knew precisely what he had to do to fulfil the job – and when he had to do it.

4

DINNER AT DIMITRI'S

Dimitri's, the most acclaimed restaurant in the Rethymno region, looks down on Agia Galini from high above the harbour. Seen from the sea, it sits perched on the upper elevation of the shops and apartments that rise behind the beach, layer by layer, like an elaborate wedding cake. On this Monday evening, newly opened after the winter break, it was three-quarters full. As usual, Dimitri Limnios himself was there, moving amongst the diners, dispensing bonhomie to accompany the delicious food and wine. Tonight's menu included lamb with chicory, rabbit stew, small fried pumpkin pies and an array of freshly caught fish – grouper with purslane, grilled red mullet and dorado in white wine. Dimitri's two helpers were left to do most of the fetching and carrying while their boss chatted even more animatedly than usual to his admiring clientele. He was a slim man in his late forties with smiling eyes set in a large, open face. A thatch of carefully combed grey hair was gelled into place, arranged to artfully conceal the bald patch on his crown. For 'ladies who lunched', Dimitri was considered to be a better catch than his fish. None of these lady admirers were sure if he'd been caught already. During the six-month off-season, he'd disappear, presumably to the mainland, but nobody knew where – or with whom. He was ostentatious about his wealth (a Rolex permanently affixed to his left wrist), but discreet as to its source.

Louise Mangan and her daughter Chloe sat at a table near the door. There were two Mangan daughters, but only the youngest, who was in her final year at the University of Kent, had been able to accompany her mother on this hastily arranged ten-day break in the town where they'd been holidaying since she and her sister were tiny. Back then, her mother and father had been together, the separation coming as Chloe was preparing for GCSEs; her father's second marriage commencing as she began studying for her A levels.

Michelle, the older sister by two years, had a better relationship with their father than Chloe, but neither of them blamed their parents for the break-up. It was just something that had happened to them – as it had happened to most of their friends. At least they'd been too old to have to experience the push-me-pull-you trauma of allocated weekends or court-determined periods with one parent or the other. Their father now lived happily in Devon with his new wife.

The girls had enjoyed a happy childhood, of which Agia Galini had been a significant part, although they'd not been back for a while, and had never stayed in a hotel, as Louise and Chloe were doing now. Their family holidays had always been spent on campsites or in rented villas.

'How long have we been coming here?' Chloe asked her mother as they finished their main course.

'Oh, I don't know,' Louise replied. 'Let me think now; we first came before you two were born, when I was still a police constable and your father had just been promoted to sergeant. One of his colleagues at Croydon, where he'd been posted, recommended that we try the south of the island when your dad told him how much we'd enjoyed our honeymoon in Crete on the north coast.'

'Bet it was different back then,' Chloe observed.

'Yes, horse-drawn carts and bathing huts. I'd go down to the sea in my crinoline petticoat. I'm really not that ancient, you know.'

Chloe laughed. 'You are, but you've worn well. Forty-six seems pretty ancient to me. Now, what about your new job? You've hardly said a word about it.'

Louise had been promoted from detective super-intendent to assistant commissioner the previous year, and this was the first time the pair had been together for any length of time since.

'I'd rather not. I needed this break to get away from it.'

'Dad said you wouldn't like it.'

'Oh, did he now? Tell me precisely what he said.'

Louise had married Tom Mangan when they were both police constables, and his silent resentment when her more rapid promotions overtook his was something that had soured their relationship: that and the fact they rarely saw one another, as their lives became increasingly dominated by work.

'Nothing derogatory. He just said that you'd miss the day-to-day involvement in catching villains – that being an assistant commissioner in the Met was more about managing than policing. What was that phrase he used?' Chloe paused to search her memory. 'Oh yes, he said you were more inclined towards overworking than overseeing.'

'How clever of him,' Louise said, miffed that her ex-husband knew her so well.

'But is he right?'

'Yes, I suppose I do miss the front line.'

'The extra money must help,' Chloe observed.

'I don't have much to spend it on,' Louise responded. 'There's only so many clothes you can wear, cars you can buy, holidays you can take.'

'Excellent. You just carry on building up our inheritance,' her daughter said, pouring them both another glass of white wine. 'So, what do you actually do?' she asked.

'Well, there are four of us ACs, and we're responsible for creating a vision and setting the direction and culture of the service as part of the management board . . .'

'Boring,' Chloe interjected, a hand hovering in front of her mouth in an imitation yawn.

'You did ask,' her mother said.

'I so wish I hadn't. Let's talk about something else. What do you make of Simon?'

Louise had yet to meet her eldest daughter's new boyfriend, but he sounded like a nice, well-brought-up lad who shared Michelle's love of music and was equally unsure about what to do with the degree in English literature he'd acquired. After Michelle had graduated, she'd continued to live in her university town of Brighton, working as an agency temp while deciding what career to pursue.

'Chelle adores him,' Chloe announced.

'Right, just like she adored his predecessor before she dumped him.'

'Henry was too quiet for her. She needs someone who's extroverted to keep her entertained.'

'Someone who quotes Keats and Shelley all day? I don't think so. Hopefully she's just playing the field. Surely neither of you is even remotely thinking of a lasting relationship yet?'

'Well, I'm not, but Chelle is older, and these days if you find someone who's compatible, you can't help but worry about the consequences of not hanging on to them for fear of being left with the dregs.'

'How depressing,' said Louise. 'I thought that my generation had paved the way for girls today to be less reliant on simply marrying the right man.'

'It's not about reliance. We're genetically pro-grammed to seek out the best father for our children, regardless of whether we're ready to have children or not. Chelle can't escape her physiology.'

'And what about you?' Louise asked. 'Are you searching for a life partner?'

'No way,' Chloe answered. 'I'm polyamorous and intend to stay that way.'

'Polyamorous? Isn't that the word for a parrot who gets fruity?'

Although her daughters were close, Chloe had a very different personality to her older sister – less cautious, more spontaneous and unpredictable. She was studying modern languages, but longed to be an actress. Michelle, on the other hand, seemed to have inherited more of her mother's character, along with the chestnut-brown hair, green eyes and tall stature. Chloe was smaller, with her father's blue eyes and mousy blond hair, which she'd had cut short for this holiday.

'And what about you, mother dear? Any men in your life?'

'Lots – but they're the ones I work with.' Louise poured them both another glass of wine, sensing that her inquisitive child was preparing to pursue the subject further. They were beginning to feel the loquacious effect of the half bottle already consumed.

'I suppose you've got used to living alone and become set in your ways, as they say,' Chloe opined.

'No. I really miss you two. It was a wrench when you both left for uni. But I have no desire to be polyamorous – or even mono-amorous.'

'But don't you miss the sex?' Chloe asked, leaning forward and lowering her voice. She knew she was pushing the boundaries, but was determined to use this opportunity to raise the question that she and her sister had long wanted to ask.

Louise paused, gazing down at the pale gold liquid in her glass and giving serious consideration to the question. 'I suppose what I miss is the intimacy,' she said slowly, 'but not so much the physical contact; just the way I used to be able to talk to your father. I think one of the vital differences between most men and most women is that we ascribe much more value to conversation, although that sounds too formal a word to use. You know what I mean – the yapping, the chatter, the ability to say whatever you like to your partner, even if they're not particularly talkative – and believe me, your father wasn't. But it doesn't matter if you don't get much back, so long as they listen. That's what I miss.'

At that moment, Dimitri seemed to materialise out of nowhere. 'Ladies, how was your meal?' he asked obsequiously.

They had already polished off two courses and, determined not to have a third, asked for the bill while expressing their genuine delight with the food. Dimitri responded with complimentary glasses of raki and a plate of freshly cut melon.

'Please enjoy. I am so pleased to see you again.'

It was nine o'clock, and those conforming to Greek mealtimes were just arriving as Brits and Germans (the two nationalities most heavily represented amongst the visitors) were already thinking of their beds.

'He fancies you,' Chloe said under her breath as their host walked away.

'Don't be daft. Dimitri is being a good host.'

'I'm telling you, Mum. He's been looking over all evening, and I'm pretty sure he's not trying to make eye contact with me.'

'Perhaps he's checking to make sure we're not nicking the cutlery,' Louise said.

'You could do worse for a holiday romance.'

'I'm not looking for a holiday romance, thank you very much. If I was, I certainly wouldn't have brought you with me.'

As Dimitri came from behind the counter to bring them their bill, he stopped to welcome two new arrivals.

'Look who's just walked in,' Chloe whispered. Her mother looked up, but didn't recognise the couple who were being led to one of the better tables, one with an uninterrupted view of the sea.

'It's Lord Whatsit. You know – the government minister.'

Louise caught the eye of Miranda Bellingham, and the two women smiled in the cursory manner required by an accidental glance.

'Well, Lady Whatsit is very attractive, I must say, but I still haven't got a clue who you're referring to.'

Her daughter was consulting Google, holding her phone below the table out of sight of the other diners. 'Bellingham,' she announced, more loudly than she meant to. 'Lord Bellingham. I just looked up Foreign Office ministers. I happened to see him the other week on *Question Time*. He was very good, particularly on the Middle East.'

'How interesting. I had heard that there was a peer in the vicinity. One of the ex-pats at that yoga class I've been going to mentioned it. I'd have thought he'd be confined to barracks, what with the election and everything.'

'Perhaps he formed an escape committee. Anyway, finish your raki, and I'll make you a coffee when we get back to the hotel.'

'Such a thoughtful girl,' Louise said, as she picked up her handbag. 'A credit to her parents, I'd say.'

Sharron checked again to make sure the twins were asleep before going down to let her lover in through the big kitchen window. Hassan had calculated a way to get in and out of the Bellinghams' villa without being seen on the security cameras. It involved waiting in a spot he'd found higher up on the sloping ground, from where he could see the terrace and everyone on it without them seeing him: a perfect observation post. Then, coming down to ground level, he'd walk through the cypress trees and crouch under the canopy where the rubbish bins were kept. Once there, he'd pause until the rotating camera had clicked into a position facing away from the bins. This allowed him two minutes to get to the kitchen window, which Sharron would have already opened in preparation. Hassan would then hoist himself up and in, wriggling across the draining board like a performing seal before being helped down by his amorous accomplice.

Sharron and Hassan had met the previous year, not long after 'Nanny' had arrived with Lady Bellingham and the twins for their summer sojourn on the island. The weather was stormy, and one day, as Sharron was walking back to the villa from the little produce store a mile away, it had begun to rain heavily. Hassan had pulled up in his battered old Renault to offer a lift. He was a Libyan who claimed to have rowed across the sea to Crete to escape the fighting when Gaddafi was overthrown. He told Sharron he was lodging with three other Libyan refugees, earning his living doing odd jobs around Agia Galini. Sharron eventually persuaded her employer to take him on to do a bit of gardening now and again. Back home, he'd been a photographer, and the only things he'd brought with him when he fled were his prized possessions: a Konica vintage film camera and a small digital Nikon which he always carried in a back pocket of his jeans.

He was short (although an inch or so taller than Sharron), with thick black hair that matched the colour of his soulful eyes, and Sharron thought him the handsomest man she'd ever been out with. Restricted by her inability to leave the twins unattended, they'd quickly worked out a way to take advantage of her employers' frequent absences. The Bellinghams had no idea that Nanny was using the villa as her love nest.

After Hassan had made his dramatic entrance through the kitchen window, they crept through the house and into Sharron's bedroom, careful not to wake the twins sleeping in the room opposite. They made love frantically, removing each other's clothes as if impatiently unwrapping Christmas presents. Afterwards, the lovers lay across Sharron's single bed, blowing smoke from their cigarettes out through the open window.

'You deserve better than to be a slave to these people,' Hassan said.

Sharron had been complaining about the extra work she had to do when Lord Bellingham was in residence – washing and ironing his clothes, cleaning the room he used as an office, and changing the bedsheets daily in accordance with his fixation on clean linen.

'I wouldn't mind if they showed a little appreciation,' she said. 'But I don't think he knows how to say thank you. And as for her, Lady Bloody Muck, she's so high and mighty.'

'She is good-looking woman,' Hassan pronounced before carefully stubbing out his cigarette. 'If I was back home in Tripoli, I would offer to photograph her and sell to magazines.'

'I suppose she's quite attractive, if you like that kind of thing.'

'I like *this* kind of thing,' Hassan said, caressing a plump breast through the thin sheet that Sharron had pulled over her.

'You're not the only man to fancy her,' she said. 'I'm sure she's having it off with someone.'

'You mean she is seeing another man?' Hassan asked distractedly. 'How you know that?'

'Because of how she acts on the phone sometimes;

not just here, but in London too. The lowered voice, the way she laughs with whoever it is. Women know when something's going on. We read the signs. For all her airs and graces, I bet she's at it more than we are.'

'I do my best to compete then,' Hassan said, pulling back the sheet to plant a trail of kisses across his lover's naked midriff.

'That was a lovely meal,' Miranda said, as she drove them home from the restaurant.

'Did you think so? We're used to eating in better places than that,' her husband answered.

'You're such a snob, Edward. Of course we are, but not on a relatively poor island catering for holidaymakers in a country where the economy has been shot to pieces.'

'I prefer a restaurant with starched white tablecloths.'

'Says the starched white Lord Bellingham,' Miranda teased.

The distance home was less than three kilometres, and it wasn't long before they were on the winding drive leading up to their villa.

'Dimitri was very attentive, as usual,' Miranda observed.

'Bit of a ladies' man if you ask me.'

'Well, I didn't – but you're right, he is. You are so ungrateful, though. That man spent more time with you than with me. He practically set out the route for you to take across the White Mountains step by step.'

Her husband indicated his reluctant acknowledgement.

'Anyway, it must be hard not to be a ladies' man when you look like Dimitri,' Lady Bellingham continued. 'Are you sure you're not the tiniest bit jealous?'

Edward responded with a grimace as they pulled up in front of the villa. 'Okay, I accept that he's more likely to be mistaken for George Clooney than I am, but if there's any jealousy around, it emanates from him, and the cause is my beautiful wife,' he said, running his hand across Miranda's thigh. She pushed it away irritably, getting out of the car to climb the ten steps leading up to the front door. At that moment, unseen by the Bellinghams, the kitchen window opened and, under a sky thick with stars, Sharron whispered farewell to her sweetheart, who lingered for one last kiss before disappearing into the cypress grove.

5

BACK TO WORK

Back in London after her spring break in Crete, Louise Mangan returned to her usual routine. As an assistant commissioner, she was detached from everything she loved about policing. She felt she was more of a management consultant than a copper. Mangan's area of responsibility was 'professionalism', which seemed to attract all the boring minutiae that the other three assistant commissioners didn't fancy dealing with.

At least her hours were more predictable than when she'd been a detective. And she was back in uniform, which removed the daily dilemma of what to wear. On the other hand, she'd enjoyed the unpredictability of a varying schedule, and, as for the uniform, she'd always had an aversion to black tights.

Mangan had no capacity for self-pity, but was aware that this latest promotion had contributed to her increasing sense of emptiness. She would come home at around 6pm every evening, pour herself a vodka and lemonade, remove those damned tights, put on a dressing gown and spend the evening watching TV or listening to the female singers she loved – Sheryl Crow, Joni Mitchell, Lucinda Williams – alone, always alone.

The flat in Brixton, which had been full of merriment and feminine companionship before the girls went off to university, was now devoid of life and laughter. Both Michelle and Chloe had used it as their London base after leaving for uni, but as their lives had developed in Brighton and Canterbury respectively, those visits had become less frequent. They were the times Louise looked forward to the most.

She still worshipped at St Mary's Church in Brixton every Sunday, but it seemed as empty as her flat, having lost most of its congregation to evangelicals and the Grim Reaper. Religion remained a great source of comfort for Louise, but it couldn't provide a cure for her loneliness. Since the amicable divorce from Tom, there had been no love interest. Louise faced the unwelcome prospect of turning fifty alone in that flat. In contrast, Tom had married again – to another policewoman he'd met on a health and safety course, moving into her house in Exeter and transferring from the Met to the Devon and Cornwall Police.

How idealistic they'd once been, Louise and Tom; two young police officers convinced they could put the world – or at least their little bit of it – to rights. For Louise, joining the Met was an extension of her religious beliefs. It facilitated the moral code by which she tried to live. There was evil in the world that had to be confronted, but she knew that very few of the people who did bad things were evil in the biblical sense. She'd been convinced their souls could better be saved through the guidance of a police officer than the ministrations of a priest. At least, that was how she and Tom had felt at the start of their police careers, when they were young and in love. On holiday once, when it was still just the two of them, somebody had asked Louise what she did for a living. They'd made a pact not to say they were police officers because of the disquieting effect it seemed to have on their fellow holidaymakers. On this occasion, she'd answered by saying she was a welfare officer, and for Louise, it was the best definition of what she'd joined the service to do. For years afterwards, she and Tom would toast each other with the mantra: 'What do we do? We administer welfare.'

But if the police force had helped to bring them together, it had also played a major role in driving them apart. Louise hadn't taken much maternity leave when she had the girls. It was difficult enough to progress through the ranks as a woman without the added handicap of long periods away. At first, Tom tried to do his bit by sharing childcare responsibilities, but this waned over time. Being a detective was exciting, but it was also exhausting, particularly when there were children to care for as well. Tom's work as a station sergeant was equally debilitating. They were both so constantly tired that on the few occasions they had the chance to spend time together, all they wanted to do was sleep.

Then there was Tom's ill-disguised jealousy about Louise's promotion to detective superintendent. That was what finished them off, although in truth they'd separated emotionally long before. The divorce had been finalised six years ago, and although they'd stayed in touch while Michelle and Chloe were still young, once they'd grown up, even that residual relationship ended. There was no longer any reason to stay in contact; no visits to organise for the girls to see their father, no concerns to be shared about their daughters' perilous passage through adolescence and early adulthood. The mechanics of a shared existence had been dismantled, and Louise was becoming so used to living alone that she was trepidatious about ever allowing a man to intrude into her life again.

Returning to her office at New Scotland Yard, recently relocated from Victoria to the Embankment, Mangan found the usual backlog of bureaucracy demanding her attention. However, in amongst the routine dross was something of much greater interest. She was being asked to coordinate the policing arrangements for a couple of important but unconnected visits to the UK.

The first involved a bit of regal flummery. King Felipe VI of Spain, along with Queen Letizia, would be paying their first state visit (the first by any Spanish head of state for thirty years). Their majesties would only be in Britain for a couple of days in July, and would only travel outside the jurisdiction of the Metropolitan Police once, to go to Windsor. Mangan had been asked to oversee the security arrangements, making sure things ran smoothly between the Met and Thames Valley Police. There wouldn't be much to worry about: a few diehard Spanish ex-pats who'd lived in Britain for years and were too old to pose a threat, even if the flame of their youthful republicanism still burned as brightly as it once had; and some Catalan separatists with links to the IRA, who'd gone quiet since their comrades in Ireland had entered the peace process. As with all such state visits, nothing would be left to chance. Louise was expected to liaise with the Spanish Guardia Civil and wished this could be in sunny Madrid rather than murky old London.

The second visit was more complex. The Turkish novelist Burak Bayram would be coming to London in September. Bayram had fled his country in 2016 to avoid arrest for criticising President Erdogan. Exiled in Berlin, he had continued to commentate on Turkey's slide toward authoritarianism. Bayram's latest novel, a searing critique of a thinly disguised Erdogan, had been banned in Turkey, and the writer was touring Europe, promoting the book – and its message that the secular state welcomed into NATO in the 1950s had changed, and was now in league with NATO's enemies.

Bayram would be in Britain for two weeks, spending much of it outside London. He had agreed to reveal his itinerary to the German authorities, who would in turn share it with the Met. Assistant Commissioner Mangan's role would be to make sure there was a police presence at all Bayram's rallies and public meetings. She'd also need to work closely with the security service to ensure the writer's personal safety throughout the visit. Bayram had powerful enemies, and while he wasn't considered to be in any imminent danger, this could change by September.

This coordinating role would pitch Mangan back into the policing world she knew and loved; something tangible rather than theoretical, to do with policing rather than human resources; a defined task rather than the kind of woolly, abstract concepts that she was becoming depressingly accustomed to wading through.

6

MANNY'S

Manny's had been a fixture on Stoke Newington Road for as long as anybody could remember, its marble tables and black-and-white tiled floor unaltered by the passing years. Today, amongst the artisan bakers and coffee-house chains, it continued its incongruous existence, specialising in what it had always specialised in – salt-beef sandwiches, chopped liver and toasted bagels.

On most mornings from Monday to Friday at around eleven, Brady could be found at a back table near the kitchen, drinking strong coffee with his sufgani-yot, the jellied doughnuts that were another of Manny's specialities. This weekday morning in mid-June was no different. Brady had walked here from his house, through the maze of quiet streets that ran between Stoke Newington Road and Hackney Downs. Cathleen, a teacher at Dalston Academy, had to be at school by eight-thirty, leaving her husband in front of his computer, where she believed he spent his working day trading gilts and bonds. Perhaps at some point in the afternoon, he'd move to the well-stocked and extensive work room he'd established in the basement to pursue his hobby of carpentry.

Brady had met Cathleen on his second day in England – at the Pied Bull, a pub close to the digs he'd found in Stoke Newington, where the Irish diaspora mixed and mingled. Cathleen's parents had emigrated here from Cork in the early sixties, and she'd been born ten years later in north London. Brady could remember thinking, in those early days in the city, how strange it was that people so divided by religion that they had to be fenced off from each other in Belfast, could live, work and socialise happily together here. Most of them in this district were from the Republic of Ireland, but even the divide of different nationalities hardly seemed to matter. Just as with the Irish rugby team, it was as if partition had never happened.

On arriving in London, Brady had cast aside his old identity like a snake discarding a skin. Cathleen knew him only through the one he'd assumed, an identity that she'd solidified by marrying him. Apart from a religion neither of them had followed, the only thing they shared was the life they had created for themselves: the teacher and the international trader.

Except that Brady had never traded in gilts and bonds. When Cathleen had left that morning, he was working instead on the aspect of his true occupation that he enjoyed the most: the planning stage. He was determining exactly how he'd meet the commitments he'd taken on following that phone call in Clissold Park, and later the conversation he'd had with the man in the pink shirt. For each job he'd established a rough outline in his head that aligned with the specifications his customers had given. These would be reviewed and refined, leaving nothing to chance. It was a lonely pursuit, and the habitual trip to Manny's had become an essential part of Brady's routine. For a man who spent so much of his time alone, it offered a vital connection with the outside world, like a diver coming up for air. Brady would arrive after the breakfast rush had subsided, but before the lunch queue formed; a time when the pace slackened, and the owner was ready to take a breather.

'Manny' Jacobs was a Glaswegian Jew who'd arrived in north London forty years ago to work in the café for his uncle, the original 'Manny'. The name had been attached to him for so long now that his given name, Joseph, had become redundant. When he'd mentioned this to Brady during one of their early conversations, the Irishman was amused by the similarity with his own situation; the name each man had assumed (in Manny's case accidentally, in his case deliberately) was the one everybody now knew them by. Brady, who considered having friends to be an occupational hazard, realised that Manny had now become the closest thing he had to one.

Their relationship had developed to the point where every morning's visit followed the same pattern. Having personally served Brady's unchanging order of coffee and doughnuts, Manny would take off his apron, pour a cup of the strong black tea he preferred and settle into the seat next to Brady, leaving his assistants to run the café for an hour or so. Neither man had any interest in prying too deeply into each other's business or extending their companionship beyond the walls of this café.

They'd originally struck up a rapport over Celtic FC. Brady had grown up following the Scottish football champions, supported in Catholic west Belfast, where he was born, as fervently as they were in the East End of Glasgow, where they were based. He'd been surprised to see a replica green-and-white hooped shirt, together with a photograph of the famous 1967 European Cup-winning team, on the wall of Manny's the first time he'd gone there fifteen years ago, and he'd never forgotten Manny's response when Brady asked why he supported Celtic.

'If a billion Catholics can follow one Jew,' Manny had asked, 'why can't one Jew follow eleven Catholics?'

Manny had once asked if Brady had ever been to Glasgow. He said he hadn't, but that wasn't true. Glasgow was where he'd first killed a man. The para-military organisation that recruited him at sixteen decided to deploy him two years later. A drug-running operation had been bringing heroin and cocaine into Belfast from Scotland, masterminded by a Glaswegian gang leader who needed to be disposed of. Brady naively believed that he would be performing a service to his community; that this was a moral crusade against drug dealers. He later came to realise that the only reason why the Glasgow operation had to be stopped was because it interfered with the lucrative drug-running that the paramilitaries were engaged in. He'd travelled on the ferry from Larne to Cairnryan with two much older men to carry out what they described as a 'clean-up operation'.

He'd known this marked the end of his apprenticeship, of watching and learning while others fired the shots. It was as if being under eighteen had imposed an age restriction in the brutal world of the paramilitaries, just as it did in normal society.

The mission in Glasgow came two days after his eighteenth birthday. His natural patience had been reinforced in training, but he'd needed every ounce of it as he waited for seven hours on a rooftop in the Springburn district, before the victim finally stepped out of a car in the street below and Brady was given the order to shoot – and to shoot again as the victim's accomplices returned fire, trying to discern their attackers amongst the chimney pots and TV aerials high above them. Brady was told he'd killed three men that day. He'd never forget his visit to Glasgow – a visit that must never be mentioned. Another of the secrets that burned inside him like coal in a furnace. So no, he'd told Manny, that time he asked – he'd never been to Glasgow.

The years of sitting together had bred in Manny and Brady a familiarity that carried no obligation to converse. Manny would ease himself into the seat next to Brady with a heavy sigh, as if some great weight had been lifted, and they'd sit in comfortable silence, reading the newspapers that were always available on a rack next to the counter. A conversation would usually only begin after the morning news had been digested along with the sufganiyot.

Short and portly, Manny remained corpulent even though he must have burned off a substantial number of calories bustling around the café every day. Despite the additional money he could make, he refused to open on Saturday, which was his 'shabbat'. In all else, he was secular, criticising many of his neighbours in Stamford Hill for their orthodoxy.

'Those frummers are living in the Middle Ages,' he'd once told Brady. 'Sure, we have our traditions and they're important, but we can't be so observant that we become a cult rather than a religion.'

'I don't care if you're in a cult or a religion, so long as you keep serving up those doughnuts,' Brady had replied.

On this particular morning, Brady had finished eating, and was in the course of expounding his views about the problems that Britain's exit from the EU would cause in Northern Ireland when he noticed that Manny's attention had wandered elsewhere. Following the proprietor's line of vision, he saw three young men walking in. They were the only other customers. Brady recognised one of them as the kid with the razor-cut partings with whom he'd had the altercation in Clissold Park.

'Look at that bastard; if he was chocolate, he'd lick himself,' Manny was saying, almost under his breath.

'Do you know him?' Brady asked.

'Aye, I know him alright.' Despite the many years he'd spent in London, Manny's accent remained pure Glaswegian. 'He marched in here a couple of months ago offering "protection". Told me that for a hundred quid a week, he'd make sure my place was safe from the Dalston Crew, who were trying to muscle their way into the area.'

'Did you call the police?'

'Of course not. I got Osman from the kitchen to tell him in Turkish where to stick his "protection". You've seen Osman – six-foot-six of muscle and bone. Only a fool would mess with him.'

'So, what happened?' Brady posed his question while watching Razor Parting stare over at the table where they were sitting.

'They buggered off. The two guys with him tried to pretend they were just having a laugh, but that one never joined in; just eyeballed us with that sneer you can see now. Excuse me a moment.'

Manny rose abruptly and walked across to where the men were ordering coffees.

'Hey, you three – out,' he shouted, pronouncing 'out' as 'oot'. 'You're barred. Go and get your coffee somewhere else.'

The trio adopted a pose of defiant nonchalance as Manny, an old man three times their age and half their size, replaced the cups that his staff had begun to distribute. While two of the men looked askance at Manny, their leader, Razor Parting, leaned back on the counter, smiling.

'Listen, Grandad,' he said. 'I'm giving you one more chance to accept my business proposition. If you don't, this café won't be here to serve anyone – you understand?'

At that moment, Osman came out of the kitchen carrying a meat cleaver. The two underlings moved towards the door, shouting expletives and making hand gestures designed to salvage some dignity from their retreat. But Razor Parting didn't join in.

'Have it your own way,' he said, sauntering slowly to the door and turning to fix one last hostile glare – on Brady.

'Yes, they are Turkish,' Osman said in response to Brady's question, having joined the table next to the kitchen at Manny's insistence in the aftermath of the confrontation. 'But not typical. Almost all the Turks in this country live within a two-mile radius around here, and they are good citizens – obey the law, pay their taxes.'

Osman explained that he had been born in Stoke Newington, his parents having arrived from southern Cyprus in the 1970s after the island was partitioned.

'I doubt if those punks know anything about Cyprus, or Kurdistan, or Syria. They are part of a minority over here who support Erdogan's Justice and Development Party in Turkey, the AKP, in basically the same way your football hooligans follow England.'

The conversation turned to whether Manny should tell the police about this clear case of attempted extortion.

'Why should I involve the police?' asked Manny. 'We've seen them off, they won't be back. They'd deny demanding money, anyway – claim they were just messing about.'

'What will you do to protect this place if it all turns nasty?' Brady asked.

'Make sure Osman stays in my kitchen,' Manny said succinctly, putting his apron on to go back to work.

7

AN OBSTINATE GERIATRIC

Edward Bellingham pushed his way through the crush of humanity that swarmed around the barriers of Oxford Circus Underground station. The usual herd of commuters was augmented by summer tourists, and Bellingham thought how much more comfortable he'd have been travelling in his air-conditioned government car. However, this trek across London on a stifling July morning had nothing to do with his position at the Foreign and Commonwealth Office (retained following the Conservative's narrow victory at the general election back in June). This journey was in pursuit of private interests rather than public service.

The government car had left his house in Putney that morning with only the ministerial red box on board. As one of Bellingham's civil servants had mentioned when he'd first entered government, the car was provided precisely for that purpose. The nightly red box contained all the important documents that needed ministerial approval, together with correspondence (which he'd had no role in formulating) requiring his signature. It wasn't that the civil service did all the minister's work for him, this instructive civil servant had been at pains to explain, more a case of them chewing it up so that the minister could swallow it more easily. The red box was lead-lined so that if the car should be consumed in a ball of flames, the minister may perish but the precious documents would survive. The red box was indispensable; the minister wasn't.

Bellingham was currently the sole occupant of his Putney house. Miranda and the twins had remained in Crete, where he intended to join them in early August for a proper month-long holiday. Not that he was in desperate need of a break. Bellingham's responsibilities for Britain's overseas territories required little in the way of strenuous effort. There was the occasional trip to somewhere pleasant, such as Bermuda or Gibraltar, as well as to destinations not quite so pleasant, such as the Falklands.

A peer of the realm occupying an important govern-ment position, happily married and with two adorable children, Lord Bellingham had every reason to be pleased with the way his cookie had crumbled – and yet, as he pushed his way up the station steps, his mood was distinctly less sunny than the weather. He was bathed in sweat from the endurance test otherwise known as a journey on the tube in summer. On the escalator up from the bowels of the earth, he'd wiped his face with a handkerchief, careful to smooth his prized thin moustache, which had been newly trimmed that morning.

He'd taken this detour to meet his solicitor, Quentin Kane of Chesterton, Kane and Palfrey, about one of the

most troublesome projects that Bellingham Developments had ever undertaken. Several streets of dilapidated
houses in the old Docklands area of London were
being cleared to construct a hotel/casino/conference
centre complex. The brownfield site had been ear-
marked in the initial transformation plan of the 1980s,
but local campaigners had secured an injunction, and
the original developers had backed off. Now, many
years later, after Bellingham Developments had taken
up the cudgels and, with all the properties but one lying
empty, the long moratorium was over, and the bulldozers had moved in.

Opposition had coalesced around the one occupant
who'd refused to leave his property despite all the
blandishments, court orders and threats to send in the
bailiffs. Stanley Brewer was in his nineties. He'd been
a docker, like almost all the original occupants of the
area. Having lived in the house for sixty years, his stated
objective was to die in it. One by one, his neighbours
had succumbed to offers of re-housing, plus substantial financial compensation, but Mr Brewer remained
implacable. The several streets had been reduced to
one, with Stanley now the only resident.

In accordance with the ministerial code, Lord
Bellingham had stepped back from the day-to-day
running of his business and placed all his investments
into a blind trust. A new managing director had been
appointed at Bellingham Developments, with Bellingham himself installed in an honorary position. But
everyone knew who still pulled the strings. Bellingham's

ministerial role at the Foreign Office didn't present any conflicts of interest, and left him enough time and energy to devote to helping run the business. He'd never faced any controversy over his continuing involvement, but this happy situation was now threatened by Stanley Brewer's intransigence. The development was a major one, secured in the teeth of fierce competition, and worth a great deal, both financially and reputationally, to a business that would provide for Bellingham and his family long after his ministerial career was over.

The old man's stubbornness hadn't yet attracted nationwide attention. There'd been a small piece in the *London Evening Standard* cribbed from a local Docklands news sheet, but Bellingham Developments had been careful not to be heavy-handed, working around Brewer's house in the hope that the Grim Reaper would eventually solve the problem for them. Now that the foundations for the hotel were being laid, the row of terraced housing that included Stanley Brewer's home needed to be demolished for completion. The stand-off had come to a head, and Quentin Kane had contacted Bellingham the previous day, asking to see him urgently. It was for this reason that the minister had informed his office of some private business he needed to attend to on his way to work this morning.

Quentin Kane collected Bellingham from reception at the impressive offices of Chesterton, Kane and Palfrey in Marylebone, not far from Broadcasting House. After some preliminary chatter, the solicitor cut to the chase.

'Two things: first of all, Brewer's daughter rang me yesterday – Janice, the one who emigrated to Australia years ago and hasn't had much to do with her father since. Unlike her brother, who is frankly a pain in the arse, she's always been unsympathetic to her father's stance. In truth, I think she's thinking of the large amounts of money that her father would receive for cooperating with us, and its implications for her inheritance.'

'Sounds like a sensible woman, but does she have any influence on her father?'

'Not much; but she thinks you might.'

Kane paused to allow the tea to be distributed. He was one of those men whose appearance identified his profession. Put him in an identity parade and ask someone to pick out the solicitor, and they'd choose Kane every time. It wasn't just the inevitable pinstripe suit. Kane was tall and languid, with a shock of thick, grey hair that he wore brushed back from a high parting in a very lawyerly way. In fact, apart from the way it was arranged, his hair wasn't dissimilar to Bellingham's. If it wasn't for the moustache and Kane being at least three inches taller, the two men could have been cut from the same mould – but the apparel clearly showed which one of them had been to law school.

The two men had actually been at Winchester together, although Kane had been three years below Bellingham and they hadn't known each other at the time. They'd met when Chesterton, Kane and Palfrey succeeded in their lobby of Bellingham Developments to become their legal representatives. And as Kane had been the one to introduce Edward to Miranda, both Lord and Lady Bellingham considered him a close friend.

After the tea-server had left the room, the solicitor said: 'Janice Lloyd, nee Brewer, tells me that her old dad is a dyed-in-the-wool, working-class Tory who worshipped Thatcher, and before that Enoch Powell. Claims her father was on that dockers' march in support of Powell in the late sixties. He is apparently also a man who respects a title. Janice says that to him, a knighthood or a peerage is akin to being a minor royal.'

Bellingham looked quizzical. 'All very interesting, Quentin – but so what?'

'Don't you see? Throughout this saga, Stanley Brewer has dealt with us; he's never met anyone from Bellingham Developments, least of all Lord Bellingham of South Ormsby, peer of the realm and minister in Her Majesty's government.'

'No, and I sincerely hope he never does. I've got better things to do than waste my time with an obstinate geriatric.'

'The trouble is, old chum, the lid will come off this very soon. We're at a point where our options are to either send in the bailiffs or waste shedloads of money hanging around waiting for the old curmudgeon to die. Everything that can be done with him in situ has been done. Stanley may well live to be a hundred; Janice tells me that his mother did. And furthermore, the local branch of rent-a-mob is likely to be picketing the site very soon. The only reason we've escaped that pleasure so far is that they've been too busy with Brexit and the general election.'

'So, what exactly are you suggesting we do?' Bellingham asked, putting his feet up on Kane's leather-bordered desk while balancing his cup and saucer precariously on his chest. Kane left his seat and walked around the desk until he was standing over his friend.

'Come with me to meet him.'

Bellingham looked aghast, sitting up so quickly that some tea tipped into the saucer.

'Janice will set up the meeting,' the solicitor continued hurriedly. 'We can't make any noise on the site after 6pm anyway, so as not to disturb old Brewer's evenings, so there will be nobody around, and we can visit him discreetly. You can turn on the charm, give him some political insights, do all the House of Lords stuff.'

'Perhaps you'd like me to dress in ermine,' Bellingham said, sarcastically.

'That's not a bad idea, actually. Look, I know it's a pain, but it must be worth a try. Do you want this on your mind all through the rest of the summer? Can you imagine the optics of trying to evict a ninety-six-year-old, salt-of-the-earth pensioner from the house he's lived in all his life? The protests? The media coverage? The ramifications for you, personally, as a government minister? What we've already offered would allow

Stanley to live out the rest of his life in luxury, with substantial resources to pass on to his children and grandkids, but we're at the point of a final offer – and it needs to be you that makes it.'

Seeing Bellingham's resolve visibly weaken, Kane pressed on. 'When do you go back to Crete?' he asked.

'Next week; the Lords goes into recess on Friday and I'm straight off on Monday. July thirty-first can't come quickly enough for me.'

'So, that's a week away. I'll set everything up through Janice, and we'll arrange to pay Stanley a visit on Friday. Agreed?'

Bellingham pondered the suggestion, taking a phone from his inside pocket and checking his commitments for the week ahead. 'Okay, but it will have to be fairly late; I've got a debate in the Lords that evening.'

'Perfect. It will need to be late anyway. If Janice tells him you're coming straight from the House of Lords, it will enhance the regal nature of your visit. No doubt Stanley will be able to find a window in his busy diary.'

'You'd better meet me at Parliament. I can't use the government car service for this, so I'll drive you across in my car. What was the second thing you wanted to tell me?'

'Ah, a bit more sensitive, I'm afraid. This came in an envelope addressed to the firm,' Kane said, moving back to his desk and passing something across to Bellingham. It was a cheap touristy postcard with a photo of Tower Bridge on the front. On the back, scrawled in capitals, it said:

YOU KNOW WHAT YOU DONE TO ME.
SO WILL EVERYONE ELSE IF I TEL THEM.
SAW YOU ON TELY. YOU HAD YOUR FUN.
NOW YOU HAVE TO PAY FOR IT.
– TRUDY

Bellingham read the card before tossing it casually on the desk. 'Some tart, or her boyfriend, trying it on,' he said, dismissively.

'Of course, but I thought you'd better see it. Might be wise to report it to the police. If it follows the usual pattern, there'll be another missive soon saying how much they want.'

Bellingham said he would report it, and asked Kane to save anything else that arrived until he got back from Crete.

He didn't tell Kane how well he remembered Trudy and what had occurred between them.

The sun was now at an angle where it shone directly between the half-drawn blinds of Kane's office window, casting a shadow across the desk that looked very much like prison bars. With a shiver of apprehension, Edward Bellingham put the postcard in his pocket and left.

8

A BANG IN THE NIGHT

The bomb exploded at 2am. Three hours later, Louise Mangan was awakened by a call to her mobile.

'Sorry to disturb you, Ma-am,' the voice at the other end said nervously. 'There's been an explosion in Stoke Newington, and counterterrorism thought you should be informed.'

'Anyone hurt?' asked Mangan.

'Not sure yet, but it's unlikely. So far as we know, the café where the device was planted was empty, but it's still alight. Forensics say it will be midday before they can search through the ashes. The building's been completely destroyed, apparently.'

'Okay. Arrange for a car to pick me up at six, please.'

By half past seven, Assistant Commissioner Mangan had convened a meeting in the smallest of the three second-floor conference rooms at New Scotland Yard, a room which had a splendid view across the Thames, sparkling in the early morning sunlight. Two counter-terrorism officers, a man and a woman, were briefing Mangan and her team. They had already explained that an accident, such as a gas explosion, had been ruled out.

'As soon as the owner, Joseph Jacobs, known as Manny, told us about his run-in with some Turkish lads, we suspected the involvement of the Bombacilar gang.'

'But given Manny's religion and what's happening in the Middle East right now, isn't it more likely that a Palestinian group was responsible?' Mangan asked.

'Too nondescript for them. An empty café in the middle of the night – hardly the Twin Towers, is it?' the man from counterterrorism said, a little too cockily for Mangan's liking. 'Mr Jacobs told us he'd been approached for protection money by these guys, but that he and his staff had seen them off.'

'But didn't you tell us just the other day that Bombacilar was a Hackney gang whose main preoccupation is a turf war with their Tottenham rivals?' one of Mangan's team asked.

'That's how things stood when we briefed you about Turkish organised crime. As we said then, these characters are mainly obsessed with killing and maiming each other, and we don't think they pose a threat to that writer guy when he comes over from Germany. We still hold that view, but this does add a different dimension.'

Listening intently, Mangan had to force herself to keep remembering that she didn't have operational responsibility for investigating this explosion. It was for others to apprehend the culprits – her interest was confined to any threats to Burak Bayram, the distinguished Turkish novelist due to visit the UK in September.

The first part of her coordinating role had gone well, with the state visit of King Felipe VI now completed.

The king, along with Queen Letizia, had arrived on 12 July and left two days later. The arrangements had gone smoothly, although Mangan was aware that there hadn't been a security threat worthy of the description. The Catalan independence referendum wasn't due until 1 October, and while hugely controversial, with the Spanish government challenging its legitimacy through the courts, none of this disputation seemed to involve the Spanish royal family. Mangan had ensured that all the various UK agencies – the Met, MI5, MI6, Buckingham Palace and Thames Valley Police – had worked together seamlessly, particularly in relation to the king's excursion to Windsor Castle. She'd even received a handwritten letter of congratulation from the commissioner himself, a gesture from a more mannered age that she thought charming.

Two weeks after that visit, all her attention was now focused on Burak Bayram's upcoming tour, which she hoped would be similarly incident-free, although it would be much longer. This bombing, in the part of London where almost the entire British Turkish community was situated, didn't bode well.

'Do we know what caused it yet?' Mangan asked.

'It was malicious, if that's what you're asking,' said the cocky counterterrorism officer, who had riled Mangan once already.

'Why don't you try not to guess what I might be asking and simply answer what I've actually asked. I'm perfectly aware it was malicious. I didn't think it was an exercise in pest control.'

The female counterterrorism officer intervened, realising what a poor impression her colleague was making. 'Our specialists suspect they used Semtex, Ma'am. It was probably hidden somewhere earlier in the day when the café was open, and activated later with a timer or a key fob.'

That's better, Mangan thought, giving this more respectful officer her full attention and encouraging her to continue.

'The irony about Bombacilar's possible involvement is that despite their name – Turkish for bombers – it would be the first time we've known them to actually plant a bomb. Their style is more Skorpian sub-machine guns than Semtex. I'd be surprised if Bombacilar posed any threat to your novelist. The thing that motivates them isn't politics or religion, it's heroin.'

'Thank you,' Mangan said, picking up her papers. 'That's been very helpful. I'm going over to Stoke Newington, just to get my bearings. I'd be grateful if we could reconvene there at around eleven.'

Arriving for his regular coffee at the usual time, Brady found a smouldering heap where Manny's used to be. The shops on either side, a boutique and a baker's, had also suffered damage, so fiercely had the fire blazed. As soon as Brady saw the fire engines, the crowd of onlookers and several uniformed police officers, his instinct was to turn on his heels and walk away. His life was by necessity lived quietly, avoiding dramas such as this. But seeing Manny crying openly as two women, presumably his wife and daughter, tried to comfort him, made Brady hesitate. Some firefighters continued to hose down parts of the wreckage, while others were beginning to pick their way gingerly through the rubble. As Manny turned away from the blue-taped barrier, guided by his wife's gentle prompting, he saw the man he'd usually be drinking coffee with at this time of day.

'Look what those bastards done. It was those kids – I know it was.'

Brady knew who Manny was referring to. Looking into the huddle of spectators that had been gathering in greater numbers throughout the morning, he'd spotted Razor Parting about three rows back, surrounded by his acolytes, exactly as he had been during that spring morning confrontation in Clissold Park. Brady could almost feel the searing defiance of his gaze. For a second, he was tempted to point him out to Manny, but that was bound to alert the police officers close by. The last thing Brady wanted was any involvement with the Metropolitan Police. He needed to slip away as soon as he decently could, but by now Manny was next to him, clinging to his arm for support.

At that moment, Assistant Commissioner Mangan arrived, accompanied by the officers she'd been meeting with earlier, and Detective Inspector Jack Cairns, who'd been assigned to the case by Borough Command.

'Mr Jacobs?' Mangan introduced herself to Manny. 'I know how traumatic this must be for you and your family. Detective Inspector Cairns wants to ask you a few questions, if that's alright? We've got somewhere quiet, and you can bring your family along with you.'

Brady, realising he'd been mistaken for a relative, extricated himself from Manny's grip, telling him quietly that he had work to do.

'But you heard those guys,' Manny said. 'You know it must be them. I need you to back me up.'

Detective Inspector Cairns intervened. 'If you did witness anything that could be instrumental, it would be helpful for us to take a statement,' he told Brady.

'Sure,' Brady replied. 'I just need to sort a few things out, then I'll join you. I presume you're based at the police station on the High Street?'

Having received confirmation, and avoiding any further interaction, Brady walked away. He turned to take another look into the crowd of spectators, but Razor Parting and his pals had disappeared.

Later that afternoon, Brady was in his basement workshop, finishing a little glazed jewellery box he planned to give to Cathleen for her birthday. He usually devoted a couple of hours every afternoon to carpentry, which he considered much more than a hobby. It was a form of therapy that he'd acquired from his father, who'd passed on the necessary skills before his violent death.

All the stresses and strains of his perilous life seemed to dissipate during an afternoon of sawing and chiselling and dovetailing in this windowless haven. But today, Brady was finding it hard to relax. He was anxious, and anxiety was an emotion he was unfamiliar with.

His current cause for concern was being in such close proximity to a detective inspector and another officer whose seniority had been obvious from the insignia on her uniform. They hadn't asked Brady for his name and address, and Manny certainly wouldn't be able to provide it. With a bit of luck, he'd hear nothing more. He didn't intend to make that visit to the police station. There were other witnesses to Razor Parting's malicious behaviour – Osman, for instance. Why should Brady take the risk?

His assumed identity had withstood every test it had been subjected to so far. He'd used it to become a viable member of society. Having acquired the driving licence, passport and marriage certificate, he'd even thought about applying for a gun licence, before deciding that it would attract too much ongoing police monitoring. But he was realistic enough to know that he was protected only against the casual interest of those with no deep suspicion. If there was ever a rigorous identity check, the kind that would be inevitable if he was suspected of a serious crime – murder, for instance – it would reveal who he really was, just as a comprehensive search of this workshop by people who knew what they were looking for would be bound to reveal the weapons hidden there.

All these thoughts fed Brady's apprehension concerning today's events. He worried most about his emotional response to the destruction of Manny's café. The entirety of his settled existence depended on avoiding such reactions. The only way he could survive in the line of work he'd chosen was by treating it as a profession. When he took a life, he did it with the dispassionate skill of a surgeon. Both were artisans: one taking lives, the other saving them. But the surgeon didn't need the same levels of discipline and constraint that Brady required for his work.

His manufactured identity had imposed a manufactured personality. To be sure, he'd always had a calm temperament, but eventually every spark of impetuosity had been extinguished. Or at least, he'd thought it had. But now he found himself thinking about Manny having his life wrecked by the disdainful, cocksure hooligan with the razor parting. He'd come into the proximity of a senior police officer at the same time as he was having thoughts that could only be described as reckless.

Most worryingly of all, Brady couldn't stop himself from contemplating revenge.

9

PERSUASION

The weather had turned. Low cloud, darkly threatening, filled the evening sky. Bursts of frantic rain had sweetened the Docklands air by the time Edward Bellingham's car pulled up on the periphery of the building site where Stanley Brewer lived.

'Can't we get any closer?' Bellingham asked, fearing they'd be caught in a shower.

'Afraid not,' Kane replied. 'We've had to ensure a road to the old bastard's front door, but it's narrow. If we park on it, the emergency services wouldn't be able to get through.'

'Right. We wouldn't want to prevent him being whisked away in an ambulance, would we?' the minister said, getting out of the car and preparing to follow Kane's lead on the walk to Brewer's house.

The rain had stopped, leaving an aroma of saturated earth mixed with mechanical odours of grease and engine oil. As they passed through the site, Bellingham thought how much it resembled a battlefield from an old Second World War newsreel. Great hulks of machinery – diggers, bulldozers, cherry pickers and cranes – stood idle, like a stalled tank regiment. As they got closer to the house, a vast crater added to the battlefield illusion. The conference centre was already in the early stages of construction. This giant hole was where the hotel/casino would be, and it was big enough to demonstrate the seriousness of Bellingham Development's intent without being so big that it destabilised the two-up, two-down terraced house that the men were walking towards. A couple of unoccupied houses had had to be left standing on either side of Stanley Brewer's home to provide structural support. Part of the pavement also remained intact, upon which stood the last remaining lamppost, casting an egg-yolk yellow light to illuminate their approach.

Mr Brewer had agreed to this meeting reluctantly (according to his daughter) on the condition it was finished in time for the *News At Ten*. Stanley prided himself on being well versed in current events. He always watched the evening news and, on Thursdays, *Question Time*, before taking himself to bed. The front door was opened by Stanley's grandson, introduced as Keith. Taller even than Kane, he was to maintain his broad-shouldered, shaven-headed presence throughout the meeting.

'Keith was in the military,' Stanley Brewer announced proudly in his introduction. 'Fourth Rifles Battalion – served in Iraq and Afghanistan, didn't you, son? He's my security guard. Makes sure nobody takes me away against my will.'

They were in the tiny sitting room, its gas heater alight despite the hot weather. Stanley was in an armchair on one side of the boarded-up fireplace, and Keith sat himself down on an identical one opposite, sitting so close to his grandfather that their knees almost touched. Bellingham and Kane were forced to squeeze on to a matching settee. A small television in the corner next to the settee was switched off. Stanley Brewer was remarkably lucid and articulate for a man born in 1921.

'Now, let's be clear,' he said by way of preliminaries, 'I'm only meeting you 'cause Janice and Peter say I should. They're my kids, and I love them, but I know what they want out of this, and it ain't what I want – or what Keith, Peter's son, wants – is it, Keith?'

Keith grunted in affirmation, keeping his eyes on Bellingham and Kane.

''E's on my side, is Keith. All his old grandad wants is to be able to die in the house he was born in. I ain't leavin' other than feet first. Now, what have you got to say for yourself?'

Bellingham was full of confidence at this early stage of the proceedings. His attitude was magisterial as he prepared to address this loyal supporter of the Conservative and Unionist Party, a breed of person that Bellingham had always regarded as being the salt of the earth – people who knew their place. Stanley may be an awkward old bastard, but the peer had been assured he had a healthy respect for authority. And so, Lord Bellingham of South Ormsby adjusted the jacket of his expensive herringbone suit so that the blue satin lining was exposed to what he expected to be admiring glances, tweaked his carefully cultivated moustache, and explained how he'd come straight from the House of Lords, where he was one of Her Majesty's loyal ministers, emphasising a long association with the party that Stanley Brewer supported. He was beginning a long paean of praise for Mrs Thatcher when his host interrupted.

''Ow did you vote?'

'Well, peers can't vote in general elections, as you know,' Bellingham said, with an air of *de haut en bas*, 'but I would have voted Conservative, of course – as I always have.'

'I ain't talkin' about the election,' the old man responded. 'I mean Leave or Remain?'

'Yes, we were allowed to vote in the EU referendum, and I voted to . . .' Bellingham paused, feeling Kane's leg pressing against his as if to convey a warning. He suspected that Brewer was not a man who'd be keen on pooling sovereignty with our European friends and neighbours, but it was too late; he had already embarked on his stock response. '. . . remain, but I very much respect the decision of the electorate – and, as the Prime Minister herself has emphasised, Brexit means Brexit.'

'Load of old bollocks,' Stanley opined.

'But as a Conservative supporter, you'll appreciate that it was we who gave the British people the chance to . . .'

'Let me stop you there.' The old man actually held up his hand as if directing traffic. 'I was a Tory supporter, but not anymore. I'm with Nigel now – and so's Keith, ain't you, son?'

Keith nodded, and Lord Bellingham, his confidence shattered, began to realise the futility of his mission. He ploughed gamely on, and by five to ten had made what he described as Bellingham Development's final offer. As he'd been complaining to Kane earlier, it included enough money to enable Stanley Brewer to buy the house next door to where Bellingham lived in Putney, one of the most expensive and exclusive areas of London, with enough left over to provide Keith with a pied-à-terre in Knightsbridge. But he understood that the offer had to be made if this impasse was ever to be broken. It was met by silence. Stanley coughed and Keith blew his nose, but neither said a word.

Kane spoke into the void. 'You may need to chew this over for a day or two, but we do need to lay these foundations by the end of summer, and we do have the law on our side. We'd be delighted if this could be settled amicably, by agreement, and I know that your children Janice and Peter want that as well. Why don't you discuss this offer with them to get their advice? But please understand it really is a final offer, and if you turn it down, we'll proceed anyway.'

Keith gave what could only be described as a snarl, and Bellingham worried that they were about to be attacked. But Stanley broke the tension.

'Wasn't you on *Question Time* a few months ago?' he asked Bellingham.

'Yes, I was,' the minister said, instinctively preening himself for an inevitable compliment.

'You was fuckin' awful.'

Stanley Brewer concluded the meeting.

10

CATHLEEN

Dalston Academy glittered in the morning sun. It was a new, modern building, where glass had replaced concrete as the main feature of its construction. Its predecessor school, the notorious Dalston Comp, had been a squat, ugly building nicknamed 'The Bunker', mainly due to its appearance, but also to reflect the fact that education and enlightenment needed a refuge in this part of London, where kids had traditionally been expected to fail. The old concrete monstrosity had been demolished in the first few years of the twenty-first century, a decade in which investment in school buildings and what went on inside them had transformed educational attainment across the capital.

Cathleen had taught English here since qualifying as a teacher in the nineties. She was one of only two teachers who'd survived the journey from comprehensive to academy. Many of the staff she'd originally worked with had joined campaigns against the change, but Cathleen could see no advantage in campaigning to preserve a system that had failed so many.

The school was multi-ethnic and worked hard to preserve a sense of cultural identity amongst its students while also instilling integration and racial harmony in all aspects of school life. Dalston and the surrounding boroughs had a large African-Caribbean population, as well as substantial Turkish, Greek, North African, Portuguese and Vietnamese communities. Cathleen's red hair and freckles marked her out as part of the Irish diaspora, although like most of those she taught, she was first-generation English. The cohort she was particularly concerned about as a teacher were the white working-class kids whose families had lived in Dalston for generations but had never developed the educational aspiration that was so prominent amongst some other ethnic groups. A few years ago, she'd asked a citizenship class to do a project about their cultural heritage. Her year nine pupils, thirteen- and fourteen-year-olds from Hackney, Islington and Stoke Newington, had produced some wonderful work; not just stories about their parents and grandparents, but colourful illustrations, either hand-drawn or cut from magazines, depicting the clothes worn, the food eaten, and the villages, towns and cities of those from whom they were descended. There was one Cockney lad in the class who had produced nothing at all. When Cathleen had questioned him as to why he hadn't participated in the project, he'd replied without rancour or cynicism: 'I'm from round here, Miss. I ain't got no cultural heritage.'

This experience had troubled her, and Cathleen had considered it a triumph when she'd persuaded this lad to read Dickens and Defoe as part of her effort to prove he had a cultural heritage every bit as rich as that of his classmates.

Cathleen had met Brady on his second night in London and married him three years later. He was the only man she'd ever loved (spiritually or physically) up to that point, and it had pleased her parents to see their daughter settled with someone who shared their religion and was from what her father always referred to as 'the old country', albeit the north, where the Troubles were happening, rather than what they regarded as the liberated south. She knew Brady had been involved in sectarian conflict, but little else about his past. She'd still never met or communicated with any of his family. His parents were dead, his siblings estranged. When she'd met this tall, attractive man, he was alone in an unfamiliar landscape. It had been part of the appeal. And she'd continued to find his otherworldliness alluring for at least the first few years of their marriage. He was a loner, she told herself, adapting to a status forced upon him by the tragic circumstances of his childhood, like a wild animal required to fend for itself. His work as a bond trader (whatever that was) demanded little in the way of personal interaction, and she'd often thought of trying to persuade him to find an occupation less isolating, but his job provided an income that allowed them to live at the wealthier end of the borough, to take expensive holidays, to live well together – and yet apart.

She had no interest in his work, and he seemed to have no interest in hers. It wasn't just that he never came to school events or was inattentive as she enthused about her pupils; it was more fundamental than that. Literature was the most important thing in her life, but of no importance whatsoever to him. Early in their relationship, she'd tried hard to interest him in the authors she loved – Dickens and Hardy, John Banville and J. M. Coetzee, Hilary Mantel and A. S. Byatt. At first, he'd shown willing, but the same recommended book would lie unopened for months on his bedside table, until Cathleen discreetly returned it to the bookshelf.

Which was why she was so surprised when he'd recently shown an interest in one of her favourite modern authors, the great Turkish writer Burak Bayram. She'd wandered into the living room one Sunday morning to find her husband examining the bookshelves, running a pointed finger down the spines, searching for a particular volume. When he'd told her whose books he was looking for, she'd assumed he'd taken an interest because he'd heard that Bayram was coming to Stoke Newington in September. He'd probably heard about it at Manny's, the café he visited every morning while she was at work. Cathleen had never crossed the threshold of Manny's, let alone met the man himself, but she knew it was her husband's main connection with the outside world – and another feature of their increasing separation.

She'd handed him a copy of *The Crescent Moon*, Bayram's most famous and accessible novel, and he'd taken it into his bedroom, from which it had yet to emerge. She thought it might be one book that he was actually reading, but couldn't be sure: for six years, they'd slept in separate rooms, ever since Cathleen had been ill with a nasty cough and high temperature, and Brady had moved into one of the two spare bedrooms to ensure they could both sleep undisturbed. He'd never moved back.

They still made love, every couple of months on a Saturday morning – always a Saturday morning, and always as part of the same ritual. He'd bring her a cup of tea at around seven-thirty, climb into bed and begin to stroke her hair. On seven Saturdays out of eight, there would be no hair stroking, and no cup of tea.

There was no need for contraception. They'd realised in the first five years of their marriage that they would never conceive. They never tried to discover why – if the problem lay with him or her. Nor was the issue ever discussed. It stretched like a long, high wall between them. Cathleen had wanted children but accepted the situation. What she found harder to accept was her husband's obvious satisfaction with their child-less state. Once, on holiday, he'd remarked on the bad manners of a child who'd been at the next table in the hotel restaurant.

'Thank God we'll never have that problem,' he'd said, after the family had left.

'That problem' was something Cathleen was desperate to have, and his callous remark had made her deeply unhappy. But Brady never noticed, just as he didn't notice her disquiet when he went away a couple of times a year without her. He'd even been away over the previous Christmas. These trips were apparently integral to his job, but Cathleen realised how little she knew about the man she'd married. The things she'd once found attractive, she now found irritating: his dark, brooding intensity, his air of self-sufficiency, the hours spent in his workshop, a masculine haven from which she felt excluded, his secretiveness and propensity for avoiding conversation – with her as much as with anybody else.

Cathleen often dwelt on her dissatisfaction without contemplating resolution. She'd never considered separating from the man she'd married. It would be contrary to the culture in which she'd been raised. Her work gave her solace and satisfaction. The children she taught gave her purpose and pride. Brady wasn't involved in any of the things that really mattered in her life, but on this fine July morning at Dalston Academy, with the long summer break to look forward to, she felt that the exotic holiday she'd soon take with her husband was a good enough substitute for a deep and meaningful relationship. Brady had become peripheral to her happiness – particularly since she'd begun an affair with a fellow teacher.

Benjamin Abiola was from a Nigerian family who had come to England when Benjamin was a baby. Ten years her senior, he'd arrived at Dalston Academy eight years ago to teach maths. He and Cathleen had become good friends. She found his soft, low, mellifluous voice comforting, his strong presence reassuring. After a few years, they began confiding in one another. They'd go to the pub with their colleagues for the regular Friday early-evening get-together that had become a tradition, but the two of them would stay later than the others. Benjamin was married to his childhood sweetheart, and had two children who would soon be old enough to come to the Academy. But he was restless and dissatisfied – increasingly so as his friendship with Cathleen deepened.

They'd first slept together on a school trip to Paris four years ago. They were there to supervise the year tens through a week-long programme arranged by the European Commission to give British pupils a more thorough understanding of what the European Union was, and what it wasn't. Dalston Academy had participated in the programme, along with many other UK schools in both the state and private sectors. It was a cold February evening, the final night of their stay, and the two friends had gone to a bistro for a quiet drink together after the boisterous final dinner with the students. As they walked back to their hotel through the broad boulevards of the Latin Quarter, they both knew they wouldn't be spending the night alone. It was unspoken but predetermined. It was a physical expression of their friendship that neither could resist, even if they'd wanted to. One of their students had made a little presentation at the dinner, handing each of the four teachers a beret as a thank you gift. It had been a wonderful evening, in which pride in their pupils had been expressed in laughter and joy as the teachers vied with one another over who could look most ridiculous in their new headgear. Benjamin and Cathleen were still giggling as they fell through the door of Benjamin's hotel room. Cathleen had been invited in for a nightcap, but as soon as the door closed behind them, they fell into a passionate embrace and caressed with unrestrained intimacy, playing out the fantasies that both had created about the other through their years of friendship. As dawn broke over Paris, they found their way to the bed, where whispered endearments preceded a third round of lovemaking.

Since then, they'd spent many afternoons and evenings together; in a flat that Benjamin borrowed from a friend, in hotels in central London, and in the back of Benjamin's car. But they hadn't spent another night with each other, and knew they never would. This affair was important to them, but it was the sex they needed, not an upheaval in their lives. Their time together enhanced their time apart, and made their existence full and more endurable.

These lascivious thoughts were percolating in Cathleen's mind as she stood alone in the staff room, gazing across the playing fields that stretched beyond the security fence towards the entrance to the school. A police car turned in off the main road and, ten minutes later, Vanessa, the school receptionist, came in to tell her that two police officers were asking to see a teacher whose name they didn't know, but who, from their stated aim of finding a teacher who worked here and was married to an Irishman, Vanessa felt may well be Cathleen.

11

ONE OF OUR MINISTERS IS MISSING

Louise Mangan savoured her second coffee of the day. It was half past eight on a dull August morning and the commissioner had asked to see her at nine. They'd known each other for years, since well before he'd risen to the illustrious position he now held, and Louise had always appreciated his quiet, deliberative style. It had earned him respect across a wide swathe of political opinion, despite his refusal to bend the knee to politicians, whether they be mayors or prime ministers. In a position notorious for its high turnover, he'd survived for almost five years.

Mangan liked Commissioner George Irvine, and knew Commissioner Irvine liked her, but she also knew he wouldn't be there for much longer. She didn't enjoy being one of his assistant commissioners – the rank he'd promoted her to – but it had its compensations. The higher salary would considerably enhance the pension she'd be eligible to retire on when she reached fifty in a little over two years. Dealing with a new boss would only add to her unhappiness at work, particularly if that new boss was the current deputy commissioner, with whom she'd always had a strained relationship.

With this in mind, she'd recently decided that she would go when Irvine did. But the more she thought about it, the less attractive the prospect of retirement became. Louise couldn't escape the conclusion that all that awaited her in retirement was a solitary existence devoid of purpose. She'd never been one for morbid introspection, and while she still refused to wallow in self-pity, she had begun to paddle at its edges.

She'd drunk one glass of Sauvignon Blanc too many the previous evening and found herself singing along mournfully to Joni Mitchell's *Blue*, playing it over and over again. Her favourite track – 'A Case of You' – was sung with the greatest gusto, wine glass lifted to the ceiling with each line of the chorus. It was only when her phone had rung that the lachrymose atmosphere evaporated. Louise had been shocked to see her reflection in the hall mirror as she answered. Tears were running in rivulets down her face, leaving dark tracks of diluted mascara. She'd thought about ignoring the call, but found herself robotically lifting the receiver even as the thought occurred – which was just as well, because the commissioner had been at the other end of the line.

'Can you pop in to see me first thing tomorrow?' he'd asked, dispensing with any preliminary niceties.

'Of course. What about?'

'Actually, Louise, I'm up to my eyes right now. Can I tell you in the morning? I've got a bit of a mission for you, but don't worry – it's one you'll like.'

They'd agreed to meet at nine, but it was ten past before Mangan was ushered into Commissioner Irvine's dark office, its highly polished mahogany reeking of masculinity – and Johnson's Pride.

Two besuited men she didn't recognise passed her in the outer office, coming out as she was going in. Mangan guessed from their demeanour that they were senior spooks.

'How do you fancy a few weeks in the sun?'

Mangan barely had time to settle into the brown leather armchair she'd been directed towards before the commissioner surprised her with this question as he stepped out from behind the desk, which she had once jokingly observed was roughly the size of a helicopter landing-pad and walked towards her. The long table on the far side of the huge office, that Louise had clustered around many times at team meetings, had obviously been the scene of a recently concluded conclave with the men in suits who had just left. The teacups had yet to be cleared and a large atlas lay open in the centre.

Mangan didn't think the commissioner's question required an answer. He knew she was a sun worshipper and so she just smiled sweetly as he took the facing armchair. As usual, his uniform was immaculate and complete. He'd never been known to remove the tunic, even in the confines of his office. As for his shoes, they shone like solidified molasses.

'One of our ministers is missing on the island of Crete.' The commissioner was well known for his Cumbrian directness, and Mangan didn't expect him to waste time on small talk. Nevertheless, the bald statement took her by surprise.

'I presume you mean a government minister?'

'Well deduced, Louise. It's actually a lord, but temporal rather than spiritual.'

'Which one?'

George Irvine rearranged his tall frame in the seat, adjusted his tie and ran his fingers along the sharp crease of his trousers before crossing his legs. It was a little ritual that Louise was familiar with. Those trouser creases were always so perfect, she wondered if they were sewn in rather than ironed.

'Lord Bellingham,' he answered eventually. 'Went hiking last Wednesday, hasn't been seen since.'

'Today's Tuesday,' Mangan said unnecessarily. 'Almost a week. I'm no hiker, but those who hike in Crete usually take much longer than that. What's the problem?'

'This was supposed to be a one-day affair. Apparently, he did it often, crossing the island at its narrowest points, about fifteen miles or so. He never went in for marathons, or even overnight camping. On this occasion, I'm told he went into an area known as the White Mountains, arranging for his wife to pick him up from a pre-determined point that evening. They were due to go for dinner together before heading home. He wasn't even supposed to be away for one night, let alone six.'

'I saw him,' Mangan said, distractedly.

The commissioner looked up in surprise.

'Lord Bellingham,' she continued. 'I saw him in Crete when I was there with my daughter a few months ago. We were in the same restaurant.'

'Well, there you are, that is precisely why I asked to see you. You've mentioned taking your holidays in Crete often enough over the years, and we need to send someone over to liaise with the Greek police. Lord Bellingham lived in Putney, so there are no complications at this end – he's a Met responsibility. As he's a government minister, we need to send someone more senior than a detective sergeant or even an inspector, which is the highest rank I'd usually consider for a job like this. Having said that, it is a bit below your pay grade, so I'd understand if you'd prefer me to send somebody else.'

Mangan didn't need time to consider. 'No, of course not,' she said. 'August in Crete, what's not to like?'

'Quite a lot, if you're fair-skinned like me. I prefer to do my ambling in the Lake District.'

The commissioner proceeded to give Mangan a full readout from the meeting he'd just had with two operatives from MI6. There was no suspicion of a terrorist plot, and there was consensus between the Greek and British security services that Bellingham was either lost or had had an accident.

'He flew out on Monday 31 July. His wife picked him up from the airport, and his private office had a text exchange with him that evening before going into holiday mode, agreeing they'd only contact him if an emergency arose.'

'They do like their long summer breaks, these ministers,' Mangan observed.

'Yes indeed. He was due to be away for the whole

of August. Best Susan and I ever manage is a fortnight in September.'

'So, why haven't I heard anything on the news?'

'The press hasn't picked up on it yet, and we're considering what line to take when they do. The authorities in Crete are worried about any negative publicity that might make people think the island is dangerous and damage the tourist industry, so the Greeks haven't gone public, but we can't keep this to ourselves much longer. There's a substantial search operation underway, for a start, and that's bound to attract attention from Brits on holiday there.'

'What about his family?' Mangan asked.

'Lady Bellingham is out there. Spends all summer there, apparently. But their two kids are back in England, staying with their grandparents.'

'When do you want me to go?'

'Straight away. We'll get the RAF to take you if you can't book on to a flight. This is an issue of national importance. We may not be the country we once were, but when a minister in Her Majesty's government goes missing, we can still rise to the challenge – although you don't need me to tell you that the Greeks are in charge, and we mustn't put their noses out of joint. I presume there's nothing you're doing that can't be postponed.'

Mangan wanted to say that there was nothing an assistant commissioner ever did that wasn't postponeable, but thought better of it. 'No,' she said. 'We've done the King of Spain, so to speak, and everything's in place for the visit of that Turkish writer in September.'

'What's the latest on the explosion in Stoke New-ington?'

'It's a serious policing issue, obviously, and I've been over to talk to Jack Cairns, but we think it's gang-related rather than political. Burak Bayram, the writer, is due to have a big meeting in the area, but we don't believe the bombing of that café constitutes a threat to his well-being, and I can pick up the coordinating role again when I get back – hopefully with Lord Belling-ham alive and well.'

'Yes, Jack's one of our best men – you won't have any worries there.'

'Oh, I know that,' Louise responded. 'The word on the street is that he would have risen much higher in the Met if it hadn't been for the Danvers stuff.'

She was referring to an incident that had taken place twenty-five years before. Billy Danvers had been one of the most vicious criminals in London, specialising in armed robbery. He and his three sons had been respon-sible for attacks on safe deposits, security depots, banks and bond couriers all over the city. For sheer brutality, the Danvers heists had earned a notoriety that few could match before or since. In September 1992, Jack Cairns, then a young detective constable with the Flying Squad, had been involved in a carefully planned oper-ation to catch Danvers and his sons in the act and end their barbarous regime. Having learned of the gang's intention to rob a Barclays Bank in south-east London, the Flying Squad set a trap. There was a shoot-out, in which a machine gun was used against the police for the first time in mainland Britain. One officer was lucky to survive after being hit by a ricochet when the gang was cornered.

Billy Danvers and two of his sons were captured, but the youngest son, Sam, had escaped into a multi-storey car park. Jack Cairns was one of three officers who pursued him to the top floor, where Sam, having failed to hijack a car, stood on the parapet, threatening to jump to his death if the police didn't back off and allow him to walk away. Two members of the public testified that they heard Cairns respond by shouting, 'Go ahead and jump, you piece of shit.'

Whether he jumped deliberately or simply lost his footing, Sam Danvers, Billy's favourite son, fell ten storeys on to concrete and died immediately. A subsequent inquest found that he was high on drugs and, in the words of the gang's legal representative, 'highly vulnerable'. Jack Cairns' invitation for Sam to kill himself was seen as a significant factor, and Detective Constable Cairns was taken through the Met's disciplinary process in a highly controversial case. The tabloid press reflected public opinion by championing the young officer and comparing his commitment to public service with the way of life chosen by his contemporary, Sam Danvers. In the end, no disciplinary action was taken, but everyone in the Met knew that the incident had blighted Jack's career. Billy Danvers, serving a twenty-five-year sentence, even tried to launch a private prosecution against the Met from his prison cell for what he claimed to be the 'execution' of his son

– an attempt that failed. Cairns had risen to the rank of detective inspector, but knew he'd go no further.

'Jack did not have a fair rub of the green, that's for sure,' the commissioner said. 'I was involved in planning that operation as a detective sergeant, working behind the scenes, and it certainly helped my career. Jack risked his life, and it's adversely affected his. Still, nobody promised fairness when we joined, only servitude. Okay, Louise, let's crack on. Jack will keep you updated about Stoke Newington while you're out in Crete. Get yourself booked into a reasonable hotel – nothing too lavish, mind.' The commissioner rose to return to his desk.

'How long shall I check in for?'

'I'd prepare to be over there until the end of August. Even if we find him soon, there's bound to be stuff to clear up.'

'Does that mean I can spend any spare time on the beach?' Mangan asked with a smile.

'This is the Metropolitan Police, not *Miami Vice*,' Irvine replied with mock horror. He knew Mangan well enough to know that relaxing on the beach was the last thing she was likely to indulge in if there was a job to do. 'In any case, I don't want you getting too used to being a detective again; I might never get you back in uniform.'

12

CAPTAIN DIAMANTAPOULIS

Assistant Commissioner Mangan was at Gatwick Airport the following morning. Her office had not only secured a seat for her on a scheduled flight with BA, but they'd also managed to book her into the hotel she'd requested – the Crystal Beach in Agia Galini, where she'd stayed with her daughter in May. She suspected that the Foreign and Commonwealth Office might have used their influence with the Greek government, given the speed with which these arrangements had been put in place.

Mangan could hardly believe her good fortune. The prospect of a turgid August ploughing a bureaucratic furrow had suddenly transformed into what might be as long as three weeks on the glorious island of Crete. There was a pang of guilt as she pondered this change of fortune, a concern that she was benefitting from the misfortune of others. However, considering that a police officer's professional life was mostly about dealing with other people's mishaps, she didn't have much trouble putting things into perspective.

The commissioner had decided that she was to undertake this task alone. He'd explained his thinking in their final conversation the previous day. 'In normal circumstances where there's a case abroad involving a Brit, we'd send a couple of detective sergeants and badge them as liaison officers, but in this case . . .'

'. . . you have the chance to save money by sending one person instead of two,' Mangan said, finishing the sentence for him.

'Exactly, although I'll be trying to save even more by ensuring that the Foreign Office pays for this particular luxury excursion.'

Arriving at Heraklion airport, Louise Mangan looked nothing like an assistant commissioner. Having escaped those tortuous black tights, she'd applied some overnight fake tan with the intention of remaining bare-legged for the duration. Her tall, slim frame was covered by a light blue, sleeveless summer dress, gathered at the waist. She'd worn a light jacket for the journey, but had placed this in her hand baggage before she'd left the plane. Her thick, dark hair was brushed back to offset the sunglasses purchased in the departure lounge at Gatwick.

Mangan may have looked like a holidaymaker, but she was aware of how serious this mission was. A hastily arranged briefing on protocol had stressed the necessity of not antagonising the Greeks by appearing in full dress uniform. She was there to liaise, not to lead, and it would be best if she wore civvies and reserved the uniform she'd packed for any ceremonial occasions that may arise. There was even a bit of her printed briefing that highlighted possible leisure activities for when she was off-duty, but Louise had no intention of relaxing in the sun. The most exciting prospect for her was reconnecting with proper detective work, however temporarily.

She was to work with Captain Petros Diamanta-poulis of the Hellenic Police, who'd been sent from Athens to lead the investigation. Mangan read the scant biographic details provided in her brief, which included a helpful phonetic version of his surname (*Día-man-ta-poo-loo*). Although he'd been born in Crete in 1969 (and so was a year older than her), he'd left the island to attend university in Athens, and had lived there ever since. He'd joined the police straight after graduating, working his way up to the sixth-highest rank. There was no further information – not even a photograph.

After grabbing her solid wheeled case from the carousel, Louise walked out into the arrivals hall to see a placard bearing her name. The unshaven, denim-clad man holding it muttered something she couldn't understand before leading her to his car in silence. He held open the front passenger door, but Mangan insisted on sitting in the back, where she would be better able to doze discreetly in preparation for her important rendezvous with the British ambassador, who was coming to meet her at the hotel that afternoon. She wouldn't have her first meeting with Captain Diamantapoulis until the evening.

Driver and passenger remained uncommunicative throughout the hour-long journey. Mangan gave up on a couple of attempts to engage in conversation, preferring to admire the glorious views instead. She'd been here often enough to know the characteristics of the typical Cretan taxi driver, and this one was no exception; he drove too fast and played the radio too loudly. Any attempt at sleep would be futile. When they arrived at the Crystal Beach Hotel, the driver wasted no time in yanking her case out of the boot, and was already wheeling it towards reception before Mangan even had time to gather her things from the back seat, ready to disembark.

'Thank you so much. I'll take that,' she said, catching up and reaching for the case, while simultaneously searching through her purse for a five-euro note to offer as a tip. 'I have to meet a Captain Diamantapoulis this evening. Have you been given a message about where I should meet him?' Mangan asked, proffering the five euros towards the driver as she spoke.

'I am Captain Diamantapoulis,' the man in denim announced, pushing the note away as if it was a toxic substance.

'Oh, my goodness. I'm so sorry. But you didn't say anything.'

'I did. You didn't listen,' he said, wheeling the case through the swing doors and depositing it at the reception desk. 'I will meet you this evening at six-thirty, in the bar.' With that, he turned and left, leaving Mangan still holding the five-euro note, which fluttered in the airstream of his rapid departure.

The ambassador, Sir Ralph Evans, was sitting in the hotel lounge, accompanied by his vice-consul for Crete.

As the two men stood to shake her hand, Mangan asked why they hadn't picked her up from the airport.

'We wanted to,' said the ambassador, 'but Captain Diamantapoulis was adamant that *he* should welcome you. We don't want to upset him, do we?'

'I fear I just have,' Mangan said, with a sigh.

13

MENDING FENCES

'We have a hundred and fifty officers looking for Lordship Bellingham, plus sixty civil guardsmen, fifteen dogs, three drones and two helicopters,' Captain Diamantapoulis was explaining.

Mangan decided that now would not be a good time to tell him that Bellingham was a lord, not a lordship. She was on a charm offensive. The captain had arrived at the hotel bar on time, but his mood seemed to be just as dark as when they'd parted. Having refused a drink, he'd embarked on this inventory in response to Mangan's cheerful 'How's it going?', which had been meant more as a greeting than a request for information.

Having spent many years dealing with the ego of the British male, both privately and professionally, she doubted the Greek version was much different. The captain needed to have his primacy recognised, his masculinity acknowledged. She needed to assure him that she presented no threat. Putting herself in his shoes, she did accept that she'd be miffed if a senior officer from an overseas force arrived to oversee an investigation she was leading, and even more miffed if he'd mistaken her for a taxi driver. But her indignation would be contained; she certainly wouldn't be in a visible strop about it, as he seemed to be. Then again, he had come to the airport to greet her personally, and she must have seemed distant and arrogant. He should have been clearer in his introduction or driven a marked police car. It wasn't entirely her fault, but she did feel it was her responsibility to try to repair the damage. All these thoughts had conspired to deprive her of sleep during the two hours she'd had to herself between meeting the ambassador that afternoon and the captain this evening. After getting showered and dressed, she'd come down to the bar, hoping that a drink and a smile would help to establish a reasonable working relationship with this difficult man. But not only was he not drinking, he wasn't smiling either.

'Look, Petros,' she said, using the form of address he'd told her he preferred. 'I'm not here to interfere, only to assist. Your government and mine both think it may be helpful to have somebody from the Metropolitan Police here for you to liaise with.' She lifted her glass of ouzo from the small round zinc table at which they were sitting, facing out across the Libyan Sea. A gentle breeze scented with faskomilo and thyme drifted in through the double doors that opened on to the terrace. 'I'm so sorry about what happened earlier. Can't we be friends?' she asked, giving what she considered to be her sweetest smile.

'I'm sorry, but I have to go now, or else I would have dinner with you to tell you more. We now have something of the lordship's that we can give to the dogs to help them, and I promised to be there this evening. You need sleep tonight, and tomorrow we start work.'

'At least have a beer before you go?'

'Not when I drive – but of course we are friends,' he said, with no conviction whatsoever, as he got up to leave.

'The lordship set off from here, to walk to here.'

It was early on the day following Mangan's arrival and Captain Petros Diamantapoulis was pointing out the course that Lord Bellingham had been following the previous Wednesday. They were in the tiny head-quarters of the Port Authority in Agia Galini, which had been commandeered to be Diamantapoulis's inves-tigation HQ. It was only a couple of blocks away from the Crystal Beach Hotel, but the captain had insisted on walking her here rather than just giving directions. She wasn't sure if she was being accompanied or chap-eroned. Now he stood in front of a large map of the island, using a long piece of cane as a pointer.

'From Hora Sfakion here, up to Georgioupoli,' the captain was saying, 'where his wife was to pick him up at 8pm. They had planned dinner in Amari on the way back to their house, which is about three kilometres out-side Agia Galini. He was dressed in shorts, a thin shirt, light jacket and walking boots. A distinctive red safety helmet was on his head, and he was carrying a small knapsack containing only bottled water and his phone.'

'Have we tracked the phone?' Mangan interrupted, and immediately wished she hadn't.

Captain Diamantapoulis gave her a look of surprise mingled with disdain. 'Of course, we tracked the phone,' he said, eventually. 'Do you think we are primitives here?'

'I didn't mean any offence,' Mangan said, apologetically. 'It's just that in England it took a long time to adapt to the digital world we now live in,' she added, stretching the truth in the service of diplomacy.

An ancient ceiling fan, the room's only defence against the already claustrophobic heat, creaked round a few more times before the captain spoke again.

'I was sent here from Athens on Friday 4 August. By next day, we had located the phone here.' He pointed to a mountainous area on the map. 'His wife tells us he liked to stop to take lots of photographs to record his journeys. His phone was found on the mountainside. There are two possibilities; he stopped to take a photo and fell, dropping his phone on the way down, or he dropped the phone and walked on.'

'Nothing found in the vicinity?'

'No, but it's very difficult terrain: wild, overgrown. Good for goats but not for people. We concentrated on this area for four days and found nothing. But can I honestly say we scoured every inch? No, I cannot. It took a while to get something of his to give the dogs a scent. Lady Bellingham is not the easiest woman to deal with. Yesterday evening, she gave us one of his sweaters, and it gave the dogs a scent, but is very difficult. This is not your Hyde Park, as you will see, because we go there now; then I take you to meet Mrs Bellingham – the ladyship.'

They set off in a police jeep, with Diamantapoulis driving and his British visitor in the front passenger seat. He had made a point of asking Mangan if she'd prefer to travel in the back, but she'd ignored this acerbic reference to their trip from the airport and climbed in next to him. Were it not for the vehicle's police nomenclature, Petros and Louise could easily have been mistaken for holidaymakers setting off on an exploration of the island.

The captain wore the same blue denim jeans as on the previous day, with a fresh short-sleeved checked shirt. He was the same height as Mangan, with a thick thatch of dark, wiry hair. His hazel eyes were deep-set, and with those jagged cheek bones, Mangan thought his craggy looks matched the contours of the landscape. She wore beige shorts with a brown sleeveless vest, her hair pulled back and bunched. She'd been told to dress for comfort, and given the extreme August heat, was happy to comply.

Mangan had driven across many mountainous regions of Crete on holiday over the years, but always on main roads. Rudimentary as these sometimes were, they were like autobahns compared with the dirt tracks they were speeding down now. Diamantapoulis drove in silence, ignoring his passenger, who eventually decided to at least have a stab at conversation.

'Your English is perfect. Did you study in Britain?' she asked.

'No, I never set foot in England. I went to Athens University. Study your language there.'

'But you were born in Crete?'

'Yes, I am Cretan. Born in Sitia, in the east of the island. None of my ancestors ever leave. I left when I was nineteen and never lived here since.'

'But it's not as if you went abroad. You stayed in Greece,' Mangan observed.

'You are right, of course, but for Cretans, Greece is another country.'

'What about your parents? Are they still here?' Mangan asked, eager to continue her interview, which was helping to distract her thoughts from the vertiginous feeling in her stomach.

'My father was a teacher here, my mother a nurse. Both are dead now. I have a brother in Sitia and a sister in Chania, so I come here to see them sometimes.'

'With your wife?' Mangan flushed even as she asked this unnecessarily personal question. 'I just wondered if you came on family holidays here. I do; I first came twenty years ago,' she added hastily.

The question remained unanswered as the captain took a tight bend while simultaneously speaking in Greek to a colleague on the two-way radio attached to the dashboard. Mangan flinched as the vehicle skirted the edge of yet another sharp bend. They seemed to have been ascending for ages, but the track was now beginning to level out, and Louise could see a cluster of police cars and yellow emergency vehicles ahead. A helicopter was flying low over the valley below. It seemed so long since she'd asked the question that the answer, when it came, seemed more like a random statement.

'Once I came here with my wife, but now I am divorced,' Diamantapoulis said, pulling into the side and applying the handbrake without glancing at the woman beside him.

It was 10am, and the sun was already high as Mangan looked down from the edge of the mountain track where they were standing. Below was a vast, sumptuously verdant valley; in front of them, the stark beauty of the Lefka Ori, the White Mountains, rising majestically through the heat haze.

'From where the phone was located down there,' Captain Diamantapoulis said, pointing to a staked-out area about seventy metres further down the slope, 'we calculate it must be here that he stopped to take a photograph.'

'It's certainly a view worth capturing,' Mangan said.

Looking down at the many uniformed officers scouring the land below, she could see that the drop wasn't sheer. The terrain sloped away gradually from the road into the bushes and trees that covered the mountainside. It would be possible for somebody to lose their footing and remain upright until they reached the first clump of bushes. Their problem would be getting enough purchase in the loose scree to climb back up again, particularly if they'd been injured. A search of the area surrounding where the phone had been found had yielded nothing. This implied that Bellingham's momentum had carried him much further down the mountain. The other alternative, Mangan thought, was that he'd searched in vain for the phone before deciding to move on without it. She was in the middle of relaying these observations to the captain as carefully as she could, desperate not to seem like someone giving a demonstration of egg-sucking to their grandmother, when she saw someone in a white uniform marching towards them: a small, overweight man whose tunic carried an array of badges and stars. A retinue of underlings scampered behind him.

Accosting Diamantapoulis with a volley of rapid-fire Greek that seemed to sap his strength, the man looked even smaller by the end of the tirade than he had at the beginning. Diamantapoulis, towering above his assailant, replied softly in the same language, before switching to English in order to introduce his guest.

'This is Assistant Commissioner Mangan from New Scotland Yard,' he announced. 'Miss Mangan, allow me to present Inspector General Kostar Pelkas.'

Mangan held out her hand, which the inspector general ignored, refusing to look in her direction as he began firing off what sounded like a fresh barrage of invective. The captain listened patiently, hands on hips, looking down, his face turned away from his persecutor, half towards Mangan. To her surprise and delight, she saw him send a surreptitious wink in her direction.

Back in the jeep, on their way to see Lady Bellingham, Captain Diamantapoulis explained that Inspector
General Pelkas was the senior officer responsible for
the whole of southern Greece, covering regions like the
Peloponnese and the Ionian islands as well as Crete.

'He is a ridiculous man, promoted on patronage and
seniority rather than ability.'

'He certainly seems to resent my presence,' Mangan
said.

'Let me assure you, he resents *my* presence. The
added problem here is that Kostar Pelkas is Cretan. The
old Cretan Gendarmerie was fiercely independent and
had a proud history prior to the Hellenic Police being
created about forty years ago. So even if that little fat
fellow wasn't the inspector general, the local police
would still resent us being here.'

'He's of a higher rank than you?'

'Oh yes, much higher. There is an inspector general
for the north and one for the south, and there are very
few ranks above them. The problem for Kostar, though,
is that I am here on the authority of the commander
himself.'

'And what were you being lectured about, if you
don't mind me asking?'

'Of course, I don't mind you asking, so long as you
don't want word for word. I wasn't listening for half
the time. But in short, he thinks I am looking in the
wrong place. He believes we should be concentrating
over towards Lake Kournas. One of the drones picked
up a lone man heading down off the main road towards

the lake. I have tried to explain that the timeline is all wrong. That drone footage was two days ago. If Bellingham was on the main road so long after his disappearance, we would not need to be searching for him. If he was at Lake Kournas, he wouldn't be lost. It is a big tourist destination.'

'And your inspector general knows where the phone was found?'

'Yes, but for Kostar it is still the 1970s, and mobile phones do not exist. He doesn't understand its significance.'

'Where is the phone?' Mangan asked.

'Safe under lock and key. I have to go back to Athens tomorrow. I plan to take it with me for our forensics people to examine.'

'Can I have a look at it?'

'Yes, of course. You may well understand the things on it better than me. I'll arrange this for you and get it sent on to Athens afterwards.'

Mangan was relieved that the captain had accepted her request with no sign of resentment.

'One thing I tell you now, though, in case it's what you were thinking. If he stopped to take a photograph, he either dropped the phone or lost his footing before he could take it, because there isn't a photo of that view on the phone. It was the first thing I check.'

After ten minutes of driving in silence, the captain said: 'You have seen where phone was found. Is there anything you want to ask?'

'Where's the nearest habitation?'

'Apart from some shelters that the shepherds use, there's nothing for miles. As you could see, we have men looking everywhere in the valley, but it's like that phrase you use, a needle in a haystack? It is entirely possible for somebody to disappear completely in this land.'

'And why are you going back to Athens tomorrow?'

'I will only be gone for few days. I must attend court on a case I was involved in, but my deputy on this search, Lieutenant Despina Nati, will be looking after you. She is a very experienced officer, and I specifically asked for her to assist me here.'

'It's good to know you have women in senior positions here,' Louise said, as they pulled into the driveway leading up to the Bellinghams' villa.

'Not here in Crete, no. A woman like Despina can rise through the ranks on the mainland, but here is more traditional.'

'More backward,' Mangan suggested.

'More traditional,' the captain said again.

14

A VISIT WORTH MAKING

Assistant Commissioner Mangan's immediate impression of Miranda Bellingham was that she could have stepped straight from the pages of one of those posh women's magazines like *Tatler* or *The Lady*. She was a few years younger than Mangan, but they were of the same generation, having both grown up in an age of expanding horizons for women without most of the extraordinary restrictions their mothers and grandmothers had had to face. But Louise sensed that this woman belonged in a different age. She had mingled with enough aristocrats to know that Miranda Bellingham wasn't one, but her superior demeanour and understated elegance made the assistant commissioner in her shorts and the captain in his jeans feel as if they had come to clean the swimming pool.

Mangan introduced herself, explaining her role and making clear that it did not in any way usurp the command of Captain Diamantapoulis. She felt that emphasising this was as important to her relationship with him as it was to making sure Lady Bellingham appreciated the importance the Metropolitan Police placed upon this case.

'I've already told your colleague here as much as I know about the route Edward took. What more can I say?'

They were sitting under the shade of an enormous parasol on the wide, sun-drenched terrace. The captain finished explaining the extent of the search and conveying the disappointing news that they'd found nothing so far. Sensing that she was given licence to intervene, Mangan took the initiative. 'Just for my benefit,' she began, 'could you run through the events since your husband arrived back here.'

'Since he arrived, or since he set out for his hike last Wednesday?'

'Since he arrived, if you wouldn't mind.'

Lady Bellingham gave a little sigh of exasperation. 'Edward arrived back on Monday, and I picked him up from the airport as I always do.'

'What time?' Mangan asked rather abruptly.

'Oh, I don't know. Let's say 4pm. Time passes very slowly here and we're not slaves to our watches and clocks. It was the usual time for his plane to land, and I brought him straight back here.'

'And then?'

'Well, then we chatted over a drink before I cooked the dinner, and we went to bed at around ten.'

'And on Tuesday?'

'I really don't see the relevance of this at all,' Lady Bellingham complained. 'The captain here didn't ask me all these silly questions.'

She'd turned in her seat to face Diamantapoulis,

probably expecting him to back her up. But he sat impassively watching the two women with no obvious intention of intervening.

'I'm so sorry, Lady Bellingham, but it's important for me to understand your husband's state of mind; to know if anything happened that might throw a light on his disappearance,' Mangan explained patiently.

'Absolutely nothing happened. Edward was tired and stressed, as he always is when he gets back from London. All he wanted to do on Tuesday was chill out. He's had problems with a development his company is involved in, and that's been playing on his mind, but he'd made some progress on that before leaving England and, as usual, the more time he spent here, the more the tension drained out of him. Early on Wednesday, I drove him to Hora Sfakion and off he went. This is all so distressing. Surely your time would be better spent looking for my husband,' Lady Bellingham concluded, turning her face away from her visitors to gaze over the forest of cypress trees towards the sea.

'And you arranged to meet again in Georgioupoli that evening?' Mangan pressed on, ignoring her host's open display of exasperation.

'Yes, we've done this a lot. I've never hiked in my life and don't intend to take it up now, but Edward loves it. I take him to wherever the route starts, and I'm there to pick him up where it ends.'

'And what did you do in the meantime?'

'With the greatest respect, Assistant Commissioner Mangan, I do not see the relevance of that question.'

'I was wondering what would have happened if your husband decided to abort his plans for some reason – where would you have been? At home?'

'No. As it happens, we have some friends in Hora Sfakion, and I went to see them before taking a leisurely drive across to the place we were due to meet, a five-star hotel on the beachfront at Georgioupoli. There's a spa there, and I was planning on getting some treatments.'

'And I suppose he would have had trouble calling you, having lost his mobile phone,' Mangan added helpfully.

'Yes – what's been happening with the mobile phone? Surely you should be concentrating your search on where that was found,' Lady Bellingham snapped back.

'We are, but this is the first time we meet since we traced it,' Diamantapoulis said to her gently.

'And I'm very grateful to you, Captain, for ringing to tell me. It gave me some hope.'

Mangan could tell that their host much preferred dealing with men, and that her arrival wasn't entirely welcome, but that it was nothing personal: just the same old bias towards the masculine that she'd grown used to in police work over the years.

'Are you here alone?' Mangan asked.

'Yes. My mother came to pick up the twins the other week. They've gone back to England to stay with my parents for a few weeks. The idea was for them to come back next week, so that Edward had time to wind down properly before we spent the rest of August together as a family. I'm entirely on my own. Can't even offer you a cup of tea, I'm afraid, because I haven't got any help at the moment, either.'

Mangan felt like asking what was so difficult about sticking a tea bag in a cup and pouring boiling water over it. Instead, she asked: 'Don't you normally have an au pair to help?'

'Yes, we had a nanny – Sharron, an English girl from Newcastle who'd been with me and the twins since they were a year old. We've spent every summer out here together since then, but unfortunately I had to dismiss her.'

Lady Bellingham explained how she and her husband had discovered that Sharron Fuller was bringing her boyfriend into the villa and using it for her romantic trysts. 'I had cause to search through the rubbish one day, looking for something I feared I'd thrown out by mistake, when I found a used condom. We don't use them,' she said, adding more information than was necessary. 'Edward was already suspicious, because he'd noticed some scuffing on the worktop in front of the kitchen window. It turned out to be where lover-boy was coming in while we were out. This place has security cameras everywhere. The Foreign Office insisted on it when Edward became a minister. This chap of Sharron's had found a way to evade the one at the back by scrambling in and out of the kitchen window.'

'Do you know who he is?' Mangan asked.

'Oh yes, we identified him alright. Edward fitted a hidden camera in the kitchen, focused directly on the window. When we came back from dinner one night, we checked the footage, and there was Hassan.'

'Who?' the two officers asked simultaneously.

'Hassan. I'm sorry, I don't know his surname. He's a Libyan lad who Sharron persuaded me to take on to do a bit of gardening. He'd certainly been doing plenty of seeding with her.' Lady Bellingham's bawdy chuckle seemed completely inappropriate given the circumstances.

'Can we see the film?' Diamantapoulis asked.

'Of course, but why? What's this got to do with Edward's disappearance?'

Mangan interjected. 'Probably nothing, but you'll understand that we need to examine every possibility.'

'And you actually believe it's possible that Hassan could be involved in my husband's disappearance? That's ridiculous. Edward is lost, and my fear is that he's fallen into that gorge near the spot where his phone was found. It's where he liked to stop, because there's a really good view of the White Mountains, but it's a sheer drop into the valley. He must have fallen – and if he's fallen, he'll be injured . . .' Lady Bellingham's voice trailed away as she turned her attention back to the view across the cypress trees. Mangan, suspecting that a tear may have emerged behind the designer sunglasses, reached over to pat the other woman's arm, which was immediately jerked away, leaving Mangan in no doubt that her sympathy was unwelcome. There was an uncomfortable silence.

'Do you know where this girl Sharron is now?' the captain asked eventually.

'Yes, she popped back to collect some stuff she'd left behind – last Tuesday, as it happens, while Edward was here. She's up in Chania working as a waitress. She gave me the name of the restaurant so that I could forward any letters. She was very contrite, and I was almost tempted to take her back on, but Edward would never have agreed. Besides, she's still with Hassan. He'd driven her over, and she told me he was outside waiting. I was not going to allow my house to be used for sordid purposes again.' Lady Bellingham rose from her chair. 'I'll get you the address of the restaurant and that footage of Hassan that you wanted,' she said, moving gracefully across the terrace.

'Just one final question,' Mangan called towards Miranda's retreating back. 'Was this route one that your husband devised?'

'No. It was one suggested to him by Dimitri, the restaurant man in Agia Galini.'

As they drove away, the assistant commissioner and the police captain compared notes. They agreed that Diamantapoulis would check the clear image of Hassan climbing through the kitchen window against police records in Athens the next day, and that Lieutenant Nati would take Mangan to Chania to speak to Sharron Fuller. In the unlikely event that Bellingham's disappearance had a sinister motivation, both Sharron and the phone could provide important clues. They both felt that Dimitri Limnios, the restaurant owner, should be asked to help. If he knew the route well, he would know the parts that may be particularly dangerous.

'Well, that was certainly a visit worth making,' Mangan said. 'We make a good double act.'

If she hoped this would provoke a cheerful rapport with the man next to her, the ploy failed dismally. Diamantapoulis stared straight ahead, his brow knitted, without so much as an acknowledgement.

'Is something the matter?' Mangan asked before adding a cheery: 'Was it something I said?'

'There was something – but not what *you* say,' he replied as they were driving into Agia Galini. There was a delay as the captain appeared to grapple with his thoughts before continuing. 'It was something *she* say. I don't know yet – I have to check.' He steered the jeep into the car park of the Crystal Beach Hotel before adding, 'But you're right.' Just as she thought he was agreeing with her comment about them making a good double act, he finished, 'It *was* a visit worth making.'

As he turned to face her, Mangan noticed he was smiling. It seemed to her as if a soft light had been switched on in a dark room.

15

COAST TO COAST

Lieutenant Nati told Mangan how she'd insisted that the two women undertake this mission to Chania unaccompanied. 'I don't know how it is in Britain, but here the police believe that unless a man is there to guide woman officers, they will be, what's your saying, damsels in distress?'

They were driving across the island with Nati at the wheel of the little police jeep that Captain Diamantapoulis had left in her charge. Soon, they'd be on the main E75 highway, skirting the sea all the way to the metropolis of Chania. It was another glorious day, the dense heat broken only by the occasional cooling breeze becoming stronger the closer they got to the north coast.

Louise was surprised to see that, in contrast to the captain the day before, Lieutenant Nati was wearing police uniform: a blue blouse with her police badge pinned to the breast pocket, navy trousers and a light zipped jacket. Mangan also noticed a pistol strapped to Nati's belt.

It was difficult to hear each other speak above the noise of the engine as they drove, all windows down, with the flapping canvas roof in place to protect them from the sun.

'I don't think I've ever been described as a damsel, but some men in the Met have certainly caused me distress,' Mangan responded, straining to be heard. 'I have to say, your captain caused me some the way he drove down these mountain roads yesterday. You are definitely a big improvement, Lieutenant Nati.'

'Please, call me Despina.'

By the time they turned on to the main highway, the two women had bonded. Despina Nati was seven years Louise Mangan's junior, and a good inch shorter for each year. Her thick black hair was cut short, framing a face that, with its dark eyes and clear olive skin, was strikingly beautiful. Overweight, particularly around the hips, the lieutenant was clearly more comfortable behind the wheel than she had been on foot. Even the short walk from the hotel to the jeep that morning had caused her to puff and wheeze.

Nati explained that the perfect English she spoke was the result of two years spent at a language school in Brighton as part of her education. Married to a fellow Athens police officer, she had a four-year-old daughter.

'Without my mother looking after her, it would be impossible for us both to work.'

'And you work with Captain Diamantapoulis in Athens?' Mangan asked, hoping that she'd got the pronunciation of the captain's name right.

'Yes, Petros and I work together. He is not one who causes me distress.'

'I fear that the captain and I didn't get off to a good start,' Mangan said, and explained how she had mistaken him for a taxi driver.

Lieutenant Nati roared with laughter. 'That wouldn't have helped,' she agreed.

'No, and I guess he was bound to resent my presence here.'

'Yes, frankly. But it's nothing to do with you being a woman. It's natural. The Crete police resent us being sent here from Athens, and we resent you coming from London. It's nothing personal, and Petros is a realist. This man who is missing is very important, yes? A lord no less. If a Greek politician was missing in England, nothing would stop us sending someone to you.'

They drove in silence for a few minutes before Mangan asked, 'Do you like Petros?'

'I like him, and I respect him. We all do. Petros should be major general by now. But I am one rank below him, and there are five or six above. His problem is, he defends the ones below and argues with the ones above. If people are fools, he tells them. That is not a good thing to do in the Hellenic Police Force.'

'He told me his marriage broke up.'

'Did he?' Nati said in surprise. 'He doesn't usually talk about it.'

'Well, he wasn't exactly effusive on the subject. I had asked a leading question.'

'Did he tell you about his daughter?'

Mangan said he hadn't, and for the next five miles of the journey, Lieutenant Nati explained how

Diamantapoulis and his wife had tried to start a family for many years, resorting in the end to a type of IVF treatment known as intracytoplasmic sperm injection. He'd persuaded his wife to undertake the treatment and she'd conceived, but their daughter was born with severe mental deficiencies.

'Petros insisted that they try to care for the child at home, and they had all kinds of modifications made to accommodate her, but the poor kid can't speak or hear, and as she got older, the burden became too much. Little Delia had to go into care and the marriage broke up. Petros goes to see his daughter every day when he can. He'll go there today after the court case; it is the main reason he goes back. But Maria, his wife, never visits the child. She blames Petros for persuading her to have the treatment, and resents him being at work for so much of the time when she was looking after Delia at home. She has remarried and wants to forget their time together. It's very sad.'

By now, they were in a stream of traffic heading through the bustling outskirts of Chania towards the seafront. In the spring, when Mangan usually took her holidays in Crete, the waterside cafés and restaurants of Chania were fairly busy; now, at the height of the season, they were a jostling mass of tourists, mainly German and British, but with lots of Swedes and French and a sprinkling of Americans.

The policewoman parked the jeep in a side street, and they joined the throng strolling leisurely towards lunch. Restaurant after restaurant in a wide crescent around the walled Venetian harbour touted for custom. Along the seafront itself, modest fishing vessels were moored alongside luxury yachts, bobbing gently on the placid waters. An elderly accordionist sat in the shade of a boat shed playing the same tune repeatedly as his cap, strategically upturned in front of him, accumulated coins.

The Amphora, where Sharron Fuller worked, was one of the most popular restaurants, specialising in seafood and traditional Cretan dishes. It was one o'clock, the hour at which the lunchtime trade was reaching its peak. In her light skirt and top, Mangan looked like any other holidaymaker, but the lieutenant was incongruous in her police uniform, albeit with the jacket removed. When they reached the Amphora, Nati went straight to the kitchens to speak to the proprietor, while Mangan stood near the menu board of the open-fronted restaurant amid a small knot of holidaymakers, who were scrutinising the fare and deciding if it was worth queueing for a seat. Amongst the six or seven waiting staff, Sharron self-identified almost immediately, her Geordie accent discernible above the hubbub as she laughed and joked with a tableful of Brits she was serving.

Mangan saw a short, heavy-set man, obviously the proprietor, emerge at the back and beckon Sharron across while holding open the long Perspex strips that separated the kitchens from the dining area. As Lieutenant Nati sidled into view beside him, Sharron suddenly took to her heels, throwing down the pad and pen with which she'd been taking orders, and pushing through the densely packed tables to reach the concourse. Mangan, reacting quickly and kicking off her beach shoes to run barefoot, was within ten feet before the waitress even knew she was being chased, Sharron's short legs proving no match for her pursuer's athletic stride.

'It would be best if you come quietly,' Mangan murmured into Sharron's ear, guiding her firmly back towards the restaurant.

In the absence of a police station in the vicinity, Nati had commandeered a room at the rear of the tourist information centre set inside a former mosque along the harbourside. The two policewomen wanted to know why Sharron had run away. After an initial mute defiance, the girl was soon in floods of tears, admitting that she'd stolen cash from the restaurant at her boyfriend's behest. When she'd seen Nati, she'd assumed the theft had been discovered and that the police had come to arrest her.

'Is your boyfriend's name Hassan?' Mangan asked gently.

Sharron nodded.

'How much did you steal?'

'Not much; thirty euros or so. I took ten a day over three days last week and gave it straight to Hassan. I knew he was using it to buy drugs, but what could I do? He's all I've got, and he said he'd leave me if I didn't do it. I tried to convince him to sell his cameras instead, but he wouldn't – he obviously thinks more of those bloody cameras than he does of me.'

'Well, it was a foolish thing to do, but it's not what we came to see you about. Where's Hassan now?'

It took a few more minutes and many more tears to elicit from Sharron that Hassan had abandoned her anyway.

'I spoke to Lady Bellingham yesterday,' Mangan said. 'She told us all about the circumstances of your dismissal, and that you went back to the villa last Tuesday. Was Hassan with you?'

'Yes, but he stayed in the car at the bottom of the drive. He wanted me to pick up the things I'd left behind, like my radio and hairdryer, so he could sell them. After I was sacked, me and Hassan had come up here to the big city, and I got this job straight away and a flat in the old town. I never wanted to see the Bellinghams again, but he insisted I go back for those things. He was acting strange from the minute I got back to his car after seeing Lady Bellingham. The next day, he was gone.'

'How were the Bellinghams?' Mangan asked.

'She was the same patronising bitch she's always been. Didn't see much of Edward. He was out on the terrace, taking the sun, and she took me into the kitchen, almost as if she wanted to remind me how Hassan used to come in through the window.'

'You arrived unannounced?'

'Oh no, it was her who suggested I come over on that Tuesday, after I'd texted her to ask if I could collect my stuff. It's really terrible that Edward has disappeared.'

'You know about that?'

'The whole island knows about it. I knew he was planning his walk for August, but I never thought there was any danger in it. I won't be going on any walks in the White Mountains, I can tell you. I don't like Lord B, but I wouldn't wish that upon him.'

It was obvious that Sharron had little respect for her former employers.

'But why did you stay with them so long if you disliked them so much?' Mangan asked, purely out of interest.

'I love the twins and I love this island and I loved Hassan,' was her succinct response. 'I don't think she'd mind too much if they never find her husband,' she added.

Mangan, surprised by this blunt statement, sought an explanation.

'I'm pretty sure she's having it off with someone,' Sharron said.

'Who?'

'I don't know, but I heard her on the phone once when she thought I was out. She was being very affectionate to somebody, and it certainly wasn't her husband. She never spoke to him like that. No, this person, whoever it was, had her all lovey-dovey. I disturbed her a couple of times – not deliberate, like, I'd just walk into a room where she was, and she'd go all red and rush out on the terrace with the phone glued to her ear.'

Sharron was surprised to learn that she hadn't yet been replaced as 'Nanny' and general dogsbody. 'There's a thousand girls who'd jump at the chance of a job like that. The pay's okay, you get to live out here for six months of the year until the kids start school, and those twins are really sweet.'

Mangan mentioned that the children had gone back to England for a few weeks.

'Really? I've been working for the Bellinghams for three years out here, and the kids never go to stay with their nana until late September. I always got the impression that Edward insisted on them being here for the whole of August with him.'

When Lieutenant Nati asked Sharron what she planned to do now, there was another explosion of tears.

'I don't know,' she sobbed. 'I can't go back to Newcastle because Hassan took my passport, and if I lose my job for raiding the till, word will spread and I'll never get another waitressing job here.'

Mangan took Nati to one side for a consultation. 'Of course, Despina, I have no jurisdiction here, but do we really want to criminalise this girl?'

The lieutenant shook her head. 'We don't need her in custody, but we do need Hassan,' she said. 'Not just for Sharron's passport. Petros sent me an email while you were questioning the girl. He has run Hassan's image through police records. His real name is Mohammed Tatanaki. He's already spent time in prison and is now suspected of being involved in trafficking large quantities of cocaine from Benghazi, through Crete and on to the mainland to be distributed across Europe. It looks as if Sharron's boyfriend is a very bad man.'

The two women drove back down to Agia Galini that evening. With Lieutenant Nati's agreement, Louise Mangan had given Sharron fifty euros, telling her to surreptitiously restore it to the restaurant's coffers.

'They probably balance up fortnightly or even monthly, so if you return whatever you took, nobody will be any the wiser,' Mangan suggested. 'I've given you more than you need. Spend anything left over on yourself.'

Sharron Fuller was pathetically grateful, swearing that she would repay the money and never do anything like it again. Mangan told her that she'd be staying at the Crystal Beach Hotel in Agia Galini, and made Sharron promise to contact her or Lieutenant Nati if Hassan showed up again.

'He's dangerous,' Nati had emphasised. 'If you help, we can get you home to England whenever you want to go, whether you have a passport or not.'

Before leaving, the lieutenant had gone to the restaurant with Sharron to tell the owner a story she'd invented about Sharron being in an abusive relationship and not wanting her boyfriend to think she'd reported him to the police. This explained the waitress's sudden flight and Nati emphasised that it was the boyfriend they were after not Sharron.

During the journey to Agia Galini, the two women reflected on their decision to help the girl rather than arrest her.

'I hope I haven't created problems for you in the future, Despina. I just sensed that making a criminal of Sharron wouldn't do anyone any good.'

'I don't know what it's like in England, but here almost every woman in prison would be better to be outside. Of course, that's true for many of the men as well, but so many girls like Sharron are in trouble because of what a man makes them do,' the lieutenant said. Then, after a few more miles, she added: 'Anyway, it has cost you fifty euros, not me.'

Louise smiled. 'Money well spent. I've got a feeling everything will go fine for Sharron – unless Hassan turns up again.'

16

ANOTHER DINNER AT DIMITRI'S

After returning to Agia Galini to drop off her passenger, Lieutenant Nati departed to alert colleagues to the recent presence of Hassan/Mohammed in the Chania area and ensure that the local police in every prefecture of the island were on the lookout for him. She also planned to return to the main search site, having received an initial report that a lot more ground had been covered with still no sign of Lord Bellingham.

'Petros will be back to resume command tomorrow, so I suggest you relax for the rest of the day. You must need to recover from your sprinting,' Nati had said as she dropped her passenger at the Crystal Beach Hotel.

'I wasn't the hundred metres sprint champion at the Metropolitan Police Athletics Day for nothing,' Louise told her new Greek friend.

She decided to use the afternoon to look at Bellingham's mobile phone; the captain had left it at the port authority office for her to examine. There'd be a couple of hours spare before she was due to receive a call from the commissioner, which was arranged for 6pm. Captain Diamantapoulis wouldn't return to the island until late that evening and they wouldn't meet until the morning, so Mangan thought she might try to get a Friday night table at Dimitri's, albeit a table for one. She was in a celebratory mood but unsure why. There wasn't anyone to feel celebratory with, but that was nothing new. It had gone well that day; a bond had been forged with Despina Nati, and not being sure how much longer she'd spend on the island, it seemed acceptable to visit her favourite restaurant, which was only a short walk away. She had to eat somewhere, she reasoned to herself, and she might pick up something useful about the route that Dimitri had devised for Lord Bellingham, although she knew she couldn't do any formal questioning of the restaurateur in the absence of the captain.

At the little port office, she was subjected to a fair degree of bureaucracy before being able to get her surgically gloved hands on Lord Bellingham's phone. She had an uncomfortable feeling of intrusiveness about scrolling through the private emails and text messages, but knew it was a job that had to be done. Forensics in Athens would examine the DNA and fingerprints as well as recovering deleted items. Mangan therefore confined herself to checking the call history and listening to the voicemail messages. Most recently, they were a mixture of bland office calls from civil servants in London, left before they knew their minister had gone missing, and increasingly frantic calls from Lady Bellingham as she waited for her husband to arrive in Georgioupoli at the end of his hike. Louise checked the photographs. The captain had already told her there weren't any from where the phone was found, but she'd expected to see a few from the first part of the walk and was surprised not to find any.

By six o'clock, she was in her room at the hotel and speaking to her boss.

'We've had to give details of Lord Bellingham's disappearance to the media,' the commissioner told her with a sigh. 'It'll mean you have lots of reporters getting in your way over there, but after nine days, we really had no choice. Do you think there's a chance he's still alive in those mountains?'

'I think if that's where he is, he could well still be alive.'

'What do you mean "if"? Surely there's no other explanation?' the commissioner said.

'In all probability, he's lost in the White Mountains, but abduction and even murder can't be ruled out,' Mangan said.

'Why do you say that, Louise? I was hoping this would be a calming phone call at the end of a frantic week, and here you are telling me a government minister may have been bumped off.'

Mangan, worried that she may have over-speculated, sought to reassure him. 'I'm only emphasising the unlikeliest possibility because nobody's found a trace of him yet. But you're right, the most probable explanation is that he's fallen or got lost or both. The search is impressively thorough, but it's hard-going in such densely planted shrubland over such a vast area. As one of the police officers I'm working with says, it's "needle in haystack" territory.'

'How are you getting on with our Greek friends?'

'Well, you know me – ever the diplomat.'

'And you've met the real diplomats, the ambassador and his team?'

'Yes, I have. Sir Ralph Evans is a bit pompous, but it was a perfectly pleasant meeting. There's a consulate here on the island and I'm working closely with them.'

'I believe it's a vice consulate actually, Louise, although I can't imagine there's much vice to deal with over there.'

Mangan smiled, pleased that George Irvine was sufficiently relaxed to be jocular.

'I'm not so sure. I've only been here two days, and so far, as well as a missing peer of the realm, I've encountered a theft, an intrusion and a drug smuggler.'

'You just concentrate on the missing peer. I'll leave it to you to judge when your presence there is no longer necessary, but I never envisaged you being in Crete beyond the end of the month.'

'Message received and understood, Boss,' Mangan said. 'I'll try not to start enjoying myself.'

It was difficult for the assistant commissioner not to enjoy herself that evening as she ate al fresco at Dimitri's. She had managed to book a table on the understanding that it would be vacated by nine. The early reservation suited Mangan. She was happy to make way for others to commandeer her table at a more traditional time for dining on Crete, and for Dimitri Limnios to get a double booking.

The restaurant's owner was giving his usual performance – extravagantly welcoming regular customers at the door, taking the bill to those he chose to converse with, flirting with the more attractive women, displaying a macho jocularity towards their husbands and boyfriends. *So much for Chloe's nonsense about him fancying me*, Louise thought, as Dimitri, reeking of cologne and with his shirt cuffs pulled back so the Rolex was on full display, silently ticked off her name before delegating a young waitress to lead her to the table. Louise wasn't surprised that he hadn't acknowledged her; she knew an insincere show-off when she saw one. It was Dimitri's restaurant she'd come to admire, not the man himself.

At the height of the season, the restaurant had to extend into the garden area. The table allocated to Louise was at the periphery of this additional space. While it offered a lovely view across the sea in one direction, to her right was a view of the rubbish bins and a ramshackle array of abandoned outhouses. In different circumstances, she might have asked for another table, but she felt privileged to even be here and was in no mood to be argumentative. A soft breeze floated up from the sea, carrying the scent of honey blossom; the sky was a blanket of scattered stars. On such a night, in such a place, she felt she could easily put up with the occasional disruption as staff from the kitchen came out to empty rubbish into the bins.

Hers seemed to be the only single-occupancy table. The others were full of tanned holidaymakers in groups or couples. She was used to dining alone, but found herself imagining what it would be like to share a table with Captain Diamantapoulis. It was not an unpleasant notion, and was less unlikely, Mangan felt, because they had now begun to have a reasonable working relationship. She'd been moved by what Lieutenant Nati had told her about the captain's commitment to his severely disabled little girl, feeling that it went some way towards explaining his dour demeanour.

She turned her mind to Lady Bellingham and what Sharron had said about her having a secret lover. Girls in Sharron's position rarely had much affection for their employer. The relationship was too much like mistress and servant for it to be anything other than distant. And what if Miranda Bellingham did have a lover? She was an attractive woman who spent most of her time alone on this gorgeously sensuous island. An extramarital affair was hardly unusual in such circumstances. Why should it raise any suspicions about the missing government minister? Unless the secret lover was Dimitri, the man who had calculated the route on which Lord Bellingham had gone missing. Louise wondered what it was that Lady Bellingham had said that Captain Diamantapoulis had found so interesting. Whatever it was, it hadn't registered with her. Perhaps she'd been less attentive than she should have been. On and on her thoughts ran, as she sat cocooned in the scented warmth of a lovely evening.

She had finished her meal and poured the last of her half bottle of rosé when she heard raised voices from the kitchen area. An old, battered Renault had been driven up from the road, trailing a cloud of dust as it screeched to a halt. She saw a young man in tattered shorts and flip-flops emerge from the car and run into the dilapidated area behind the bins, disappearing from her sightline only to return ten minutes later just as Dimitri appeared at the kitchen door. The restaurant owner, obviously furious about something, began haranguing the young man. It was incongruous to see the normally smooth and stylish Dimitri engaged in such an altercation. Few of the other diners were able to see what was happening, and those who could were too engaged in their own conversations to pay much attention.

Mangan wished she could understand what was being said as the lad in shorts seemed to be forced back into his car by the barrage of abuse that Dimitri was directing at him. Instead of driving away, he sat motionless at the wheel as his assailant strode back into the kitchen, only to emerge five minutes later with a large open box of what looked like produce, which he placed in the car before it was driven off in another swirl of dust and sand.

Mangan's interest was sufficiently aroused to seek an explanation from the waitress when she came over to settle the bill. 'Do you provide a take-away service?' she asked her.

'No, madam, we don't. There are plenty of pizza parlours around if you need take-away.'

'Oh, it's just that I saw a car pull up outside the kitchen and drive away with something.'

'That was one of the Libyan boys. Dimitri was very angry, because he'd taken off his expensive watch to do something in the kitchen and couldn't find it again. When he saw that boy, who is known for stealing, he thought he'd sneaked in and taken it. He insisted the boy stay in his car while he searches some more, and he finds his watch fallen into a vegetable rack; he has made mistake. Dimitri has an allotment ten kilometres from here where fresh food for the restaurant is grown. He is happy to give some of the produce to these boys from Libya, but from allotment – he hates them coming here to restaurant because it disturbs, and we are busy here. But he gives this boy some produce to say sorry for accusing him, but he doesn't want to see him come here again.'

Mangan decided to try her luck. 'Does Hassan come here?' she asked.

'Do you know Hassan?' the girl said.

'Yes, he worked at the villa of a friend of mine on the island.'

'Well, you should know, that was Hassan who came just now.'

Louise hadn't seen the image of Sharron's boyfriend that Lady Bellingham had handed straight to the captain and so said something about not being able to see the boy clearly enough. The girl handed back her debit card and there was no further conversation. Louise texted Despina Nati to tell her that Hassan was back in the vicinity of Agia Galini. As she left, she noticed the waitress in deep conversation with Dimitri at the rear of

the restaurant. She thought she saw a nod in her direction, as if the girl was pointing her out. For the first
time that evening, the restaurant owner appeared to
be taking an interest in the woman who'd dined alone.

As soon as Louise returned to her hotel room, she
went back to work. There were some 'assistant commissioner' tasks that needed to be done, and as Crete
was two hours ahead, it was still only half past six
in London, so those she needed to be in contact with
would probably still be at their desks. Realisation of
the harmful health effects of a culture of long working
hours had yet to permeate New Scotland Yard. Louise
kicked off her shoes and knuckled down to an hour or
two of administrative work, feeling a subliminal need
to justify the lovely dinner she'd just enjoyed.

Most of what she had to do involved routine texts
and emails, in accordance with the bureaucratic nature
of her more exalted position, but there was also a phone
call to make. It was to Detective Inspector Jack Cairns,
who was leading the investigation into the arson attack
in Stoke Newington. Mangan got the boring stuff out
of the way before stepping out on to the large terrace
to gaze over the calm, moonlit sea as the call was con-
nected. She was calling Cairns to discuss whether any
changes needed to be made to the plans already in place
for the visit of Burak Bayram to Stoke Newington on
the evening of 21 September. The incident at Manny's
café had necessitated a rethink. If it was gang-related,
the arrangements need not be disturbed. But if it was

politically motivated, she may have to tighten security, change the venue, or perhaps even try to convince the organisers to postpone the event altogether. The writer's notoriety amongst Turkey's political leaders had been highlighted by a denunciation of his new book by President Erdogan himself, who accused Burak Bayram of being associated with 'communists and anarchists bent on overthrowing the Turkish state'.

When the call was put through, Mangan found Jack Cairns in ebullient mood. He was at the Emirates Stadium. It was half-time and Arsenal were winning two-nil. Mangan and Cairns had worked together a few times in their Met careers, and Cairns had always had an affectionate if irreverent attitude towards Louise that hadn't changed with her promotion, but it never morphed into the misogyny that Mangan had experienced from a minority of colleagues throughout her career. She also felt a great deal of sympathy for Jack because of the way he had been treated over the Danvers business.

'On a junket, are we?' Cairns said, when Mangan told him where she was.

'I wish. This is proper police work, Jack; the kind I trust you're fully engaged with when you're not at the football.'

When they got down to the serious stuff, Cairns was adamant that Burak Bayram's public meeting should go ahead as planned. 'We're confident we know who was responsible for the explosion at the restaurant. It's a bunch of yobs who've probably never read a book in their lives. They don't have any political motivation, and I doubt they know who Bayram is.'

'Is this the gang that was running the protection racket? The ones who call themselves something with "bomb" in it?'

'Yes, the Bombacilar gang. Our problem is we don't have anything on them that would stand up in court.'

'No witness statements about them threatening the café owner?' Mangan asked.

'We've got them from Manny, the proprietor, and his chef. They would testify that these guys were demanding money with menaces. I'm sure they're telling the truth, but the gang leader, a guy by the name of Taylan Ayhan, just says it was a misunderstanding, that he and his mates were fooling around, and it got misconstrued.'

'Strange sense of humour. Don't we have enough for the prosecutor? After all, the café was destroyed just as they threatened, jest or no jest.'

'No. We can't prove they're part of Bombacilar. It's all circumstantial, and there's nothing linking them to the explosion. Indeed, the Turkish lads are claiming to be the injured party, saying that Manny had a grudge against them because they are Muslims, and that he'd refused to serve them. More annoyingly, another potential witness who was in the café when Taylan Ayhan was supposed to have made these threats, one of Manny's friends, says he didn't hear or see anything. Manny wanted us to find this guy, so we did, but he turned out to be no help at all. You might remember him: the one who was with Manny when we arrived at the scene.'

'The tall, dark guy? I thought he was one of the family.'

'So did I, but when he failed to come to the station like he said he would, we went back to Manny. Turns out the guy is a regular customer, but the only thing Manny could tell us about him was that he was Irish and married to a teacher at the local school. So we went to all the schools in the area, asking if there was a teacher married to a man fitting that description. Eventually we came up trumps at Dalston Academy. The guy's teacher wife gave us their address, and we went straight round. All in vain, I'm afraid. This bloke, Brady, said he wasn't close enough to hear the conversation, so could neither verify nor refute Manny's version of events. Really disappointing, but don't worry. As I say, that Bombacilar mob have never had a political thought in their heads, and in any case, we'll probably find some reason to take their leader into custody, even if it's just for the day of Bayram's meeting.'

'That's reassuring. Thanks, Jack.'

'No problem. Have to go. The game's just kicked off again. See you when you get back from your holidays.'

Louise wondered why this Brady chap had made himself so difficult to find. But it was a fleeting thought that vanished in the gentle lapping of the Libyan Sea against the shore below.

17

A MEETING IN THE RED LION

The Bellingham story was headline news in London that Friday. The front page of the *Times* reported it as 'Minister Vanishes on Mountain Walk', while the *Sun* carried a photograph of 'The Disappearing Peer'. The story was a godsend for the papers in what was usually regarded as the 'silly season', when inconsequential items were given undeserved prominence for lack of any substantial news.

One journalist who had a particular interest was Chris Finch, who'd been working on an exposé of Bellingham and had reached the point where he had a story ready to go to print once it had received the necessary legal clearance. A freelance reporter with a fearsome reputation for uncovering the dark secrets of prominent politicians and celebrities, Finch had previously caused the resignation of an ex-defence secretary when he unveiled the politician's acceptance of a substantial gift from an arms manufacturer. The gift hadn't been registered, and would have been disallowed if it had. Finch had worked for months on the story before finally producing the damning evidence in a front-page exclusive for the *Sunday Times*.

That was five years ago, and it had made his name (which was Christopher Finch when he wrote for the broadsheets, and Chris Finch in the tabloids). After that, people with a score to settle had been attracted to Finch like iron filings to a magnet, and he became the grateful recipient of all kinds of juicy gossip. The newspaper he wrote for most often, the *Daily Candour*, a downmarket rag with pretensions, had even provided him with a couple of assistants to sift through all the leads he was receiving in order to sort the lucrative wheat from the more voluminous chaff.

It was Chris Finch who broke the story about a prominent gameshow host having a predilection for hardcore pornography; who exposed the minor royal who'd travelled to Thailand incognito for nefarious purposes; who uncovered the truth about the happily married business tycoon who'd had to resign as President of the CBI over an all-expenses-paid affair with his secretary; who revealed that a senior police officer had covered up a shoplifting offence committed as a juvenile.

For Finch, the disappearance of Lord Edward Bellingham presented a dilemma. He'd been contacted a few months before by a reliable source in the House of Lords, who'd seen evidence that Bellingham was being blackmailed by a woman who claimed that the noble lord had forced himself upon her when she was fifteen years of age. Although Finch had traced the girl involved, the story had yet to attain the level of substantiation required to convince the *Candour* to risk a libel suit by publishing.

Now was undoubtedly the best time for the story to land. Reports of Bellingham's disappearance meant the peer of the realm had reached maximum newsworthiness. This was bound to diminish rapidly as public interest waned and other stories pushed it down the news agenda. Publish the exposé too early and Finch risked his reputation; too late, and it may just make an inside page halfway down. Fears were growing over the minister's safety, and it was important to break the story before a body was found. To publish such revelations in the wake of the discovery of a corpse would be considered bad taste even by the *Daily Candour*.

Such was the quandary facing the intrepid reporter as he sat alone in a corner of the Red Lion in Whitehall. This was his regular workstation. It was perfect for picking up titbits from loose-tongued civil servants and politicians, as the pub lay a matter of yards from Derby Gate, one of the entrances to the Palace of Westminster. It was here in the Red Lion that he'd first heard about the defence secretary's gift, and here that he had been tipped off by a civil servant about the minor royal's journey to Thailand. It was here, too, that he'd acquired a House of Commons pass one evening, when a tipsy MP, keen to ingratiate himself with a reporter whose discretion he may one day need, offered to register Finch as a member of staff. That pass was a godsend, allowing Finch to wander practically anywhere within the sprawling neo-Gothic structure on the north bank of the Thames, a freedom he'd only just returned from exercising. Parliament was in recess and almost empty, but there was often someone around worth talking to, and Finch had been keen to pick up some reaction to the news about Bellingham's disappearance from the people who worked most closely with him in the Lords. It had proved to be a wasted journey, however, and he'd returned sweating from the exertion that even this gentle stroll in the early August heat had caused him.

Finch had never been slim, but over the past few years his waist had seemed to expand with every new front-page story. Swarthy and of average height, he liked to think he resembled Orson Welles, the American film star of the mid-twentieth century. For a while, he'd even grown a beard and taken to wearing a fedora, basing his look on something he remembered the great man appearing in (which turned out to be a sherry advertisement from the 1970s). That fashion phase had passed. He'd long since dispensed with the fedora, but the bulk remained. The numerous pints of Guinness consumed in the Red Lion hadn't helped; neither had the emotional trauma of his divorce. Finch had been married for sixteen years when, one Christmas, he'd arrived home from a work trip abroad to find a Post-it note on the fridge door from his wife. She'd run off with the man from the flat downstairs. The couple had no children and little to show for the years they'd spent together. It was only after his wife had left that Finch realised how fond he'd been of her. At fifty years of age, he had little interest in establishing another relationship, but remained determined to stop the dial on his scales moving beyond eighteen stone, a determination that always involved doing something unspecified at some stage in the future.

As he returned to his corner table in the Red Lion with another pint of the black stuff, his phone pinged to alert him to a new text message: 'Sorry running late will be there by 12.30.' It was from Quentin Kane, Bellingham's solicitor. He'd agreed to meet Finch that day, having spent weeks avoiding him. To get the solicitor's full attention, the journalist had resorted to a white lie hinting that he knew something about the minister's disappearance. In fact, like everyone else, he'd been unaware that Bellingham was even missing, let alone had been gone for more than a week, until the story broke that morning.

At first the Foreign and Commonwealth Office had colluded with the Greek authorities to keep the disappearance under wraps, trying to avoid what the government's communications machine described as 'unhelpful speculation'. They'd managed to keep the lid on things for a while before reports coming back from the island about a large-scale search in the vicinity of the White Mountains had made the obfuscation unsustainable. The government's line now was that the minister had gone hiking across the island, as he'd done many times before, and while it was easy to get lost in that area, there was an abundance of fruit on the trees, there were no predatory animals, and the climate was benign. It wasn't unheard of for hikers to vanish for weeks in the White Mountains, only to eventually be found unharmed.

This development provided a whole new dimension to the scandal that Finch had been carefully piecing together for a couple of months. He knew that what he regarded as typical Foreign and Commonwealth Office sophistry was already impossible to maintain. How could a government minister, albeit a very junior one, remain out of contact for so long? Speculation about Bellingham's fate was already running wild, with the *Daily Candour* leading the way. Tomorrow's edition would carry the banner headline 'End of the Peer?'.

Kane eventually arrived in the Red Lion at 12.40pm. He and Finch had never met, but, as usual, Kane's appearance – the suit, his bearing, the swept-back hair – betrayed his profession. The journalist beckoned him over immediately. With introductory small talk out of the way and a glass of Claret in front of him, the lawyer got down to business.

'We'll sue the arse off you if that rubbish gets printed,' he told Finch, as lightly as if they'd been discussing holiday plans.

'That's hardly an original response, Mr Kane. My story is very robust – and if Bellingham is dead, it doesn't even need to be. As you well know, a dead man can't be defamed.'

Quentin Kane took another sip of wine before responding. 'If he's dead, it could be years before we know. A man once vanished on Crete, and it was ten years before a body was found. You need to exploit your story now if it's to have maximum impact. You'll soon find out how good Chesterton, Kane and Palfrey are at defending against defamation.'

Finch ignored the provocation. 'How much did you know about this incident with the girl?' he asked.

'Only that I presume she was the one making crude attempts at blackmail,' Kane said, going on to tell Finch about the postcard received at his chambers.

'I've actually met her,' the journalist said. 'She's a smart girl if a little under-educated, and her story checks out – the dates, locations, what your noble friend was up to at the time.'

'What did she say happened?' Kane demanded.

'Don't insult my intelligence. You can read all about it in Sunday's paper.'

'Look, Chris – can I call you Chris?'

'Call me anything you like, so long as it's not naive.'

'Look, Chris. The only concern I have is to protect the family. In normal circumstances, Edward Bellingham would be able to defend himself, but you must realise that his disappearance is quite enough for his family to cope with. They can do without this.'

Finch continued to drink his Guinness impassively.

'I was at school with Bellingham, did you know that?' Kane asked.

'Course I did. Couple of Old Wykehamists, aren't you?'

'Yes, we were at Winchester, but we weren't in the same year. It was Miranda, his wife, who was my friend. I actually introduced them. She's at her wits' end with worry. A story like this, at such a time, true or false, would do a great deal of harm.'

'True or false,' Finch repeated. 'So, you're not sure of your ground.'

'I don't even know what he's bloody accused of,' Kane said, allowing his frustration to surface for the first time.

In truth, Finch wasn't entirely sure if he was on terra firma with this story. The girl, Trudy Smith, had stopped cooperating. Having spoken to Finch in June, she'd embarked on a negotiation, demanding more money than even the *Daily Candour* was willing to pay. Finch knew that if she was weighing up how much she'd get for the story against how much she could extract from the minister to suppress it, the multimillionaire owner of Bellingham Developments would be bound to tip the scales. She'd been playing this game for a while and was good at it. But now it looked as if the noble lord wouldn't be around for her to fleece, and Finch had a proposition to make to the languid lawyer sitting opposite. But he needed to ensure it would fall on fertile soil.

'Okay, Quentin – can I call you Quentin? Let me tell you what your buddy did,' he said, shifting his enormous frame so that he was looking directly at Kane across the wooden table, a movement that caused a small tsunami in his half-finished pint. 'Trudy Smith was a fifteen-year-old schoolgirl when she met Bellingham in a nightclub. This was ten years ago, before your mate's peerage. Bellingham Developments were involved in a big project in Southampton, and Edward needed to spend a lot of time down there. His main leisure activity seemed to be going out on the pull, even though he was with his first wife at the time.'

None of this was news to Quentin Kane; he'd rescued his client from several potentially embarrassing situations with various – usually much younger – women over the years.

'When he discovered her age,' Finch continued, 'rather than end the relationship, he took it to a new, more sordid level, insisting on Trudy wearing her school uniform so that he could take photos of her in various stages of undress. In one of those photographs, Bellingham's reflection in a hotel mirror is clear. It is incontrovertible proof, and Trudy was wise enough to keep a copy. She was a child besotted by an older man, and easily persuaded to do anything Bellingham wanted her to.'

Kane, though he had been unaware of any of this, managed to maintain an air of mild indifference, as if he was being told something he already knew.

'He made her pregnant. Did you know that?'

Now there was a reaction. The glass of wine that Kane had been lifting towards his lips was suddenly placed back on the table.

'No, I didn't think you did,' Finch continued. 'He put this kid in the family way, to use that quaint old expression. Arranged and paid for the abortion, but not before he'd persuaded Trudy to sign a statement saying that the culprit was a boy in her class, so that it would look as if Bellingham had stepped in to help a young girl in trouble. Trudy told me that she'd wanted that baby, but Bellingham wouldn't hear of it. He told her he loved her, but if she had the baby he'd be in big trouble. If she had the abortion and signed the statement, he'd divorce his wife and marry Trudy. So that's what she did, this fifteen-year-old child had the abortion, but she never saw Bellingham again – until her mum happened to have *Question Time* on the telly one evening a few months ago and there he was, pontificating about declining moral standards. She'd known him as Edward Bell. He'd told her he worked as a surveyor on that Southampton building site; she'd had no idea he owned the company. Not being a follower of my noble profession, she was not only unaware that Bell was Bellingham, she also didn't know that he was by now a lord and a minister in Her Majesty's government. When she googled him after the programme, she discovered the final betrayal: that he'd divorced his wife and married again, but not to her, not to poor lovesick Trudy. She'd always clung to the belief that one day Edward Bell would come back to marry her. Now that her illusions were well and truly punctured, Trudy Smith took against your friend with a venom I doubt she knew she was capable of. Unbeknown to him, she'd kept that one photograph. She decided to seek compensation.'

Quentin Kane drained his glass. 'Sounds like you've got all you need for the story,' he said, eventually.

'She showed me the photograph; too explicit, even for the *Candour*, but she wasn't silly enough to actually give it to me.'

'And presumably you've got her signed declaration that a boy in her school knocked her up,' Kane declared.

From Finch's reaction, the solicitor could see he'd hit a raw nerve.

'I'll be honest with you – that's the main problem. I've told Trudy that I need to get her former classmate, who's supposed to be the one who got her pregnant, to confirm that the declaration is a load of cobblers. But the lad is in the army and currently stationed abroad.'

'Well, bad luck, old chap. By the time you've got his testimony – and, no doubt, something corroborating that he never laid a hand on the delectable Trudy – your opportunity will have passed,' Kane said, as he got up to leave.

'Hang on one second,' Finch said, placing a heavy hand on the solicitor's shoulder. 'If I get this into the *Candour* now, your problem with Trudy disappears; she can't blackmail Bellingham about a secret that's already been revealed.'

Kane sat down again. 'Go on. I'm listening.'

'I need you to work on Lady Bellingham. She may be shocked by the revelation, but it all happened before she met Edward. I can't see her wanting to sue in revenge. I *can* see her wanting to close off the blackmail threat – particularly if the family's trusted solicitor advises her against litigation, which you'd be very wise to do.'

'But this will destroy her husband's career.'

'His time as a minister is over anyway, Quentin. This story will be published eventually – as it should be, because men who've done what your mate did should not be in public office. Hopefully he'll be found alive in those mountains, but he can't escape this story, even if he gives in to blackmail; if Trudy doesn't reveal it, I will.'

'What's the quid pro quo?' Kane asked.

'I'm perfectly willing to push some of the *Candour*'s accumulated wealth your way.'

'I don't want your money, but if the worst happens, it will be a while before Miranda can apply for a Declaration of Assumed Death that would allow her full access to Bellingham's fortune. The twins start prep school next year. It would be jolly decent of the *Candour* to pay their fees for a couple of years.'

Finch agreed, as long as the fees came within a parameter that he knew the newspaper had allowed for. The two men recorded their agreement on a video message, which Finch insisted upon to protect himself from any change of heart. Quentin Kane felt that this was the best possible outcome given all the circumstances. It protected Lady Bellingham from blackmail, as well as providing financial assistance to tide her over. As for Edward Bellingham, if he was alive, he deserved everything that was coming to him. And if he was dead, he'd be beyond caring.

18

LAKE KOURNAS

Captain Diamantapoulis and Assistant Commissioner Mangan were reunited in Kournas, the town that lies high above the lake of the same name. Diamantapoulis had flown back early that Saturday morning. Mangan arrived via the jeep with Lieutenant Despina Nati, who'd insisted on picking her up.

'Despina, I'm perfectly capable of hiring a car to drive myself around,' Louise had said.

'Sorry Louise, but Petros is insistent. He tells me "Make sure she is accompanied at all times,"' the lieutenant had said, mimicking the captain's deep voice. 'I think more so that he knows where you are than for your protection,' she'd added with a chuckle.

Mangan was glad to have Despina's company on the journey. She was also relieved at not having to drive on such perilous roads. She spent the first part of the journey up towards the north coast explaining what had happened at the restaurant. Despina confirmed that, after receiving Mangan's text the previous evening, she'd passed this information to the Cretan constabulary. As for Dimitri Limnios himself, the lieutenant had asked the local police if they suspected him of any criminal activity, and they had responded negatively. The restaurateur was known to be sympathetic to asylum seekers from Libya, often employing them in his kitchens to give them some income. It could be that he was simply providing Hassan with food and produce and Mangan had indeed seen Dimitri hand over a box of food. Apart from thinking his watch had been stolen, Nati suggested that Limnios may have been annoyed because Sharron's boyfriend had come to the restaurant on a busy Friday night, or because he felt his generosity was being exploited. It could also be that there was more than one Libyan refugee called Hassan on the island. Nati felt that, while it was good that Louise had been able to ascertain that Hassan was back in the vicinity of Agia Galini, what she'd seen and heard at Dimitri's on Friday evening could be innocently explained. Nevertheless, she would make sure that Captain Diamantapoulis was fully appraised of the situation.

There was a period of silence on the journey as Mangan enjoyed the view. She saw a herdsman taking some goats to a fresh pasture; an old woman, dressed in black from head to toe, picking olives; two children swinging on an ancient tree in the centre of one of the villages they drove through. Every so often, they'd pass a roadside shrine, perfectly preserved, its candle still burning. Nati said that each one marked the site of a fatal accident. It seemed incongruous to even imagine such violent deaths as the morning sunlight bathed the landscape in a thick, honeyed glow. The scenery was so peacefully pastoral that Mangan had to remind herself that Edward Bellingham was out there somewhere – dead or alive.

'Why are we meeting at this lake?' she asked, as her thoughts returned to the day ahead.

'It's not *a* lake, it's *the* lake – Kournas. The only natural lake on the island, and very beautiful.'

'So, he wanted to show me the scenery?'

Despina laughed. 'Who knows? Petros is very proud of his native island and keen to impress you, I think. But no, to be serious, the Greek army has now been called in to help search the lake. I'm told it was at the insistence of Inspector General Pelkas.'

'But I thought Captain Diamantapoulis was in charge.'

'He is, but Pelkas is senior, and it appears he took advantage of Petros's absence to convince the commander, who is our top man – the equivalent to your commissioner, I think, no?'

Mangan nodded affirmation.

'Inspector General Pelkas convinced the commander to bring in the army and to focus on this part of the island,' Nati continued. 'The captain will be very unhappy, you will see.'

When they reached Kournas at midday, the sun was at its zenith and the White Mountains were reflected on the lake's still surface like a massive mural. Tourists were being directed away from lakeside bathing spots towards roped-off areas, from where they could observe the various amphibious vehicles fanning out across the deepest parts of the lake in preparation for the search.

'In mythology, Lake Kournas is bottomless,' Nati explained. 'And while most of it is now said to be only twenty-two metres deep, the locals say that there are parts that are much, much deeper – maybe thirty kilometres. The lake was formed in prehistoric times when huge asteroids hit the earth. Some went deeper than others, which is why nobody is completely sure how far down the deepest bits go. What we do know is that there is uneven surface and rough vegetation down there.'

Captain Diamantapoulis was standing with a dozen officers from the police and military, looking down at Lake Kournas from the shade of a row of pine trees. He looked incongruous in shirt and jeans amongst all the regalia. Mangan looked for the gold-braided splendour of Inspector General Pelkas, searching the group for the fringed epaulettes and sparkling medals that she remembered from their previous encounter. But the captain's bête noire didn't appear to be in attendance. Mangan pushed her way into the male huddle. She was taller than most of the Greeks, and the captain saw her before she reached him. Did his slight smile suggest he was pleased to see her? Mangan had the distinct impression it did, and wondered why it seemed to matter so much.

By the time she'd struggled through, the captain's attention had turned towards a map unfurled across a trestle table. Large stones had been placed at either end to prevent it being carried away on the breeze that blew across the ridge like the hot breath of a mountain dragon. It was obvious that an intense conversation was taking place about the methodology for searching the lake, and Mangan was pleased when Lieutenant Nati suddenly popped up beside her to translate. The captain beckoned the two women closer, saying something in Greek to Nati as he gave a cursory nod by way of greeting to Louise. He then turned to listen intently to the military officer who was explaining how the operation below was to be carried out.

After a while, and with the explanation still in full flow, Nati took Mangan to one side and whispered, 'Petros says we are not to say anything here. He will meet us at a bar a mile or so further along this road, and we talk there.'

The captain arrived at the bar an hour or so after the two women. He ordered a beer and listened as Lieutenant Nati told him what had happened in Chania, how Mangan had apprehended Sharron and what the girl had told them about going to see Lady Bellingham. Like a relay runner passing a baton, she handed the story on to Mangan, who went over the previous evening's excitement at Dimitri's.

'It probably won't help in the search for Bellingham,' Nati said, resuming the narration for its final leg, 'but the Cretan police should have tracked down Hassan, or Mohammed, whatever his name is, by tonight, so at least we can find out what he's been up to.'

The captain leaned forward as if to reveal a secret. 'The Crete Gendarmerie will have done no such thing, because you and I, Despina, no longer have any meaningful authority on this island.'

The two women listened with increasing anxiety as Diamantapoulis explained how Inspector General Pelkas had convinced their ultimate boss in Athens to place Pelkas in charge of the search operation instead of the captain.

'The media in England now knows that the lordship has been missing for ten days. There is huge pressure on the Hellenic Police to find something,' the captain concluded.

'But how could the boss do this without even speaking with you?' Nati asked.

'To be fair, he did ask to see me last night, but there was something else I had to do.'

'You refused to meet the commander?' Nati said, aghast.

'I didn't refuse as if to be insubordinate. I had a domestic commitment and made clear that once it was finished, I would meet him; but that obviously wasn't good enough.'

Mangan guessed from what Despina Nati had told her that this 'domestic commitment' was to see his daughter. Diamantapoulis went on to say that he'd received a late-night email from the commander's office, informing him that from now on, he would be working under the command of Inspector General Kostar Pelkas. He'd heard from a sympathetic local police officer that Nati's request to organise a search for Hassan had been countermanded by Pelkas himself.

'Even though Hassan is on our wanted list in Athens, and despite what you reported about his association with the Bellinghams, Pelkas has ordered that all police activity on this island be focused on the search,' Diamantapoulis said, running his hand through his thick hair and turning to gaze into the middle distance for a moment. 'And perhaps he is right,' he added. 'He is a jumped-up little creep, but perhaps he'll have more success than I have.'

'So where is Pelkas?' Mangan asked. 'I didn't see him there this morning.'

'No, he was conducting a press conference down beside the lake. I have been instructed to meet him there, at 3pm. You should come with me, Louise.'

Realising that he'd referred to her as 'Louise' for the first time came as a greater shock than the invitation.

'You are here to liaise, no?' he continued by way of explanation, 'and I am no longer the man to liaise with – Kostar Pelkas must be your new point of contact.'

Mangan saw the obvious logic in this, but given the way Pelkas had ignored her when she'd been introduced to him a couple of days before, she doubted this would be an easy or fruitful relationship, and the way the search for Hassan had been summarily abandoned gave her real cause for concern.

'Do you think he'll find anything in Lake Kournas?' Nati asked.

'No – but then again, I suppose it's not too far off the route Bellingham was supposed to take, and the Greek government is anxious to demonstrate the lengths we go to in order to find the lordship. The lake provides good pictures, you understand. The worry for me is that with so much attention focused on Lake Kournas, Pelkas may find something – but only because he put it there in the first place.'

Seeing how shocked Mangan was at this implication, the captain warmed to his theme.

'I know this man. He is Cretan, but there are things that are bad about my island, and he is one of them. He is interested in only one thing, and that is Kostar Pelkas.'

Mangan felt a sudden urge to pat the arm of the man beside her in a gesture of affectionate solidarity. She found this disconcerting and, remembering that Diamantapoulis had talked about needing to check something after their meeting with Lady Bellingham, she asked him about it, as much to divert her thoughts as to elicit information.

'I checked if any of my colleagues back in the office has spoken to Lady Bellingham since we found the phone,' the captain said slowly.

'Why?' asked Mangan, slightly irritated that she needed to hurry the conversation along.

'I am telling you two why because you are the only ones I can trust amongst the police on this island now. I can tell nobody else at this stage.'

'Okay, I would feel privileged to have that information. What is it?' Mangan said with a hint of exasperation, which she felt was necessary to balance out the more affectionate thoughts she'd been having about the captain recently.

'When we went to see Lady Bellingham, she told us about the area where the lordship's phone was found. You remember?'

'Yes, I remember. What about it?'

The captain lifted his glass to drain the last mouthful of beer before saying, 'I didn't tell her where the phone was found, and neither did anybody from my office.'

19

A FAT MAN IN CRETE

Chris Finch had neither the build nor the constitution for a hot climate. Exiting through the rear doors of the plane at Heraklion airport felt like walking into a colossal hairdryer. Basted in sweat simply from walking the few yards from the plane to the bus that was waiting to transport passengers to the terminal, he was pleased to at least get a seat, nestling one buttock precariously on the outside edge to avoid crushing the woman sitting next to him.

Having done the deal with Quentin Kane, Finch had spent the rest of Friday preparing his fifteen hundred words for publication. In the main it had already been written, requiring only a few tweaks and a final polish before being submitted. After a tussle over which title would carry the exclusive, the *Daily* or the *Sunday*, the *Sunday Candour* had emerged victorious. Today was pre-publication day – Saturday 12 August - and while Finch wished he could have been in the UK to witness first-hand the furore his piece was bound to cause, he'd been made an offer that it would have been unwise to refuse.

The *Daily Candour*, miffed that the story was being diverted to its Sunday sister, decided they must have their journalist of the moment in Crete to focus on the reaction its readers would most be interested in – that of Lady Bellingham. The paper also wanted him to provide a sense of the drama involved in so many people searching such a vast area for such an important man.

'Paint a picture for *Candour* readers, Chris,' the editor, Tam Mackay, a grizzled veteran of Fleet Street's golden years, had said, 'like only you can. And while you're at it, try to find out what's happened to Lord Sleazy Bastard.'

The editor's theory was that Bellingham was faking his own death.

'I was a cub reporter when Stonehouse vanished,' Mackay had told a bunch of sub-editors and reporters gathered to discuss Finch's proposed mission the previous day. 'That's the Right Honourable John Stonehouse,' he emphasised, noticing the puzzled looks amongst his younger colleagues. 'Labour Cabinet minister – left his clothes and passport on a Miami beach to make it look as if he'd drowned, and then turned up in Australia under a false identity – with his secretary. Bellingham may have done a Stonehouse.'

'What, gone to Australia with his secretary?' one of the reporters piped up mischievously.

'No, you wanker; faked his own demise. This Trudy story provides a motive. He was being blackmailed; his reputation was at stake. We know Bellingham was a womaniser; come to think of it, perhaps he *was* shagging his secretary. What we know for certain is that he had the motivation to imitate Mr Stonehouse's vanishing trick.

It's only a theory, but if there's one person capable of getting to the truth, it's the big man.'

Hence the decision that Finch must go to Crete was made at the last moment, and it took great difficulty and a bit of string-pulling to get him on to an already crowded holiday flight. He'd been reflecting on Mackay's theory throughout the flight. Having expected to be moving on to a new story, he now found himself on an all-expenses-paid trip to Crete to follow up the one he'd just written. He planned to interview lots of British holidaymakers to see what they made of Lord Bellingham's disappearance, encouraging some juicy observations on the noble lord's seduction of a schoolgirl. The *Sunday Candour* had already arranged to fly in thousands of copies of tomorrow's edition to be distributed in those parts of the island where Brits tended to congregate. Mackay had even contemplated dropping copies from the air on to the beaches below, as if commanding a wartime propaganda mission. The only thing that had dissuaded him was the possibility of a sun worshipper from Basildon being knocked unconscious by the weight of the television supplement.

Finch intended to focus particular attention on the search for Bellingham. A natural believer in the superiority of British institutions over their foreign equivalents, he doubted the Greeks were up to the job. He'd been told about Assistant Commissioner Mangan being on the island, and would be sure to talk to her, but Finch doubted if one woman from the Met would be able to fairly represent English exceptionalism, and felt the urge to do a spot of detecting himself. He'd already got his little team of gossip-sifters at the *Candour* to focus all their attention on this, the story of the moment. And in relation to Lady Bellingham, who he'd now be able to interview in person rather than over the phone, he would make her his absolute priority in the busy schedule that had been formulating in his head as the journey wore on.

By the time Finch had settled his huge frame into the Audi saloon he'd hired at the airport, he'd decided to head straight for the Bellinghams' villa, the *Candour* having provided the address. His calculation was that he'd have a better chance of being granted an audience with Lady Miranda the day before his piece was published than the day after.

The Bellingham villa was set back from the road. Finch stopped the car just before the turning leading up to it. He had yet to determine the approach he would take when he got there. The paper was unable to trace a phone number for Lady Bellingham, so he couldn't ring ahead to forewarn her of his arrival. This wasn't too problematic, as the method he usually adopted in circumstances where he was making an unwelcome visit with unpalatable news was to confront the intended recipient in person. Nevertheless, he needed a few minutes to think things through. The opening remarks could lead to one of two possible outcomes: either he'd be invited in, or he'd have the door slammed in his face. He needed to ensure the former rather than risk the latter; to engineer the opportunity to deploy all his skills of apparent empathy and trustworthiness in order to secure yet another Chris Finch exclusive for Monday's paper.

A photographer who used to work for the *Daily Candour* before retiring to one of the Greek islands was available for Finch to use as and when he was needed. This snapper had been willingly pressed into service whenever the paper wanted a photo of a celebrity on a beach or a yacht somewhere in the archipelago. They were due to meet later at Finch's hotel, and he planned to bring the guy here at some stage to get pictures of Lady Bellingham – with or without her permission. But he'd calculated that to bring him along today would be counterproductive.

The heat was intensifying, and the indomitable reporter was enjoying a few more moments of air-conditioned reflection when a car nosed slowly out of the turning that led down from the villa, pausing at the junction to survey the traffic on the main road. It was a Mercedes convertible with its top down, and at the wheel was Lady Miranda Bellingham.

Finch had seen many photographs of her, but her identity would have been obvious even if he hadn't: the aristocratic posture, the flawlessly smooth skin, the abundant auburn hair, the casual elegance she exuded even at a distance of twenty metres. There was no reason why she'd have noticed Finch, whose car was in the deep shade of the cypress trees lining the route.

He made an immediate decision: there was no point going up to the house if Lady Bellingham wasn't there; his time would be better spent following the Mercedes. He guessed that Miranda had left home in a hurry. Why else would the roof be down on the convertible, allowing the fierce sun access to that perfect complexion? Although, Finch mused, if anyone was going to drive an open-top in a hot climate, it was bound to be a Brit. No Greek would be daft enough to drive a convertible.

They were passing through a string of villages with names that all seemed to begin with 'K', heading in the direction of a town called Patsos. Finch thought he'd never been required to acclimatise to a new destination so quickly. He wasn't a great traveller, and hot countries were the ones he liked to travel to the least. Chris Finch had no eye for the aesthetic. The beauty of the landscape would have been of no interest, even if he hadn't had to focus all his attention on following the car in front along unfamiliar roads, while keeping at enough of a distance to avoid arousing suspicion.

When they'd gone a few miles past Patsos, heading along a narrow country track, the Mercedes pulled in to a fenced-off compound. There were acres of olive trees and tomato vines, with several small fields dedicated to growing green produce. Finch felt he would be too conspicuous following Lady Bellingham in past the 'Keep Out' sign that she had ignored. Instead, he drove a few metres further down the track and took a turning that led him up into the hills, allowing him to watch her from above. He could hardly believe his luck. It would have been impossible to see what was happening from anywhere along the road he'd been on. In contrast, this remote spot, on what was little more than a dirt track leading nowhere, was the perfect observation post.

Leaving his car and crouching uncomfortably in the bushes, he watched as Lady Bellingham parked and walked towards a row of three huts deep in the olive grove, carrying a package that she'd taken from the glove compartment. Five men emerged from the huts, three of them carrying rifles. None of them seemed particularly pleased to see her. Nothing of what they were saying could be heard by Finch, but their body language suggested this was not a congress of old friends. The package was handed to one of the men who Lady Bellingham then proceeded to castigate, her index finger wagging and jabbing towards him like sparks from an electrode. She wore a long, flowing dress that swirled up as she turned on her heels to march back to the Mercedes. Finch thought she looked magnificent in her anger. Before she could drive away, one of the men ran over to her car and flung the package on to the back seat.

He thought it likely that Lady Miranda would now head back to the villa, and if he followed, he could interview her as originally intended. But his curiosity had been aroused. He wanted to know what this place was, what Lady Bellingham was doing here, and what was in the package she'd handed over only for it to be so unceremoniously returned. It was unlikely that such questions would be answered in an interview.

Rather than take the road back towards Agia Galini, he decided to drive into that fenced-off area towards the three huts in the middle of the olive grove. It was a decision he was to regret almost immediately.

20

CONFRONTATION AT THE TAVERNA

Inspector General Kostar Pelkas had commandeered a taverna on the shore of Lake Kournas to be his temporary headquarters. It was here that he was due to meet Captain Diamantapoulis at 3pm.

Mangan had been nervous about accepting the captain's invitation to accompany him, but his revelation about Lady Bellingham had reinforced her growing concerns about whether the noble lord was really a lost hiker or if there was a more sinister explanation for his disappearance. The order Pelkas had given to abandon all attempts to apprehend Hassan had appalled her. She was in no position to dictate who should oversee a Greek police operation, but Mangan was certain that the transfer of control to Pelkas would not be in the Met's best interests. She needed to speak to the commissioner – and, as she soon discovered, the commissioner was keen to speak to her.

The *Sunday Candour* had felt it wise to inform the government about the story they were about to publish concerning a minister having once had sex with a minor. The commissioner's peaceful Saturday had been disturbed by this information being subsequently relayed to New Scotland Yard, where it aroused a strong suspicion that there was now at least a possibility that Bellingham might have disappeared deliberately. A public figure under this kind of pressure could well have contemplated suicide or a change of identity.

When the commissioner told Mangan about the story that was about to be published, he was pleased to hear that, although unaware of the *Sunday Candour* revelations, his assistant commissioner had already been thinking along the same lines. By the time their conversation was ending, Mangan was not only fully authorised and prepared to accompany Diamantapoulis to the meeting with Pelkas, but Irvine was arranging a call to his opposite number in Athens to reinforce the strategy they'd agreed should be pursued. He had a final piece of advice to offer.

'You do have your uniform with you, don't you, Louise?' the commissioner asked.

'Yes: not the Full Monty with the medals, but the one I wear to work, certainly.'

'Then wear it to the meeting. It sounds as if you need to be at your most authoritative with this Pelkas fellow.'

And so it was that when Mangan met Diamanta-poulis, she was reluctantly trussed up in a dark blue tunic with a Brunswick star embroidered on each lapel, a chequered cravat, a bowler-style hardhat and a pair of snow-white gloves. Beneath her uniform skirt were the dreaded black tights, that were as uncomfortable as they were unsuitable in the thirty-five-degree heat.

Not a word passed between Mangan and the captain as they waited to be ushered into the great man's presence. Diamantapoulis said nothing about her uniform, and Mangan said nothing about her phone call with the commissioner. There was insufficient time, and she didn't want to exacerbate the strain that the man next to her was already under. She thought the captain looked tired and trepidatious, and wondered if he now regretted inviting her to what was bound to be a humiliating ordeal for him.

The taverna headquarters was a hive of activity. A huge search grid had been fixed along one wall, which was being systematically adhered to outside on the lake by divers equipped with grappling hooks, chain drags and expensive-looking sonar equipment. Police and military personnel were hurrying back and forth between the taverna and the lake. Along the shore, a bank of camera tripods stood like three-legged aliens from an H.G. Wells novel, as if preparing to wade into the water; present were CNN, BBC, ITV and Euro Channel, as well as a battalion of Greek TV stations.

Eventually, the call came for the two officers to enter the inner sanctum. The kitchen must have until recently been fully equipped with stoves and ovens. In their place now was a suite of computers and filing cabinets, as well as chairs and desks. Mangan wondered how they had managed to transform the place so quickly. It was impressive – and was meant to be. There were four or five men and women at desks dotted around the perimeter, but at the centre, occupying the biggest desk, was the diminutive figure of Inspector General Pelkas.

'And who is this woman, Captain?' he asked, surprising Louise by speaking in English.

'You know who she is, because I introduced you to Assistant Commissioner Mangan a few days ago,' the captain asserted. 'She is here to liaise on this search, and as you are now in charge, I thought I should bring her with me.'

Mangan suspected that Pelkas was well aware of her role, and that the importance of keeping her sweet would have been re-emphasised to him by Athens. This was a little charade for her benefit. Why else would he be speaking in English? He must be intending to engage with her rather than ignore her, as he had at their last encounter. The inspector general came round the desk to greet her. He was adorned in the same regalia she remembered from the last time they'd met, except that the medals seemed to have been given an extra shine for the cameras outside.

'I'm delighted to meet you,' he said, shaking hands with Louise as she and the captain stood like naughty children in front of a headmaster. There was a height difference between Mangan and Pelkas of at least six inches, which made him seem more pupil than master, but what he lacked in inches, he made up for in self-importance.

'I trust you appreciate the thoroughness with which this operation is now being carried out,' Pelkas said.

'Diamantapoulis here will be leaving now that I have taken charge. I called him here to tell him that I've decided to facilitate his return to Athens to catch the criminals who seem to thrive there, and to leave Crete to me.' As he spoke, Pelkas paraded up and down, hands behind his back, between the two visitors and his enormous desk. The audience of underlings seemed to be paying more attention to what the inspector general was saying than whatever work they were supposed to be doing.

'It would be enormously helpful for me if Captain Diamantapoulis remained here to assist in my lines of investigation,' Mangan said, as sweetly as she could.

Pelkas came to a halt with his back to her, like a clockwork soldier needing to be rewound. There was silence across the enormous taverna.

'What lines of investigation would those be?' he asked after a few seconds of rumination.

'There's a Libyan exile whom we believe is wanted for suspected drug offences, and for stealing a British passport, and—'

'Ah, Hassan, as he's known here,' Pelkas interrupted. 'I do not intend to have my officers diverted to pursue a petty criminal when a British government minister is missing on this island. I would have thought the Metropolitan Police would be pleased with me for this, no?'

'The Metropolitan Police have every confidence in your ability to conduct a full search for Lord Bellingham, but we think Hassan may have some important information, and that's one reason why we would be much happier if Captain Diamantapoulis remained to pursue that aspect, without disturbing the crucial work you are doing in trying to find Lord Bellingham.'

Mangan couldn't be sure if the captain supported the intervention she was making on his behalf. She was keeping her eyes firmly fixed on the inspector general.

'My dear,' Pelkas said eventually, his voice dripping condescension as he resumed his little perambulation in front of them, 'I cannot allow you to dictate how investigations are conducted in a country outside your jurisdiction. I am in charge now, and Captain Diamantapoulis's work on Crete has come to an end.'

'I think you'll find that it hasn't.' Mangan's words echoed round the taverna as if they'd been relayed over a tannoy. The tense atmosphere was only broken when one of the desk-dwellers on the periphery came forward, phone in hand, to whisper in the inspector general's ear. Pelkas took the phone and, turning his back on the two visitors, spent a few minutes listening to whoever was at the other end. There was the occasional interjection from Pelkas quietly pleading his case, at which the voice at the other end seemed to rise in volume. As the conversation was in Greek, Mangan didn't know what was being said, but when she looked at the captain, she saw that his usual saturnine expression had softened. She could swear there was a twinkle in his eye.

Pelkas handed the phone back to his underling, waving him away. Resuming his seat behind the huge desk, he feigned deep interest in a document he'd picked up, before eventually saying to the captain: 'I am instructed to ask you to stay with Assistant Commissioner Mangan and give her any assistance she needs.'

And there he sat, subdued, as Mangan and Diamantapoulis left the taverna.

Despina Nati was waiting outside at the wheel of the familiar police jeep. When she'd dropped them off earlier, the captain had expected to be heading back to Athens that evening. He'd checked out of the police billet where he'd been staying, and his travel bag was on the back seat. As they drove down towards Agia Galini, he was trying to piece together what had happened.

'It's simple,' Louise Mangan explained. 'Your boss, the commander back in Athens, and my boss, the commissioner in London, know each other very well. Apparently, they were on an international police seminar together years ago and stayed in touch. As soon as I told the commissioner what was happening, he arranged to talk to his old friend. We've just witnessed the result of that conversation; Inspector General Pelkas has been put back in his box.'

Nati let out a hearty cheer as she manoeuvred the jeep round another mountain bend.

'And I now work for you,' the captain said, feigning a disquiet that Mangan sensed wasn't entirely frivolous.

'Let's hope you come up to scratch,' she said, smiling.

When Mangan went on to tell her Greek colleagues about the story that would break in tomorrow's UK Sunday papers, neither of them expressed surprise or disgust.

'In Greece, the age of consent is fifteen, so it would not be a crime here,' Nati said.

'As for politicians having affairs,' the captain added, 'it would be more news if they didn't.'

'I know it doesn't alter the need to find him,' Mangan said. 'But many people think it gives him a good reason not to be found.'

The captain pondered her words for a minute or two before saying, 'That's a good point, Louise.'

Mangan felt another irrational stab of satisfaction. Not only had the taciturn policeman called her 'Louise' again, but this was the first time he'd offered anything approaching praise. Diamantapoulis had placed himself in the back of the jeep, with the two women in the front. As Mangan half turned towards him to acknowledge the comment, his dark eyes were looking directly into hers, and Louise Mangan knew that whatever the unfamiliar emotion was that stirred inside her, it wasn't simply comradeship.

21

LONDON CALLING

There was more activity in Stoke Newington than was normal for mid-August. For a start, the police were out in force. Ever since the explosion, there'd been a reintroduction of the neighbourhood policing teams that had largely vanished from the streets in recent years.

The badly damaged restaurant was boarded up, and Manny himself had not been seen in the vicinity for weeks. There was talk of him opening another place further along the High Street, where a Clinton's card shop had been, but those who knew him best said he was a broken man. The old Glaswegian nursed an impotent anger, complaining bitterly about no arrests being made even though everybody knew who was responsible for the explosion at his premises.

Brady had been making strenuous efforts to dispel the wrath he felt on Manny's behalf that was so damaging to his own equilibrium. He was spending more time in his workshop, crafting and shaping an intricate prayer lectern embossed with wood mosaics, which he planned to present to Manny as a gift. Brady hoped the effort would temper his thoughts and the finished product assuage his guilt. Of all the emotions swirling round his system following the violent disturbance of his placid and precious routine, self-reproach was the most prominent. He'd done nothing to protect Manny from the vicious gang that had ruined the old man's life.

Brady and his wife had just spent their usual fortnight in an expensive hotel on the Mediterranean. Cathleen's job had always dictated when they went away; the last week in July and the first week of August, as soon as the schools broke up. Although they didn't have children of their own, this was peak holiday period for those who did. In order to insulate themselves against noisy kids with overindulgent parents, Brady always booked expensive hotels, the kind with the grandeur and quiet elegance that seemed to have a tranquilising effect on any infants whose parents were rich enough to bring them. These holidays were Brady's only concession to luxury, arranged essentially for his benefit rather than his wife's.

This year the holiday had been more important, because it was an opportunity to restore harmony after a blazing row. Brady had been furious with his wife for pointing the police in his direction. Fortunately, Cathleen had phoned him to warn of the impending arrival of a squad car. As a result, he was ready when the coppers came round that same afternoon. Brady eventually conceded that Cathleen had been wise to cooperate. Had she refused to give her address when the police arrived at her school and asked for it, the consequences could have been far worse. Nevertheless, the trauma of having to deal with a visit from the police, and knowing

that his name and address would now appear somewhere on their database, had made him difficult to live
with over the past few weeks.

The two officers sent to question Brady about what
he'd witnessed at Manny's when Razor Parting and his
mates were behaving threateningly had gleaned nothing
more than a statement about Brady being too far away
to hear. He hadn't spoken to Manny since, but could
imagine how upset his friend would be. A truthful statement from Brady may have tipped the scales and helped
convict those thugs. But while being questioned by the
police had stripped away one of the veils he hid behind,
appearing as a witness in a court of law would have
been much more damaging. It was a risk he couldn't
contemplate.

His anger with Cathleen eventually subsided under
the weight of its own irrationality. He'd been trying
to make it up with her throughout the summer, but
something seemed to have crept into her personality
– an edge that he'd never noticed before, but which
remained despite his most arduous attempts at making
up. This holiday was to be the culmination of his efforts,
and Brady hoped that the objective had been achieved.
As usual on holiday (as at home), they'd rarely spent
their days together. Cathleen loved all things nautical,
scuba-diving as well as swimming, windsurfing and
water-skiing. Brady couldn't swim, and had a hatred
of beaches equally divided between sea and sand. On
each day of the holiday, they'd part after breakfast and
meet again at dinner. When Cathleen asked what her

husband had been up to that day, he'd give some vague answer, such as: 'Just pottering about.'

The day after their return, while Cathleen was dealing with the detritus of the holiday, Brady walked up to the High Street. It was a fine day with a couple of cotton-wool clouds in an aquamarine sky. He knew he should be getting on with the prayer lectern, but the weather was too good to be locked away in his windowless workshop. Besides, having avoided the scene of the crime (and the source of his disturbing vengeful thoughts) for so long, Brady felt it was time to take a stroll over to Manny's and confront his demons. Dressed in shorts and T-shirt, with a pair of sliders on his feet, he was wandering towards the burned-out café when somebody hailed him from across the street. It was Osman, Manny's chef, struggling along the opposite pavement on crutches, a plaster cast on one leg and a dressing on his bruised face.

'Hey, Osman. What happened to you, man?' Brady asked, crossing the road to join him.

'There was five of them – and if you think I look bad, you should see them guys.'

A few minutes later, the Turkish cook was easing himself behind a table in Starbucks as Brady queued for the coffees, over which Osman had promised to relay the latest news.

'The police have done nothing,' Osman said contemptuously after Brady had joined him at the table with two lattes. 'Not a damn thing. They say they haven't got enough evidence, but in the meantime Taylan and his thugs do exactly as they please, terrorising decent people.'

'Who's Taylan?' Brady asked.

'You know, Taylan Ayhan – the guy you saw in the restaurant that day.'

Brady realised he was talking about Razor Parting. So that was his name – Taylan.

'He's the leader of the pack, and it was him who broke my leg. Hit it with an iron bar – but only after I'd done serious damage to that surly face of his.'

Osman explained how he'd told the police about the way Taylan and his gang had been demanding protection money. He'd even gone so far as to take them to the park to point Taylan out.

'They're in Clissold Park most days in summer, and I got that Detective Inspector Cairns to run me up there in his unmarked car. We saw Taylan, his arse on the back of a park bench, all his disciples gathered round like he was some kind of fuckin' prophet or something. I don't think they saw me, but it must have got back to them that I'd fingered them, because the next thing they're outside where I live, mucking about, making a noise. We have a baby, eighteen months old, and there they are, five of them at around 9pm, just as my wife is trying to get the kid to sleep. They're shouting and laughing, waiting for me to come out.'

Osman paused to sweeten his drink, using one giant hand to sugar and stir his coffee, while Brady expressed some futile platitudes about not rising to the bait.

'It was a big thing for me to go to the police,' Osman

said. 'In my community, we don't do that. We fight our own battles. But everyone is terrified of these punks, and so I did it – for Manny. I then hear that those guys got taken in for questioning, then released for lack of proof. Taylan must have guessed that it was me who dobbed them in. Anyway, now they are outside my house, and my wife, she pleaded with me not to go down, to call the police instead, but I went out to face them. Not to do that would have been cowardly. I could not lift my head in my community if I had done that. I went out with a baseball bat I keep for security and inflicted serious damage, like I say. I hit Taylan across his thick skull.'

'But it was five against one; there was no way you could have come out on top,' Brady said.

'No – and as you can see, I didn't. A neighbour called the cops, otherwise they might have killed me.'

'Were they arrested?'

'I refused to press charges, so they may get a fine for – what you call it? Begins with an "a".'

'Affray?' suggested Brady.

'Yeh, that's it, affray. A fine for that, but nothing more.' All Osman's ebullient self-confidence seemed to have seeped away, like air from a punctured tyre. 'The problem now is that while I'm like this, I can't do nothing to protect my wife and child, and those bastards are still coming outside my house most nights, taunting me. Taylan with his damaged head – he still comes with more of his gang, taking the piss, disturbing my family, hoping I go out there so they can have another go.'

'Isn't there anyone else in your community who'll take them on?' Brady asked.

'No, they're all scared – especially after what happened to me.'

'Can't the police move them on?'

Osman responded with a bitter laugh. 'Two officers come by occasionally as part of the patrols that started when the café was burned down. And when they come, Taylan and his gang sit on the wall, my wall, in front of my house. They sit quietly, and you know what the coppers do? They chat with them, have a bit of a laugh. Me and my neighbours, we are trapped indoors by these bastards, and the police have a laugh with them.'

Osman went quiet and, Brady waited a few minutes before enquiring about his friend. 'Have you seen Manny?' he asked.

'No, but he calls me.'

'Has he said anything about me?'

'Only that he heard you did give the police a statement about what you saw. He was pleased about that. Says he can't understand why that doesn't help to get them prosecuted.'

Brady felt a wave of relief that Manny didn't know or hadn't registered how innocuous his statement had been. All he and Osman knew was that he'd made one.

'He'll get the insurance money, sure enough,' the chef was saying, 'but he doesn't think he can face reopening the restaurant. Says he's too old to go through it all again, and that perhaps he'll go back to Glasgow, or even go to Israel.'

'But that's so defeatist,' Brady heard himself saying.

'Perhaps that's because we've been defeated,' Osman remarked dryly.

A few miles to the east, while Brady and Osman were having their Starbucks conversation in Stoke Newington, Quentin Kane was paying what he hoped would be his last visit to Stanley Brewer. The wily old dissenter was no longer holding up the Bellingham development in Docklands, having eventually accepted the 'final' offer Kane and Edward Bellingham had made to him in July. He'd added some fresh conditions, one of which was that he be given full board at the Lansbury Hotel, an expensive establishment in Canary Wharf, while a suitable house was found for him. Bellingham Developments, keen to complete the demolition, immediately accepted, despite Chesterton, Kane and Palfrey counselling resistance.

'Why the fuck can't he live with his son, or his weird grandson?' Kane had espoused when presented with this new stipulation. 'How long are we expected to keep him in the lap of luxury at the Lansbury for? Until we've provided him with a palace built with gold fucking bricks?'

The urbane solicitor's associates, having never heard him swear before, worried that exasperation was taking its toll. Kane had already had to take an unscheduled week off at the beginning of August because of the stress he was under. Since returning, more pressure had been piled upon him by the disappearance of Lord

Bellingham in Crete and the subsequent revelations published in last Sunday's *Candour*. It was Chesterton and Palfrey who worried most about their partner. Kane was unmarried and had devoted most of his adult life to the practice. His partners understood his foul-mouthed reaction to yet another outrageous demand, but considered opposition futile when so much depended on getting Brewer out. In the end, an agreement had been reached for the old man to occupy the suite at the Lansbury until Christmas, and on this fine summer's day, Quentin Kane was presenting the final series of documents for Stanley to sign. A young woman from the legal firm appointed to represent Brewer (paid for by Bellingham Developments as part of a previous set of demands) had already scrutinised and cleared the papers separately, but had insisted on being present for these final formalities. The only other person in attendance was Keith, Stanley's grandson, whose silent hostility felt no less threatening than it had before the deal was done.

'Where's your mate, then?' Stanley asked, breaking the silence. 'Heard he's gone missing.'

'Oh, you know how the papers exaggerate these things,' Kane replied. 'He's an experienced hiker. I'm sure he'll turn up soon.'

Noticing that Keith's hard-bitten face and bare arms were deeply tanned and, in an attempt to change the subject, Kane asked if Keith had enjoyed his holiday.

'No,' Keith replied, the word dropping like a boulder, blocking any attempt at further conversation.

'He's not been away long,' Stanley interjected. 'Been lookin' after me, ain't you son?'

'Yeah,' Keith responded.

Kane wondered if Brewer's morose grandson had ever attempted a word with more than one syllable.

'Keef and some of his old regiment had a reunion for five days, but he don't like it abroad. Can't stand the food for a start, but I insisted he 'ad a break after all that time protectin' me from the bailiffs.'

Kane, who'd been adding his signature mindlessly to each piece of paper the young woman placed in front of him, was on the last few documents, and was looking forward to being able to screw the cap back on to his gold Parker pen. He was feeling euphoric at the prospect of putting this horrendous saga behind him.

'You didn't need to have Keith protecting you, Stanley. You must know that. If we planned to send in the bailiffs, we wouldn't have paid the exorbitant costs of this hotel, would we?' he said cheerily, keeping the retrospective attraction of the bailiffs to himself.

'My Keef didn't want me to accept this deal,' Brewer announced. 'He'd have fought you, wouldn't you, son?'

Keith's affirmative grunt and unnerving stare increased the speed with which Kane signed the documents. As he got up to leave, he heard the young woman from Brewer's solicitors ask where Keith had gone to get such a lovely tan. Stanley answered on his grandson's behalf.

'Went to Crete, didn't you, Keef?' he said.

22

NEVER ON A SUNDAY

The front-page exclusive in the *Sunday Candour* had scattered opinion about Lord Bellingham as effectively as a bowling ball striking pins. On Saturday, the search had been for a happily married, successful business-man-turned-politician; by Sunday lunchtime, the quest was to find a relic from the age of sleaze. On Saturday, Bellingham had been a missing minister who must be found; by Sunday, he was a fugitive criminal who needed to be brought to justice. Some callers to UK radio stations were already questioning why any more time and expense should be wasted trying to find him.

Meanwhile, the *Daily Candour* was advertising a series of articles by Chris Finch, 'The Man Who Unmasked the Multimillionaire Monster', which it said would be published over the coming week. The problem was that nobody at the newspaper had managed to establish contact with Finch since a cursory call after his plane had landed in Crete on Saturday lunchtime. By Sunday afternoon, Tam Mackay, the *Candour*'s gnarled editor, was shouting abusive messages into the reporter's voicemail.

'For fuck's sake, where are you? You're too fucking fat to disappear. CALL ME NOW.'

Finch had yet to check into the hotel where he was due to stay, and while he had a reputation for following his nose and periods of silence weren't unusual, his editor was becoming seriously concerned.

For Louise Mangan and the British Embassy officials with whom she was working, the *Sunday Candour* story hadn't eased the pressure to find the missing minister. Opinions were shifting, and there was now a majority who believed that Inspector General Pelkas was right to concentrate the search on Lake Kournas. The drone footage of a lone hiker heading in that direction wasn't conclusive either way, and, as Mangan had pointed out, whoever the man was, he certainly didn't appear to be wearing the distinctive red safety helmet that Bellingham was said to have been wearing when he set off. But as the ambassador, Sir Ralph Evans, (a leading advocate for Pelkas), now languidly opined, a man intent on suicide was unlikely to be particularly concerned about wearing a safety helmet.

This conversation took place on Sunday morning, Louise having been patched into a call from her hotel room that involved Sir Ralph Evans in Athens, the vice-consul in Rethymnon, and several embassy officials scattered across the country. She'd explained the new arrangement reached after the intervention of the Met commissioner and his old friend, the commander of the Hellenic Police. Pelkas was now in charge of the search for Lord Bellingham, while Diamantapoulis was following the trail that may link Hassan and his drug-smuggling/people-trafficking gang with Lord and

Lady Bellingham via their friend, the restaurant owner Dimitri.

'It seems a fairly tenuous link,' the ambassador observed.

Mangan explained that Hassan had worked at Dimitri's. 'I happened to see him on Friday when I was dining there. Not only do the Bellinghams use that restaurant a lot, but it was also Dimitri who'd suggested the route that Lord Bellingham was following when he vanished.'

'That's all very interesting,' Sir Ralph responded loftily, 'but your job is to liaise with Inspector General Pelkas in the search for Lord Bellingham. You must leave the drug-smugglers to the Greek police.'

Mangan could feel her colour rise. She would wish later that she'd bitten her tongue, but the words were already out. 'I'm not sure what *your* job is, but I do know it doesn't involve instructing me. I answer to my commissioner, and I'm perfectly aware of my responsibilities. I do not take kindly to being patronised. Do you understand?'

There was a shocked silence before Sir Ralph made the kind of syrupy apology that Mangan felt would be termed 'an expression of regret' in diplomatic circles. She'd made an enemy of the ambassador, and knew it wasn't a wise thing to do.

Mangan had remained in Agia Galini while Nati had driven the captain up to Heraklion early that morning to talk to the specialist drug squad based there. Diamantapoulis knew this unit well, having worked with them before, and told Mangan it consisted of the finest officers on the island. Now that Pelkas was no longer able to undermine the search for Hassan, the captain wanted to ensure the squad were up for the challenge. He and Louise were due to touch base in a telephone conversation that evening.

She'd made sure that Pelkas was aware of her availability should he wish to liaise with her, and, much to her surprise, a car had arrived at her hotel that lunchtime, sent by Inspector General Pelkas to bring her to Lake Kournas. When she arrived at the commandeered taverna, Pelkas made such a demonstrable fuss of her, she feared he might kiss the hand she proffered. Fortunately, the welcome ceremony was limited to a handshake and a couple of his exaggerated bows.

Pelkas said he'd brought her here for an important announcement. An article of Bellingham's clothing had been found in the lake. He was about to proclaim this before the waiting media and wanted Louise ('my distinguished and honourable liaison of Metropolitan Police') to appear with him. Mangan had some difficulty convincing her new admirer that accompanying him at press conferences wasn't part of her role, and she insisted instead on watching from the shade of a lakeside tree as Pelkas preened himself before the cameras. He wouldn't reveal what the item of clothing was at this stage, only that its size and condition suggested it was Bellingham's. It would be subjected to various tests and the matter would be discussed with Lady Bellingham before full details could be revealed. In a search such as this, Mangan ruminated, it was wrong to give any publicity before subjecting the item to proper scrutiny. The integrity of the operation was being sacrificed to the vanity of the man in charge.

That evening, when Mangan called Diamantapoulis, the captain was certain that the item in the lake would turn out to be the jumper he'd asked Lady Bellingham to give him in order to provide a scent for the police dogs.

'I did predict this, Louise – you recall?'

She did, but felt obliged to act as devil's advocate. 'But Lady Bellingham will see the jumper and recognise it as the one she gave to you.'

'Yes, but we both feel that she would find it very convenient for the lordship to be thought to be drowned, don't we? If we're right, she won't contradict the Pelkas version of events.'

'Hang on,' Louise protested. 'I agree that Lady Bellingham knows more than she's letting on, but that doesn't mean she's colluding with Pelkas. Do we have anyone tailing her?'

After a few seconds of silence, the captain said: 'I'm sorry, I thought we'd drawn similar conclusions when the mobile phone was found, and Lady Bellingham knows where without being told. No, she is not being tailed. Pelkas has ensured there is hardly anyone in police uniform who is not conscripted to the White Mountains, even the traffic cops. In any case, I doubt I have the authority to do that now. Pelkas is in charge of the search for Bellingham, and I look for Hassan.'

'The ambassador is suggesting I pay another visit to Lady Bellingham,' Mangan said. 'Given the revelations in the press about her husband, he thinks a "woman to woman" chat might be appropriate.'

'Sure, woman to woman, Brit to Brit; it makes sense. I am neither woman nor Brit, but I would like to be there with you – like before, just watching.'

'Any further thoughts on what I saw at Dimitri's the other night?'

'Nati thinks it can be easily explained, and I'm sure she is right,' the captain responded. 'But I'm equally sure that Dimitri Limnios is up to his neck in the smuggling from Libya. I am taking steps to keep him under surveillance.'

'What kind of steps?' Louise asked. 'If you couldn't find the men to follow Lady Bellingham, how will you keep an eye on Dimitri?'

'In ways that will impress even your sophisticated and advanced police force.'

Louise knew when she was being baited, and decided not to pursue the matter any further. It was enough to know that her suspicions about the restaurant owner were shared.

'When are you back from Heraklion?' she asked.

'Sometime later in the week. The guys here are getting close to locating the place Hassan's gang use as a hub for their operation, and when they do, I will get authority from the commander to raid it. I don't think you should rush to meet Lady Bellingham anyway. Not until I hear from Athens. My people sent the phone there after you examined it. I'm told they have retrieved some deleted items that we may want to ask her about. It's why I want to come with you when you visit. I may not have authority to visit her myself, but if I go with you . . .'

'Okay, I understand. I won't arrange to visit her until you get back and we've had a chance to put our heads together.'

Mangan was about to end the call when Diamanta-poulis said, 'I know you will need to work with Pelkas, and that this body in the lake stuff will seem more and more convenient to believe, but I know Pelkas. He's not just pompous, he's corrupted. Please trust me, Louise.'

She assured him that she did. And it was true, she did trust him. She liked him, too; she liked him more than she'd liked any man in a long while.

23

THE AMBASSADOR AND THE WAITRESS

The disappearance of the journalist who'd revealed Edward Bellingham's sordid past generated an even greater media focus on Crete. The car that Chris Finch had hired at the airport was found neatly parked on a road in Chania the day after he failed to arrive at his hotel. For a few days, the belief that he was pursuing a story in his usual reclusive way remained feasible, but by Wednesday it was clear that a second Brit had gone missing on the island.

The search for Lord Bellingham was being scaled down, and was by now confined to Lake Kournas. The item of clothing had been identified – not as the sweater that had been given to Diamantapoulis to provide a scent for the dogs, as the captain had wrongly predicted, but as the light jacket that Lady Bellingham confirmed her husband had been wearing when she'd dropped him off.

Resources were being diverted from one search to the other, from Bellingham to Finch. The missing reporter didn't have quite the same salience as a missing government minister, so they were much reduced. There was no further military involvement, for instance,

189

apart from some navy activity on Lake Kournas, where Pelkas remained intent on finding a body, despite expert opinion that the lake was too deep and difficult to offer up its secrets.

Louise Mangan spent the week travelling between her base in Agia Galini and Heraklion, where Captain Diamantapoulis and Lieutenant Nati were working with narcotics agents and customs officials, who seemed grateful to be appreciated in what they considered to be their undervalued work.

Louise recognised in this specialist unit the camaraderie and integrity that she'd delighted in throughout her career with the Met. With the disappearance of Chris Finch, she was now liaising on two fronts, and as she'd pointed out to the ambassador, the two cases were linked; not just by the story Finch was pursuing, but through Hassan.

There'd been another awkward conversation between them during the week. Sir Ralph had come to Heraklion for a face-to-face chat, and Louise could tell he was keen to mend fences after clashing with her on Sunday, but that he also found it difficult to adjust to dealing with an English figure of authority who hadn't been in the Household Cavalry and wasn't a member of White's. The ambassador was one of those men, Louise mused, who knew he was cleverer than everyone else, but was determined to do his damnedest to conceal it. She'd met many like him in her career and understood that it was an ingrained characteristic. The air of superiority Sir Ralph conveyed was as much an essential element of his personality as the colour of his eyes, and just as impossible to change. However, she was as keen as he was to put Sunday's fracas behind them.

'The Greek authorities are very proud of their record in tackling the drugs trade, and are delighted that you're taking an interest, Assistant Commissioner,' the ambassador said, carefully interlacing his long fingers over the immaculately tailored, pin-striped knee of his right trouser leg. 'But I wondered if you could enlighten me about what purpose this serves in relation to the search for Lord Bellingham, who appears to have been found in Lake Kournas, or Mr Christopher Finch, whose newspaper is becoming increasingly vociferous about what they see as a lack of progress in detecting his whereabouts.'

The words fell like honeyed rain.

'I'm glad to have this opportunity to explain,' Mangan said, smoothing her red cotton skirt and taking a swig of water from the bottle in her hand.

They were sitting in the vice-consul's office, not far from Heraklion airport. Captain Diamantapoulis was with Nati and his new comrades from the narcotics unit, questioning a prospective informer suspected of being a major player in the organised people-smuggling operation. Real progress was being made in the quest to find the location of the smugglers' main hub, and Mangan proceeded to explain the relevance of this in the search for the two missing British citizens.

'Hassan worked for the Bellinghams for a short while, and had been having an affair with their nanny.

His real name is Mohammed Tatanaki; he's a Libyan wanted by the Greek police for suspected involvement with a notorious smuggling gang. He hasn't been seen since the day before Chris Finch arrived in Crete. Hassan is also in possession of a UK passport, stolen from his girlfriend. Wherever Finch drove in that hired car, we're pretty sure it wasn't to Chania, where his car was found. The call he made to his office shortly after he arrived placed him as travelling in the opposite direction. A call between two members of the gang that Hassan was involved with, intercepted by Greek security forces on Monday, mentioned that they had captured "a big man from England". Finch is an investigative journalist. While he was here on the Bellingham case, there's no telling what else he'd have poked his nose into. He has a reputation for going off-piste. So, my liaison role, whether regarding Bellingham or Finch, has to be concerned with helping to find Hassan.'

From the way Sir Ralph was contemplating the ceiling, Louise knew he had no comeback. Nevertheless, she decided to hammer her point home.

'You may like to seek elucidation from our National Crime Agency, who I've been keeping informed on all this. They've been working with the Greek authorities for some time, because the gang that Hassan's a part of is suspected of being involved in trafficking people and drugs from Libya right across Europe, with Britain being a major destination. They say this is one of the most vicious and ruthless gangs they've ever encountered –

and they know what they're talking about,' Mangan said, leaving the ambassador in no doubt that, as far as she was concerned, he didn't.

Mangan's increasingly fraught relationship with Sir Ralph contrasted with her blossoming friendship with the captain. They worked together for most of the days she spent in Heraklion, and dined together almost every evening. There was no lapse of professionalism; they just felt increasingly comfortable in each other's company. She called him Petros, and he called her Louise, except when some of the senior drugs squad officers were around, at which times they felt duty-bound to retain an element of formality.

They spent their days being briefed on the complex web of movements being tracked between Libya and Italy, Syria and Europe, and Damascus and London. In most of these, Greece was a staging post. In some transits, particularly the refugee routes out of Libya, Crete was the terminus, while in others the destination was Athens and the land route into Europe. They were briefed on the gangs and their personnel. Mohammed Tatanaki (aka Hassan) was a minor player in a ruthless bunch of people-traffickers with a particular propensity for slaughtering their enemies, real or perceived, sometimes in particularly gruesome ways. The leaders had yet to be identified, but many of the foot soldiers had been, and Hassan was one. He'd been pinpointed when working at the Athens end of the operation, but had obviously forged a new identity after fleeing to Crete, where he'd originally arrived from Libya.

In the evenings after work, Petros, Despina and Louise would dine together. One memorable evening, they went to a taverna owned by an old school friend of the captain. It was situated in a square near the Morosini Fountain, and they ate there late at night under the stars. They talked about work, but also other things: music, the films they enjoyed, the books they'd read. Louise told them about her love of Joni Mitchell, Despina about her passion for Bruce Springsteen. Louise discovered that the captain, whose father had been a music teacher, was an accomplished pianist. He'd been raised listening to the famous Greek composer Mikis Theodorakis. Louise teased that he probably hadn't heard of Joni or Bruce, and they all laughed (although Louise suspected it was true). Despina mentioned that she was the only one who wasn't divorced, and wondered if her dining companions wanted any tips. Petros pointed out that she was ten years younger and had plenty of time to join the club. While Louise talked about the contribution her job had made to destroying her marriage, the captain revealed nothing of his marital circumstances. He was going back to Athens the next day, and Louise knew it was to see his daughter, but he said nothing about her, and Louise could see that it was a part of his life that remained out of bounds.

Late on Saturday afternoon, after spending the week in Heraklion, Louise returned to Agia Galini. When she was picking up her room keys from reception at the Crystal Beach Hotel, the manager told her someone had called to see her and had been waiting for an hour on the terrace. Going immediately to the doorway, Louise was delighted to see Sharron, sitting with a glass of what looked like pina colada in her hand, legs stretched towards a facing chair, skirt hitched high on her plump thighs, catching the last fierce rays of the day's sun. There was a yelp of excitement when Sharron saw Louise and the two women embraced, words cascading from Sharron like sparks from a welder.

A lot had happened in the nine days since they'd last met. Most significantly, Sharron had a new boy-friend who 'treats me like a princess'. He was a chef at the restaurant on the Chania seafront where Sharron was waitressing, but he planned to open his own place 'when he's saved a bit of money, like'.

'I got him to drive me down here so I could repay my debt,' Sharron said, handing over an envelope and insisting that Louise open it straight away. Inside was a card inscribed 'For a Special Friend' and fifty euros, the amount Louise had given her to replace the stolen money in the restaurant till.

'Are you sure you can afford this?' Louise said.

'I got Christos, that's my boyfriend, to borrow me the money because I wasn't sure how long you'd be over here for. You told me you were at the Crystal Beach in Agia Galini, but you didn't say how long for. I'm a Virgo,' Sharron continued in her broad Geordie accent. 'I believe in fate. Our meeting, just those few minutes, transformed my life. I could have been arrested and deported with a criminal record; instead, thanks to you, I've got a new life to look forward to with a wonderful bloke.' Sharron pointed in the general direction of the seafront, where Louise assumed Christos was wandering around until being summoned to drive his girlfriend back to Chania. 'And it's all because of the trust you showed in me.'

Louise wasn't an emotional woman, but she couldn't help but be touched by Sharron's effusive display of genuine gratitude. However, she knew she had a job to do, and that this girl was a vital component in the mystery of Bellingham's disappearance, as well as in the search for Hassan. She asked Sharron for her thoughts on the *Sunday Candour* newspaper revelations.

'I wasn't surprised, dirty bugger. I'd never trust a man with a moustache like that – so pervy, like a slug had slithered across his top lip.'

'Did he ever try anything on with you?' Mangan asked, aware that Sharron hadn't been much older than Trudy, the girl in the story, when she'd started to work for the Bellinghams.

'No, he never did, but I caught him leering at me a few times, like – you know, the way men do when they think they might cop an eyeful. I certainly didn't wander around in my nightie when he was at home, I can tell you.'

Sharron asked if Louise had discovered anything about the affair she was convinced Miranda was having, and Louise told her they weren't likely to unless they could come up with something more tangible than a suspicion. She ordered another pina colada for Sharron and a vodka and tonic for herself before moving the conversation on to Hassan, telling Sharron what she'd seen when she'd dined alone at Dimitri's the other Friday night.

'Captain Diamantapoulis, my colleague, who you haven't met, is in Heraklion, working with a specialist narcotics unit to try to find Hassan, and they think they've located the place the gang operates from. Do you think that's where Hassan might be hiding? Would that be where he came from in his car that Friday evening? What's his association with Dimitri?' Suddenly conscious of being a little too professional in the way she was questioning her visitor, Louise paused, placing an affectionate hand on Sharron's shoulder. 'Sorry, love,' she said. 'I didn't mean to bombard you; it's just the pressure getting to me.'

Sharron said she didn't mind at all. The drinks arrived, and once she'd taken a first sip, she seemed ready to respond. Dimitri had shown great kindness to many Libyan refugees, including Hassan, she explained. When he'd learned that Hassan's profession was photography, Dimitri had provided him with some rudimentary facilities. But then Hassan had gone to Athens, and when he returned the restaurateur had grown tired of Hassan's constant dishonesty and unreliability.

'I couldn't blame him, really,' Sharron said. 'Dimitri paid him for tasks that never got done, and he knew it was Hassan who was thieving from him – nothing much, just booze and the odd piece of prime meat, no money, like. Hassan was a charmer and he tried to smooth his way out of it, but the charm had stopped working with Dimitri. No wonder he suspected Hassan of nicking his watch that night.'

She knew Hassan had once lived at the cooperative where Dimitri grew his vegetables, a place up in the hills above Patsos, but by the time she'd met him last year, Hassan had told her he was dossing with three other Libyan refugees in a place along the coast.

'But I never went there. We did all our courting at the Bellinghams' when they were out or in his little car. He'd take me to beaches that nobody else knew about, and I'd watch him take photographs of the scenery and the sunsets. I didn't know anything about no drug-smuggling. He'd disappear off for days, and I never knew where he'd been, but it wasn't as if we were married, like.'

Sharron suggested that the likely explanation for what Louise had seen at Dimitri's that Friday night was that Hassan was desperate for food and shelter. 'He'd left me, don't forget, and cleared off from Chania. If, as you say, the police were looking for him, he was probably after Dimitri's help to escape.'

'Well, from what I saw, he didn't get any help,' Louise observed.

'No, but he did escape. That's the other thing I came to tell you. Hassan has gone back to Libya.'

24

A MAN IN CHAINS

'How can she be so sure?' the captain asked.

They were driving up into the hills above Patsos in the police jeep, Lieutenant Nati at the wheel, Mangan in the seat next to her, Captain Diamantapoulis in the back.

'She showed me the note he delivered to the flat they'd shared. It was put through her door, together with the passport he'd stolen. His written English wasn't great, but Sharron said he always wrote in block capitals, and she's convinced it was from him. He said he was going back to his own country because it was safer for him there than in Crete at the moment. He was sorry for deserting Sharron and hoped the return of her passport would allow her to go home as well. It was rather a sweet note; he said he still loved her and put a couple of kisses after his name.'

The captain's eyes narrowed against the strong midday sunlight as he absorbed this information. 'Our intelligence suggests he's still here, hiding out in the place we're on our way to now – so we'll soon find out.'

It was the Tuesday following Sharron's Saturday visit to the Crystal Beach Hotel. In the ensuing days, the decision had been taken to raid the compound and the operation had been planned. The jeep that Nati drove was the third vehicle in a convoy of four. Ahead of them were two trucks, each containing eight armed officers from the narcotics squad. Behind them was another, larger, jeep with six more armed men. Mangan noticed that the captain had a handgun on his belt. All three of them – the captain, Nati and Mangan – were wearing bulletproof vests, with protective helmets ready to be strapped on when they reached their destination. The captain had been reluctant to grant Mangan's request to come with him on the raid, but she'd persevered, and eventually he'd conceded – on the condition that she stayed with Nati in the jeep. It would be illegal for her to carry a weapon in Greece, so Nati would be her armed guard, and she had to agree to wear the protective equipment, which she was happy to do.

This specialist drugs unit had long suspected that the central hub of the drug transmission between Benghazi and Athens was here in the hills, close to the coast facing the Libyan Sea. Using a combination of intelligence reports and covert observation, they'd pinpointed the precise location two weeks ago, but Inspector General Pelkas had refused to authorise a raid and had insisted no further action be taken.

When Diamantapoulis was told this on his first visit to the unit in Heraklion, he'd countermanded the order and become an immediate hero to the narcotics squad, who'd been frustrated and demoralised by the inspector general's timidity. The squad was convinced that this place was also used for the interlinked people-trafficking operation, and were sure that they'd find human cargo as well as drugs at the site.

As they drove up to the compound, Nati asked if the inspector general was aware of this exercise. 'If you don't inform him, with plenty of people to corroborate that you did,' she surmised, 'he will report to the commander in Athens to get you into trouble and out of his hair. That's my worry.'

'But if he knows, he would try to stop us,' the captain responded emphatically. 'Let's leave Kostar with his lordship, who he thinks he's found in the lake.'

By now they were at the gates of the compound, passing the forbidding 'NO ENTRY' sign at speed. The leading truck pulled up abruptly half a kilometre on, in front of a row of three huts set about twenty metres apart. Some of the officers had already leapt out to aim their weapons and meet any resistance with their semi-automatics. Diamantapoulis led from the front, stepping from the police jeep, gun in hand, to run towards the closest hut. Four men followed him. A colleague was shouting into a hand-held loudhailer, instructing whoever was inside the huts to give themselves up.

Louise, determined to stay close to the action, had disobeyed the captain's instruction to stay in the jeep. She had a premonition about this place. Owing to the archaic bureaucracy of the Greek land registry, its ownership had yet to be finally established, but this must surely be the place 'in the hills above Patsos' where Sharron thought Dimitri grew his vegetables for the restaurant. Louise thought that Lord Bellingham was more likely to be here than in Lake Kournas.

The elite police platoon had fanned out to surround all three huts, weapons aimed at doors and windows. But there was no activity inside, no movement behind the doors, no silhouettes at the windows. Louise noticed the debris around the raised skirting of the huts – tins of food, a pair of gloves, cans of Coke, what looked like ink cartridges – suggesting some spillage in a hurried withdrawal.

They watched and waited. Leaves rustled as one of Crete's sudden strong winds blew up from the coast; a dog barked intermittently from out in the undergrowth; but mostly there was silence. Louise, having removed her helmet to pin back a stray lock of hair, heard something else, the sound of tapping at precise intervals – tap, tap, tap. It was faint, barely discernible even in the silence, but she heard it nevertheless – tap, tap, tap.

She drew it to the captain's attention, but he was dismissive, whispering that it was probably an animal or a bird in the olive grove beyond; too distant and devolved to be of any significance.

After ten minutes, Diamantapoulis led six of the officers into the first hut. The doors weren't locked, and there was nobody inside. It was the same in the other two huts. One contained beds and a stove, another had obviously been used for preparing and eating meals. While signs of human habitation were everywhere, there was no sign of any humans. After searching each hut thoroughly, the captain ordered his men to fan out into the acres of olive groves, fields and scrubland that stretched behind the huts. The barking dog was found tied up in a tool shed – but there was nothing else. All the signs pointed to a hasty exodus. Aside from the debris that Louise had observed, the tyre marks of several vehicles were still visible in the soft earth leading on to the road.

Mangan gestured towards Nati to ask that she join her in trying to locate the tapping that she could still hear, albeit with declining frequency. While the armed officers moved to the north of the huts, the two women followed the sound towards the latrines, set into a clearing about three hundred metres to the south. Once Mangan had persuaded her to remove her helmet, Nati confirmed that she could also hear the tapping sound. They crouched in silence, straining to hear it again. After a few minutes it resumed, appearing to come from underground. Nati ran back to the jeep, returning with a spade, one of several tools affixed to its side in case of emergencies. Digging into the loose soil, she uncovered wooden planks and, eventually, a trapdoor.

The planks had been laid across what seemed to be a huge carbon steel water tank. When Mangan opened the trapdoor, the daylight exposed a metal ladder stretching down ten metres to the floor of the tank. Nati insisted on going down first, gun in hand, with Mangan close behind. As they descended, they realised immediately that this was no storage unit. The smell of human detritus was overwhelming. When they reached the bottom and Lieutenant Nati shone her powerful torch into the darkness, they could see soiled bedding, filthy sleeping bags, discarded clothing, sandals, some children's toys. Mangan guessed this must be where migrants were kept while waiting to embark on the next leg of their journey; a staging post for people so desperate for a better life they were prepared to endure squalor and indignity on land as well as mortal danger at sea.

The two women thought the container was empty until they heard the tapping once again, now louder – and closer. Nati's torch sent a beam of light into a far corner, where first they saw a set of empty manacles, and then, next to them, the sorry sight of a badly beaten man who, like the barking dog, had been chained up to die.

This poor man had been using the chain on one wrist to tap against the insulated metal, trying to attract attention. Nati went to get help, while Mangan tried to comfort the man. She could see a stab wound in his side and the marks of excessive torture. He was barely alive. Taking a bottle of water from her belt, she held it to his lips. Despite the ragged beard and the beating he'd taken, she recognised him from the photographs she'd seen. It was Christopher Finch.

25

AN AFTERNOON VISIT TO THE
PREMIER INN

Cathleen arrived at the Premier Inn in Blackfriars at one
o'clock, and went straight up to the room on the second
floor, where Benjamin had told her he'd be waiting.
Their affair was easier to conduct during the holidays.
Unconstrained by the school day, they could pass off
trips into central London as part of their pedagogic
preparation for the new term. They took turns paying
for the hotel room – 'going Dutch cap', as Benjamin
joked. One of the things that Cathleen liked about her
lover was his unrelenting good humour.

They always used Premier Inns, principally because
they were so much cheaper than other hotels. They only
used the room for three hours at the most, but had to
book it for twenty-four. It would be extravagant to use
a dearer hotel. They'd never contemplated getting their
money's worth by spending a whole night together.
Never had done since Paris and never wanted to. They
were lovers but they weren't in love.

Another benefit of these hotels was that there were
few staff, thus there was greater privacy. In any case,
those renting rooms here were not the sort of people

to pry into the lives of their fellow guests. Premier Inns were functional hotels for functional people: the rooms clean and adequate, the walls thick enough to ensure that no sound escaped into the world beyond.

The strenuous exertion of Cathleen and Benjamin's first hotel encounter in Paris had long mellowed into a steady routine involving as much conversational intercourse as sexual. Indeed, the conversation would generally continue while they were having sex, such was the relaxed intimacy they shared. Benjamin told Cathleen that chatting while screwing heightened his enjoyment, and Cathleen said that it combined the two things she didn't get enough of at home.

The only added extra to the facilities provided was the whisky that Benjamin always brought with him. The brand was Teacher's (another of his little japes), and after making love, they'd sit upright against the headrest while Benjamin poured a few inches of the stuff into the tumblers taken from the bathroom.

On this afternoon, Cathleen told Benjamin about her Mediterranean holiday. It was as if she'd spent it alone rather than with Brady. She spoke of her swimming, the scuba dives, and her exploration of the coastline and its beaches.

'What the hell does he do all day?' Benjamin asked, placing his whisky on the bedside table as he rearranged the sheets.

'God knows. Most days, he'd take a ferry to another island, but he was usually back for dinner.'

'Has he finished reading that book yet?' Benjamin was referring to *The Crescent Moon* by Burak Bayram. Cathleen had told him some weeks ago that Brady had asked to borrow it from her extensive book collection, stressing how unusual it was for her husband to read any novel, let alone the profound political allegory for which Bayram was most famous.

'If he has, he hasn't given it back to me yet. I doubt he'll be at Bayram's event in the Assembly Rooms next month.'

'No, but we will. I promised to get you tickets and I have – wangled five for school staff, so we'll be part of a Dalston Academy delegation.'

'That's great – I'm looking forward to it, even if you're not.'

'You know that I prefer Ben Okri to Bayram.'

'Yes, but you haven't actually read any Bayram, which makes it a rather futile comparison.'

'Guilty as charged, but I'll endure anything to spend some time with you – even if there will be five of us on this date.'

Benjamin was still smiling when Cathleen put her tumbler on the bedside table and turned a serious face towards her lover. 'I've decided to leave him,' she said, looking directly at Benjamin. 'Don't worry,' she added, noticing a flash of anxiety in his eyes. 'I'm not leaving him for you – I'm leaving him for me.'

Slightly irritated at Cathleen's implication, Benjamin protested that they'd always been straight with one another about wanting an affair rather than a life together.

'I know, darling,' Cathleen said, stroking his arm. 'Unfortunately, though, all this will have to stop, at least while I get my bearings as a single woman.'

'What's brought this about?' Benjamin asked. 'Your hubby is no different now to the way he's always been, at least since I've known you.'

'It's cumulative, a process that's been gathering momentum. You're a part of it, in that I now know that a different man can give me pleasure, but it's mainly a realisation that I'd be better off alone than with him. It's not just that I don't love him anymore; it's that I'm beginning to despise him, and that's not fair. As you say, he's no different now than when I married him. He was a stranger to me then – living in his own enclosed world – and he's a stranger to me now, after all these years of marriage.'

'When will you tell him?'

'I thought I'd find some rooms to rent and bugger off, leaving him a note. Do you think that's cowardly?'

'I think you should do it in the way you're most comfortable with. When are you planning to make the great escape?'

'Before the next term begins,' Cathleen said.

'That soon? That's only a couple of weeks away.'

'Yes, my darling, that soon. This is our farewell shag. From now on, we're going back to being friends.'

'That's a shame. But all good things must come to an end, I suppose. How do you think he'll take it?'

'I'm not sure. If I don't leave a note, he might not even notice I've gone, such is the nature of our lives together.'

'Do you think he'll cut up rough?'

'Oh no,' Cathleen protested. 'If there's one thing I know about my husband, it's that he's not a violent man.'

26

BAYRAM'S BOYS

Brady had come to a decision. His chance meeting with Osman and their subsequent conversation over coffee had put the notion in his head, but it was meeting Manny again that had turned it into a firm resolution to take decisive action.

Having asked Osman for Manny's address in Golders Green so that he could deliver the prayer lectern in person when it reached its beautifully crafted and highly polished completion, Brady travelled over in a taxi, the handsome gift incongruously wrapped in a black bin liner. Unable to confirm in advance whether there'd be anyone in, Brady had warned the cab driver that he may need to be taken straight back home, but was relieved to find his friend mowing the front lawn. He let the taxi go and, at Manny's invitation, carried his still unwrapped present through the long garden and into the house, where he was stopped by a young policewoman posted inside the front porch.

'They're worried I may still be a target,' the old man explained. 'Would they want to kill me as well as destroy my livelihood?'

Manny left the question hanging. There was a camera set up inside the front porch, and the police officer took Brady's photograph, as well as his name and address, explaining that she was obliged to record every visitor, whether tradesman, friend or family. She did say that Brady was entitled to decline the photo opportunity, but he knew this would attract suspicion. His discomfort was eased by the knowledge that his details were now on record anyway, by virtue of his wife's (since forgiven) indiscretion, and that there'd be no mugshot with which his photo could be compared.

Manny was delighted with the exquisite piece of carpentry that emerged from the bin liner when they'd entered his substantial house and reached the living room. The old Glaswegian gently lifted the lectern, taking it to a big picture window to gaze at its fine detail in a stronger light. He called to Naomi, his wife, who was equally impressed. As they ran their hands across the lacquered wood, Manny and Naomi were overcome with emotion. Manny explained that the strain of the past few weeks had taken its toll on them both.

'How could this gang of thugs do this to us – destroy our lives with no come back?' Manny asked through his tears.

It was this encounter that finally convinced Brady that there had to be retribution, and that, given the absence of any alternative, he'd need to be the one to deliver it.

Brady didn't reveal anything about his intention to either Manny or Osman. They weren't to know that it was him who'd intervened on their behalf. In fact, he wasn't entirely sure if he was even doing it for them, or more for his own satisfaction. But he was very sure about the risk he was taking. With one extremely lucrative contract completed and one more to fulfil before early retirement, this would be a dangerous distraction – uncharacteristically impulsive, insufficiently planned.

Osman had told him that his home might be besieged on any night of the week, but that it was a regular feature of Tuesday evenings. Apparently, there was a weekly gym session that the gang attended, after which they'd head over to Osman's house for some light entertainment. The late summer dusk descended at around eight-thirty, and it was then that Razor Parting and his buddies gathered to continue their campaign of intimidation.

Brady had noticed an empty house being renovated a little further down, on the opposite side of the road to Osman's house. It was encased in scaffolding, providing Brady with an easy and unobserved route to a vantage point from which he could look down on the street below. He'd made a point of going there on a couple of occasions to reconnoitre, finding that the workmen knocked off at around four-thirty. One evening, he'd tested his plan on a dummy run, and found it relatively easy to climb the scaffolding at the back of the house. There was a motion-activated light and security camera, but Brady knew everything there was to know about disabling such devices.

The next time he visited the site, on the evening of Tuesday 22 August, he was there for business, dressed in dark clothes, with a backpack containing the dismantled

Remington semi-automatic, which he'd chosen over the more powerful Barrett M82. The Barrett had a vast range and was capable of bringing down a helicopter, but Brady had decided that this rabble didn't warrant such a weapon. The Remington, with its less lethal cartridge, would be sufficient. Having dealt with the security equipment and climbed the scaffolding, he reassembled the gun and positioned himself against the stone balustrade, waiting.

An hour passed, and he was beginning to think that this might be one evening when the Bombacilar gang had better things to do: completing a jigsaw puzzle, perhaps, or examining their stamp collection. Chewing steadily, he'd already discarded one piece of gum and had popped another into his mouth, when six or seven young men swaggered into view. Four of them had their hoods up, but in the lead, unhooded, was Razor Parting. The injuries that Osman had inflicted were no longer evident. What was clear to Brady was that those injuries had failed to diminish the cocky demeanour of Taylan Ayhan.

He recognised some of the others from the encounter in Manny's café. They sat along the wall in front of Osman's house, their leader encouraging them to ever louder hoots and howls. Brady had already decided on just two shots: one to wound (rather than kill), the other randomly fired, for its shock value alone. His victim for the first shot wouldn't be Razor Parting; he preferred to injure one of the princes rather than the king, in the hope that this would be enough to convince their leader that he could be next and his followers to find something better to do with their evenings. People in neighbouring houses were closing their curtains to shut out what was happening in the street. Brady hoped that nobody would call the police to complain about these yobs, but as no one had interfered in Osman's persecution up until now, he calculated that the risk was minimal.

The gang was sitting in an untidy line, calling Osman's name.

'Oh Osman, are you coming out to play?' they trilled, before switching to Turkish to yell what Brady suspected were deeply offensive insults. Eventually, they broke into a football chant: 'We are Bombacilar, we are Bombacilar,' repeated over and over – until the first shot was fired.

There was a scream as a tall, skinny lad who'd been sitting next to Razor Parting, seemingly his first lieutenant, was hit in the thigh. He writhed around on the pavement, screaming in pain, blood spurting from the wound as his mates scrambled for cover. They had no idea where the shot had come from, but knew that it couldn't have been from behind them, so they scrambled to get into the front garden of Osman's house, crouching along the wall they'd been sitting on. Two of the gang assisted their wounded comrade, while Razor Parting tried to locate where their attacker was firing from. Brady ducked below the balustrade. He'd deliberately used his bullet to extract maximum impact for minimum injury – a flesh wound that looked worse than it was. He needed his victim to be mobile enough for his friends to be able to carry him away.

The gang was settling behind the wall when Brady's second shot ricocheted off a metal gate behind them, convincing them they were under sustained attack from all directions and needed to retreat, speedily. As the dishevelled ranks of the Bombacilar gang fled in terror, Brady calmly dismantled the Remington and descended the scaffolding to slip down an alleyway at the opposite end of the street from Osman's house. By the time the first police sirens were disturbing the evening peace, Brady was on the other side of the High Street, moving between the dense maze of houses, on his way home. He'd already used a proxy app on a burner phone to tweet anonymously:

> We are the defenders of Burak Bayram and
> all he stands for. We will drive the scum out of
> our community. Tonight was a warning.
> – Bayram's Boys

27

THE DISCERNED AND THE DELETED

Assistant Commissioner Louise Mangan was informed about the Stoke Newington shooting the morning after it happened. She was in the police jeep with Captain Diamantapoulis and Lieutenant Nati, heading back to Agia Galini just after daybreak. They'd worked through the previous night at the compound, first to ensure that the man they'd found, badly beaten and close to death, was airlifted to a military hospital on the mainland, where the medics calculated he'd have at least a ten per cent chance of survival. Despite Mangan's immediate recognition of him as Chris Finch, the *Daily Candour* journalist who'd been reported missing last week, an extensive search had not turned up a passport or papers, and the man had yet to be formally named. Severely dehydrated and barely clothed, Finch must have spent at least a week manacled to the wall of his manufactured underground cell, using his final reserves of strength to tap out the sounds that she'd heard, which had led to his discovery. The second empty set of manacles next to where Finch had been held showed that the submerged water tank was not only used to temporarily house migrants, but also as a place to punish and imprison those seen as enemies.

Once the still-unconscious Finch had been despatched to hospital, the captain concentrated on overseeing a thorough search of the sixty-acre site. His officers continued to rummage through scrubland, and search through olive trees, and across fields of fruit and vegetables, as well as in the outhouses and greenhouses. The three large huts at the heart of the estate came under particular scrutiny. The captain had managed to get permission for a forensic unit to be helicoptered across from Athens after emphasising the importance of this discovery to his commander. He'd also pleaded, in the same conversation, that there should be no publicity given to the raid, despite its obvious newsworthiness. They still hadn't found Hassan, and their priority must be to capture the murderous gang of which he was a member. Obviously, the fact that they'd found Finch needed to be reported, but describing the circumstances of his discovery would only make the pursuit more difficult. Upon being told this, Mangan hoped the commander would contrast the captain's approach with that of Inspector General Pelkas, who was still conducting a self-promoting media circus at Lake Kournas.

The intelligence gathered by the narcotics unit about this being the central hub for the trafficking of people and drugs between Libya and mainland Europe had proved to be correct. The hasty abandonment of the compound suggested knowledge of the impending raid, and this disturbed Diamantapoulis, who expressed his concern to Mangan on the early morning journey back to the coast.

'Do you think Pelkas tipped them off?' Louise asked.

'Perhaps, although I did my best to ensure he was kept in the dark. None of the men has any respect for that clown, but I suppose he may have an ally somewhere.'

They planned to return to their respective hotels for a few hours' sleep and a shower before examining the analysis of Lord Bellingham's phone that the forensics team had brought with them from Athens. The team wondered why the captain still considered this analysis to be necessary. The news in Greece and around the world was that the disgraced politician had been located – in Lake Kournas.

Nati was pulling into the Crystal Beach car park to drop Louise off prior to driving a few kilometres down the coast to Matala, where she and the captain had rooms in a hotel run by a retired former colleague. Mangan was just about to get out of the jeep when Detective Inspector Jack Cairns called to tell her about the Stoke Newington shooting the previous night, and the message from 'Bayram's Boys'.

'The spooks, having told us there was no likelihood of trouble at Bayram's event on 21 September, now think there might be. I wanted to get to you before the commissioner does. I think he might be about to curtail your holiday.'

'What do the spooks know about this "Bayram's Boys" outfit?' Mangan asked, ignoring the misrepresentation of her work in Crete.

'Nothing at all; never heard of them.'

'And yet they're armed and capable of what sounds like a quite sophisticated ambush.'

'Precisely,' said Cairns. 'There could have been fatalities last night, and the worry is that there may be in the future. As that message said, it was just a warning.'

'Any clues as to who was involved?' Mangan asked.

'Well, it certainly wasn't Osman, who's the obvious suspect given how they were taunting him. Might have been someone on his behalf, or Manny's. Or maybe the local Turkish community really have had enough of these bastards.'

'Hmm. There are other ways of dealing with troublemakers that don't involve firing a bloody gun in a residential area. Do we know where the shot was fired from?'

'Judging by its trajectory, it was fired from an empty house a bit further up the road. It's got scaffolding up, and our guys are in the process of searching it, as well as looking for the bullets now it's light.'

'Okay. Thanks for the tip-off, Jack. I'll wait to hear from the commissioner later, hopefully after I've had some kip. Oh, and Jack – we've found that missing reporter. It's amazing, the things you can achieve on holiday,' Mangan said, before ending the call.

The captain headed off to Matala with Nati, having agreed to meet Mangan again at lunchtime to go through the forensic examination of Bellingham's phone. After setting up a call with the commissioner for that evening, Mangan sank into a hot bath before closing the thin curtains of her room and surrendering herself to sleep.

Her alarm went at midday, and an hour later Mangan and the captain had reunited in the little port authority office to go through the forensics report. The captain had a thin folder in front of him, from which he extracted a single sheet of paper that, he told Louise, contained the all-important summary of what had been found.

'There is no English translation, so I'm afraid you have to listen to me rather than read it yourself.'

'If I must,' Louise said, rolling her eyes and giving no indication of the pleasure she took in listening to Petros's rich bass carefully enunciating a language that was not his own.

Lord Bellingham's mobile phone was zipped into a transparent plastic bag in front of them on the desk.

'First, there are no fingerprints belonging to anyone other than the lordship. Second, there is nothing on this phone that helps us.'

Mangan gave a little sigh of disappointment before noticing a faint smile begin to dawn on the captain's stern features. 'It's what's *not* on the phone that is interesting,' he said.

Louise gave the captain a playful punch on the arm as he motioned for her to sit next to him.

'So, our people retrieved all the items deleted. There is much we don't need to look at, hours of porn videos that the lordship accessed regularly. I am not a prude, and realise this stuff is popular with lots of men, but what he watches is unacceptable. He has strong interest in young girls, but I think we know that already. So, nothing there that helps us.'

The captain pulled on a pair of disposable gossamer gloves before unzipping the plastic bag and taking out the phone. 'But something *has* been deleted that we need to think about,' he said.

Looking at the array of apps, Mangan pointed to one that had 'Home Connect' printed under it. 'These are whizzy things. They allow you to monitor your house while you're away. Apparently, there's even a mic attached, so that if you see anyone suspicious approaching your front door, you can question them as to what they're doing there from thousands of miles away. I'm thinking of getting one myself.'

From the silence beside her, Louise could tell that her intervention wasn't going down well.

'Yes, I know,' Petros said eventually. 'I have one on my phone. Even here, in this backward country, we have such things. For some reason, footage from the app has been deleted; either that, or the cameras in London weren't working properly.'

'So, nothing useful there?' Mangan asked, ignoring the captain's sarcastic barb and keen to get back to business.

'No. What is interesting is *this*.' The captain opened a travel app, and a timetable filled the screen. 'These are ferry crossings between Crete and the port of Piraeus in Athens. Most of them concern the crossing from

Chania. There's a high-speed ferry that departs daily in the summer and does the journey in six and a half hours – some crossings can take almost double that.'

'When was this downloaded?'

'On Tuesday 1 August, the day before he disappeared.'

The captain explained that the forensics team had retrieved lots of dross, but that he had focused on those few days after Bellingham's arrival in Crete, before he went missing in the White Mountains.

'Perhaps they were planning an excursion to the mainland during his holiday,' Mangan postulated, getting up from her uncomfortable chair and pacing the floor. The sleep she'd snatched hadn't refreshed her; if anything, it had pushed the exhaustion deeper into her system. Captain Diamantapoulis remained seated, picking at the buttons of his short-sleeved shirt.

'Perhaps you're right,' he responded, after a few minutes' thought. 'But why delete them? If they had such plans, they'd need that information again over the following days or weeks. A greater "perhaps" is that they were planning his departure from the island.'

Louise returned to her chair. The prehistoric ceiling fan in the tiny office whirled and stuttered, failing to do anything other than recirculate the dusty heat. She and the captain sat in thoughtful silence for five minutes.

'What you're saying,' Louise said, eventually, 'is that the Bellinghams knew he was about to be exposed, and developed a plan for Lord B to go missing, presumed dead. She doesn't drive him to Hora Sfakion aiming to meet him at Georgioupoli at the end of his walk in the White Mountains, as we were told – because there was no walk. Instead, she drives him to Chania, so he can hop on a ferry to Athens.'

'Yes, and on the way, along the route he was supposed to have hiked, they put his phone in a place it is likely to be found, and above a precipice that he might have fallen into,' the captain interjected.

'Which explains why Miranda knew where it was found, even though you hadn't told her,' Mangan concluded. 'It's a theory, but how could he do it without leaving a trail? Wouldn't he need to have his passport checked to get on the ferry?'

'No, it is going from one part of Greece to another – no need to show passports. Also, if he pays in cash to go on the ferry as a pedestrian, there will be no record of the transaction, and no security footage – that is always focused on cars.'

'For this to be more than a theory, we need to be able to prove that Lady Bellingham drove to Chania,' Mangan declared.

The captain placed a gentle hand on her shoulder. 'Of course, Louise, of course. But this is more than a theory for me already. It explains everything – her knowing where the phone was, her reluctance to talk about what she was doing between dropping him off and waiting to pick him up, the absence of any sign of him despite the biggest search ever launched on this island. He wasn't found because he's not here. You need to look for him in Athens or somewhere else on the mainland. Anywhere in Europe except this island – anywhere except Crete.'

'But with everyone now believing he's in Lake Kournas, isn't this a bit too flimsy to change their minds?'

'I agree, flimsy. Unless we can prove she drove to Chania. Which is why I'm sending Nati back to Athens. We have had speed cameras on Crete for the last three years, not many, and some we have don't work properly, but Lady Bellingham has a very distinctive car, and to get to Chania they would have needed to drive on the main road, the E75, where the best cameras are – so Nati and her colleagues will check every available film for that route on that day.'

'Excellent; that should prove your theory one way or the other. I don't suppose there's any route they could have taken to avoid the cameras?'

'There isn't, but think about it, Louise; why would they? Lots of people get lost in the White Mountains – vanish and are never found. It is the perfect cover, and the suspicion that he may have killed himself is just as good for their purpose. Who would suspect she has driven him to a ferry port? They have no need to worry about the journey to Chania, only what to do once he gets to Athens.'

'We certainly need to speak to Lady Bellingham again,' Mangan said.

'She says she is too upset to talk to us until a week's time,' the captain responded.

'Oh, does she now? I might not be here in a week's time, and seeing her is an important part of my liaison role.'

Diamantapoulis smiled, saying softly, 'Yes, is true – and I do not want to lose my liaison officer, but maybe delay is for the best. Maybe it's better to go to see Lady Bellingham after we receive Nati's report from the cameras.'

'I wasn't suggesting we arrest her, Petros,' Mangan responded, more aggressively than she'd meant to.

'I know; I'm only saying that the week she wants to delay suits us as well. If still no body is found in the lake, if the journalist recovers enough to tell us some-thing, if we find Hassan, if Despina finds something on the speed cameras . . . I can only hope that you are here with me next Tuesday when we see her.'

Louise rose wearily to her feet, pulling at her thin blouse in the sticky heat. 'I'll head on back to my room. I could do with a swim and a shower before the call with my commissioner this evening.'

'Nearly forgot,' the captain called after her as she walked towards the door. 'Lady Bellingham has insisted that her solicitor from London is with her when we see her next week.'

28

RETURN TO THE SMOKE

'I need you back here, Louise, and I need you back here now.'

Commissioner Irvine was unusually dictatorial. Mangan was surprised by his tone. In all the years she'd known him, she'd never heard him so much as raise his voice. He was a man who thrived on pressure, who took pride in his ability to remain calm in stressful situations. When she said she appreciated the pressure he must be under, it hadn't helped.

'I'm not under any pressure, Louise, and if I was, it wouldn't affect my judgement. The simple fact is that everybody except you and your Greek policeman think that Lord Bellingham has been found, and most of the public couldn't care less if he's dead or alive. I've been supporting the line you're taking about the wider issue to do with drugs and people-trafficking, and I've made sure that you've been given credit for finding that British reporter . . .'

'He does have a name,' Mangan said quietly.

'Yes, Finch, isn't it?'

'Not the reporter; I mean the Greek policeman I'm working with. The man who organised the raid that led to us finding Finch.'

'I know he has a name. It's been in all the reports I've been getting. The trouble is, I can't pronounce it. Anyway, this shooting in Stoke Newington is causing a fair amount of concern, and your task of overseeing the security arrangements for when that Turkish writer comes over is now more important than finding Lord Bellingham, who most people think has already been found.'

Having concluded that she needed to return to London, Mangan's objective in this conversation was to ensure she'd be able to then come back to Crete for the interview with Lady Bellingham in a week's time. She was in no doubt that she could combine liaising re: Bellingham with overseeing re: Bayram – if she was allowed to.

'I'll come back tomorrow,' Mangan announced, 'but please don't replace me over here.'

'I've already lined up a detective inspector,' the commissioner responded.

'All I ask is that you don't confirm that until we've had a chance to have a proper face-to-face conversation. There have been developments that strengthen the theory that Bellingham faked his own demise. I can't explain it over the phone, but if we could meet towards the end of the week, I might have some pretty incontrovertible evidence.'

The commissioner conceded, as Mangan had been sure he would. She'd known him long enough to be sure of his faith in her, and he knew how much it was reciprocated.

'I was keen to talk to you when you're back, anyway. GCHQ has picked up a scrap of intelligence about a contract killing. It was part of an exchange between a couple of dubious characters, and they don't know if it's happened or about to happen, but they think Bayram might be the target – so you can see why I'm eager to have you back, fully focused on that visit next month.'

Brady's decision to intervene to defend Osman and avenge Manny came as close to spontaneity as anything he'd done in his professional life. There'd been no meticulous planning, no careful preparation. He'd noticed the empty, scaffolded building in the road where Osman lived and made a spot decision.

It was the first time he'd shot somebody pro bono. Even in Northern Ireland, there'd been a return for his paramilitary activity, albeit non-pecuniary. Back then, he did it for a cause. On this occasion, while he told himself it was for Manny and Osman, he knew really it was just petty retribution against a guy whose attitude had annoyed him.

This was why he'd walked through the streets where he lived carrying a lethal weapon, clambered up scaffolding in a densely populated area and fired into a residential street. He couldn't have done more to draw attention to where he lived if he'd walked naked down the High Street. It had been completely and utterly irrational.

He'd chosen that particular Tuesday evening to utilise his irrationality because Cathleen was out of the way, at a school event preparing for the term that was soon to start. He'd got home ahead of her, which was just as well. It would have been difficult to explain to his wife why he was walking the streets in dark clothing with a bag on his back. Brady wasn't known for his devotion to fresh air and exercise.

He was in his workshop when Cathleen returned. The gun was back in his hidden arsenal, behind a false wall he'd constructed. He wondered what had got into him; what made him take such risks when he was so close to giving all this up. With one super-lucrative job already done this year and one more to do, the retirement fund accumulating in his Swiss bank account would soon be more than sufficient. It had been irresponsible to risk it all on a piece of petty revenge. If he'd been stopped and searched, either going or returning this evening, the game would have been up.

'What's done is done,' Brady thought to himself, but he couldn't stop the feeling of destabilisation, as if a small part of the intricate mechanism that controlled his life had broken and was about to destroy the entire machine. He could hear Cathleen pottering around the kitchen. She called out to ask if he wanted a cup of tea. At least this aspect – the comfortable domesticity of his life with Cathleen – remained stable. He didn't ask about her meeting when he eventually emerged from his workshop to pick up his mug of tea from the breakfast bar. Neither did he notice how glamorously Cathleen had dressed for a mundane work gathering with her fellow teachers.

There had been no work meeting, of course. Cathleen had been for dinner with Benjamin. They'd both used the same excuse of a pre-term get-together to go to a restaurant in the City, where they had talked with an animated intimacy that Cathleen had never experienced in her marriage. She'd told Benjamin about the bedsit she'd found and would be moving into in a couple of weeks when she left home to begin her new life without Brady.

Quentin Kane didn't usually read the *Daily Candour*. He'd always been a *Telegraph* man, although he occasionally bought the *Financial Times* on Saturdays for its weekend section. Having done the deal with Chris Finch, though, and after hearing of the journalist's misfortune, he felt obliged to keep up with the story. His *Daily Telegraph* would, of course, have contained some information about the discovery of Finch, who'd apparently been the captive of a criminal gang. It was important national news that all the papers were covering. But only the *Candour*, recording the travails of one of their own, did so with gusto, spreading the story over three pages in an incongruous combination of sensationalism and solemnity.

Kane was reading the newspaper over a cup of coffee in his office at Chesterton, Kane and Palfrey. The awful fate that had befallen Finch didn't affect the agreement they'd reached in the Red Lion. The money had already been transferred by the newspaper group into an account that Kane had specifically set up to pay the school fees for Miranda Bellingham's children. Kane had kept to his side of the bargain. He'd called Lady Bellingham to warn her what would be in the next day's *Sunday Candour*. The story had been a shock to her, but not a surprise. She'd married Edward Bellingham fully aware of his wandering eye – and his predilection for schoolgirls.

Miranda was happy with the agreement her solicitor had secured and had no intention of resorting to litigation. Why should she? Thanks to Kane's deal with Chris Finch, the money that would have gone to Trudy Smith – or, as she'd described her, 'that grubby little scrubber' – would now provide for the first few years of the twins' education. What did seem to be causing Lady Bellingham greater concern was the line of questioning being pursued by 'a Scotland Yard woman who's apparently been sent over to interfere with the perfectly adequate work the Greek police are doing'. Miranda told Quentin how much she resented being treated as if hers was only one version of events that needed to be checked and verified. Miranda was insisting on Kane going out to Crete to be with her when this policewoman, Assistant Commissioner Mangan, came to see her again.

'I've managed to put her off for a week; my husband has drowned, for fuck's sake, why are they still hassling me? I need your help, Quentin,' she'd said in their most recent conversation. Kane had agreed to go. A few days in Crete would hardly be onerous.

He'd come into the office this morning for the weekly partners' meeting, which was now due to begin. Kane put the *Daily Candour* back with all the other newspapers helpfully provided in the Chesterton, Kane and Palfrey waiting room. Picking up his coffee, Kane joined Sir Charles Chesterton and Tom Palfrey in Sir Charles's office. They could have used the oak-panelled boardroom, but this was an informal gathering of the three partners. It would be inappropriate to hold it around a table that could (and frequently did) seat twenty-five.

Sir Charles Chesterton, the senior partner, was a distinguished-looking man in his early seventies, who now spent more time on the golf course than in the office. Kane had suggested having these meetings fortnightly or even monthly, but Sir Charles had made them a feature of the practice from its early days and was hostile to any suggestions of change. He considered this Wednesday meeting to be a tradition and therefore inviolable.

Tom Palfrey was four years older than Kane. A small, stout man with more hair on his face than his scalp, he'd gone to the same school as Kane. Indeed, being a fellow Wykamist was undoubtedly the main reason why Palfrey had championed Kane's recruitment to the partnership fifteen years ago.

As they gathered in a corner of Chesterton's office, Palfrey was keen to commend Kane on his success in finally securing the completion of the Bellingham

Developments site in London Docklands. 'Looks as if you just got in under the wire before the stigma of Lord Bellingham's sexual peccadillos begins to corrode his company,' he said.

'Hardly peccadillos,' observed Sir Charles in his rich baritone. 'They weren't minor sexual transgressions. That awful man took pornographic pictures of a child who he'd impregnated – bit more serious than a peccadillo, I'd say.'

This statement brooked no objection. Kane, keen to get off the subject, sipped his coffee, saying nothing, but Tom Palfrey was in full flow.

'I suppose we shouldn't speak ill of the presumed dead,' he reflected, 'but old Eddie always was a bit of a cad. He was my contemporary at Winchester, and was forever chastising the younger boys. Weren't you ever one of his victims, Quentin?'

'No,' Kane said, rising to refill his cup from a coffee percolator on a side table.

'Well, you're lucky. I once saw him and his pals tie a small boy to a goal post on a freezing cold day, pull down the lad's pants, and offer us sixth-formers a fiver if we could hit the boy's arse from the penalty spot. The poor lad was humiliated. He had a very red backside by end of play, I can tell you.'

'And were you one of the penalty takers?' Sir Charles asked.

'We all had to take one, but I deliberately missed. I never was much good at football; always a rugger man myself.'

The two men laughed, but Kane saw nothing funny. He hadn't been one of Edward Bellingham's victims at Winchester, but one of his friends had, and Kane had been a silent witness to that boy's degradation.

29

THE INCIDENT AT WINCHESTER

The events that still haunted Quentin Kane had taken place in 1981, when Kane was thirteen years old. He was in his first year at the school, and had forged a close friendship with a Chinese boy named Bobby Cheong, whose father was a prominent Hong Kong businessman and committed anglophile. Cheong Senior had never experienced the English public school system himself, but was convinced of its superiority. This was predicated on a belief in the natural supremacy of the English aristocracy, and the conviction that cold showers and a harsh environment would be the making of his son.

Quentin and Bobby's relationship was based in the main on their mutual detestation of the school. For Quentin, this was driven by enforced separation from his three older sisters, and the fact that he struggled academically. Born in a Hampshire village, the son of two successful lawyers, he'd had an idyllic childhood – up to this point. Although educated privately from the age of four, he'd never boarded before. As his home was only twenty miles away from Winchester, he resented having to do so at this school when he could easily have been a day boy. But his parents believed that the full value of one of England's greatest public schools couldn't be realised unless their son was imprisoned within it.

Bobby's reasons for detesting the school were very different. He was the brightest boy in their year and had no problem with being away from his family. Most of his young life had been spent separated from his parents and siblings, as he had been educated privately in England while his main family home was in Hong Kong. But Bobby Cheong was being viciously bullied by an eighteen-year-old boy in his final year – Edward Bellingham.

Bellingham had a reputation as a nasty piece of work who, ever since becoming physically developed, had been an enthusiastic beater, flogger – and, it was rumoured, buggerer – of any small boy unfortunate enough to attract his venomous attention. Kane had been with Bobby when that attention had first been focused on his friend.

They were walking to a lesson along with many other boys, criss-crossing Chamber Court, when Bellingham, coming from behind with a gang of acolytes, pushed Bobby violently to the ground, shouting 'Out of my way, chinky!' to the obvious amusement of his pals. Quentin had urged his friend to report it to their housemaster, but Bobby said this would only make the situation worse.

'If I had a penny for every time I've been called a chinky, I'd be a millionaire,' he'd said, brushing himself down.

Kane pointed out that he probably was a millionaire anyway, given his father's great wealth, and the two boys walked on, laughing. Bobby thought this would be an isolated incident, but soon realised his mistake. Bellingham had found a fresh victim. Bobby's unhappiness increased the more relentless the bullying became. His state of mind was discernible by his demeanour. The easy smile surfaced less often; the infectious giggle disappeared. He became morose and introspective. Kane knew that Bobby was being targeted, but wasn't a direct witness to Bellingham's tyranny again until the friends were at something called Christian Summer Camp, which took place over the first week of the long summer holiday.

As Bobby wasn't going home to Hong Kong until the middle of August, he'd volunteered for the camp, and asked Quentin if he'd opt in as well. There wasn't much Bible bashing, and they'd be doing lots of activities that they both enjoyed: sailing on the Solent, trekking through the New Forest – there'd even be a night out in Bournemouth. Despite being called a camp, they wouldn't have to slum it under canvas; they'd remain in their own dormitories, setting off for a new adventure every day. The whole thing was run by a prominent banker, George Smythers, a lay preacher who dedicated his summers to these character-building activities at his old school.

The camp was for first- and second-year pupils (thirteen- and fourteen-year-olds), but a few of the older boys attended in supervisory roles. When the week commenced, the friends were shocked to find that one of these older boys was Edward Bellingham. Bobby told Quentin that he'd finally reported his persecutor to the master of the college (Winchester's head teacher) the previous week, after an incident in the refectory. Two of the gang had held Bobby down while Bellingham stuffed noodles into his mouth, standing over him and asking if he was enjoying his 'chinky dinner'. Bobby had run straight to the master's office, noodles down his jacket, sauce smeared across his face. The master hadn't been free to see him, and Bobby had had to relate that incident, and many others, to a bursar in an outer office, who'd promised to pass it all on to his boss.

'Why have they let him come to summer camp when they know I'm here?' Bobby asked plaintively of his friend on their first night. They were the only two boys in their dormitory to be on the course and therefore still occupying their beds.

'Well, these things take time, and it was only last week that you reported him. I suppose they'd have to check a few things out, be sure you're telling the truth; you know, like in *Starsky and Hutch*,' Quentin tried to reassure his friend.

'I reported eight separate incidents of serious bullying. You'd think they'd keep him away from me, at least while they investigate.'

By day five, Bobby was beginning to believe that something had happened in response to his complaint after all. He couldn't avoid encountering Bellingham, but there'd been no bullying during the camp. Indeed, his bête noire hadn't uttered a word to him, and had even given a smile of approval when Bobby, who had a fine voice, had sung a hymn as part of the camp concert on the third night. By Friday evening, Bobby was telling Quentin that he was convinced something had been said to Bellingham – maybe he'd even been threatened with expulsion. Why else would his attitude have changed so completely?

'I wish now that I'd reported him sooner,' Bobby said, as the lights went out on the final night of camp.

The two boys' beds were two metres apart, and during the night, Kane's sleep was disturbed by a deep voice speaking softly close by. A full moon shone through the open curtains, and he saw two figures standing over Bobby's bed. Keeping perfectly still, as if asleep, he could see from the bedside clock that it was one o'clock in the morning, and that one of the two figures standing over Bobby was Edward Bellingham. The other was George Smythers, the man running the camp.

Bobby rose sleepily at Smythers' behest, allowing himself to be manoeuvred towards the door. Kane continued pretending he was asleep, aware that Bellingham was standing over him, watching carefully. In the years since that night, he'd told himself that if it had just been Bellingham taking Bobby from his bed, he'd have raised the alarm, but the presence of an adult, a devout lay preacher, had reassured him that his friend was safe. Kane's theory as he lay awake that night, wondering where his friend had been taken, was that

Bellingham had confessed his sins to Mr Smythers and that the good Christian banker had arranged a ceremony of penitence so that the week could end in a spirit of repentance and forgiveness.

He must have dozed off, because when he next opened his eyes, Bobby was back in his bed, sobbing and shaking uncontrollably. Kane sat up and looked at his clock – it was now 3.30am. He asked what had happened, but Bobby didn't answer. He never uttered a word about that night.

Next day, the camp concluded with a service in the chapel. Bellingham was leaving Winchester for Oxford University that summer, and so the smaller boys no longer had to suffer his presence at the school. But Bobby was never the same again. The transformation that had begun when the bullying commenced reached its sad conclusion on that last night of summer camp.

Bobby's academic prowess deteriorated along with his mental health, and he left Winchester after a disastrous set of GCSE results, ordered back to Hong Kong by his father. Kane wrote to him several times, receiving nothing in return. Their friendship had faded under the strain of Bobby's illness even before their enforced separation. But Kane had persevered, sending a card every Christmas, ensuring his old school friend was always aware of his contact details as he moved through university, law school, and the various flats he occupied with successive girlfriends throughout his twenties.

Still there were no replies – until one Christmas, when a card arrived from Hong Kong. Inside was a letter in which Bobby set out, in a sprawling, shaky hand, the events of that Friday night at Christian Summer Camp.

When Bobby was woken up, Smythers had told him he'd been selected for a special service that always took place when there was a full moon. Only very special pupils were chosen for this secret ceremony. Bellingham's presence at the bedside had worried Bobby, but he'd remained convinced that his adversary had been spoken to and no longer represented a threat. Besides, he was with the respected banker and lay preacher who oversaw Christian Summer Camp. What danger could there be?

But Smythers was a sadomasochist who'd been glad to help Bellingham exact revenge on Bobby for reporting him to the master of the college. That night, Bellingham delighted in telling Bobby that his complaint had never reached the master's desk, the bursar having decided instead to deal with it himself by having a quiet man-to-man chat with the offender. This was relayed in Smythers' suite of rooms, while Bobby was being stripped of his pyjamas. Then Bellingham held Bobby down while the good Christian banker raped him, chanting liturgical psalms and begging forgiveness throughout.

Bellingham had then told Bobby that Smythers was a powerful and influential man, and that if anything was said about what had happened, it would be Bobby who was disgraced, and neither he nor his family would ever be allowed into Britain again. Bobby's letter ended by saying that Bellingham's final words to him after taking him back to the dormitory were, 'Thanks for all the fun, chinky.' The nocturnal activities of George Smythers were eventually uncovered, culminating in a scandal that rocked the famous old school. But Bobby's rape and Bellingham's involvement that night in the summer of 1982 had never been revealed.

A month after the Christmas card had been sent, Bobby Cheong threw himself from the twenty-fourth floor of the Mandarin Oriental Hotel.

'Well, I think that just about wraps things up,' Sir Charles was saying. 'You okay, Quentin? You've been awfully quiet.'

Kane responded with a weak smile, and said he was perfectly fine. He told the partners about flying out to Crete to help Lady Bellingham the following week.

'Ah, the fragrant Miranda. What a joy it was to work with her when she was here,' said Tom Palfrey. 'You're wise to look after her. She's destined to be a very rich lady.'

'Weren't you the one who introduced her to Lord Bellingham in the first place?' Sir Charles pitched in.

Kane nodded his confirmation.

'Best thing that ever happened to Eddie Bellingham, if you ask me,' Palfrey declared. 'He may have been a cad, but he was a good judge of women.'

And on that consensual note, the meeting ended.

30

BACK IN UNIFORM

Louise Mangan was back in her office at New Scotland Yard – and back in uniform. The late-August weather was being described as a heat wave, but Louise felt that, by Cretan standards, it was positively autumnal. Her focus this morning was on a meeting about the security arrangements for Burak Bayram's event at Stoke Newington Town Hall in a month's time. One of the team working for her on this assignment was Detective Sergeant Rushil Din, who'd worked with Mangan in 2015 on a case involving a Russian film-maker poisoned in a London hotel. The bravery of Din and Geoff Tonkin, the detective constable who'd worked with him, had earned them a commendation. The two were close friends and had been nicknamed Torvill and Dean at Hendon police college. The nicknames stuck. Both had since been promoted, although 'Torvill' was now working in Essex and only 'Dean' remained with the Met.

DS Din had been assigned most of the legwork on the Bayram visit, and was now sitting in Mangan's office as she prepared to start the meeting. Detective Inspector Cairns, the officer in charge of the investigation into the shooting (and the bombing of Manny's), sat next to Din at the circular table. A woman from the security service completed the quartet assembled to discuss the latest situation in Stoke Newington.

'We can't find anyone who's even heard of an organisation called Bayram's Boys,' the woman from MI5 was saying, 'least of all Burak Bayram himself. Our German partners spoke to him last night. He pointed out that everything he's ever written or said has promoted non-violence. In Turkey, he's argued consistently against meeting force with force.'

'Sounds as if they could be anybody's boys except Bayram's. What about the weapon and where it was fired from?' Mangan asked, turning to Cairns, who promptly circulated a sheet of paper.

'As you can read for yourself, two shots fired, but only one bullet retrieved, the one that hit that lad in the thigh. I suppose you could call that the first bullet point.' There was a collective groan as Cairns moved on. 'The cartridge was a 22.3 Remington, so the gun was, in all probability, a Remington Model 700 bolt-action rifle. Needless to say, we're checking out everyone who has a licence for that model, but it could also have been fired from a Remington semi-automatic. They're illegal in this country. In any case, it would be unusual for a gun used in a hit like this to be licensed. We're in gangland territory here, and the guys who populate it aren't known for their adherence to licensing laws.'

'So, we're pretty sure the posting by "Bayram's Boys" was an attempt to divert attention – but from what?' Mangan asked.

'As we were discussing when I rang you in Crete, it could well be that the local Turkish community has had enough of Taylan Ayhan and his bunch of thugs, and have decided to do something about it themselves. To be honest, we weren't very effective at stopping this Bombacilar gang from disrupting their lives.'

'Taylan Ayhan; is that the surly character we suspect of planting the Semtex in the café?' Mangan asked.

'Yeah, the one with the interesting hairstyle. We couldn't put a restraining order on him because he hasn't been involved in any court proceedings, so we were looking at dealing with his gang under the antisocial behaviour stuff – but, as you know, it's been watered down considerably,' Cairns said. 'In the meantime, this rabble has been terrorising decent, law-abiding citizens in their own homes. Not our finest hour. Although we could have done more if Osman Erkin had been prepared to name them as the ones who beat him up.'

'Is Osman not a suspect?' asked Din, immediately wishing he hadn't.

'Only if you think a guy so badly beaten he probably has trouble climbing into bed, could get himself up forty-five feet of scaffolding,' Cairns sneered.

'I think Rushil was suggesting he may have arranged for somebody else to do it on his behalf,' Mangan interjected, keen to defend her loyal detective sergeant. 'Getting back to the paper in front of us – you are certain the shot was fired from the top of that scaffolding?'

'No doubt about it. The trajectory of the shot, the distance over which it was fired – it all fits.'

'But nothing found on the scaffolding?'

'We've been having dry weather, so there were no footprints or mud marks; nothing except a piece of gum. Apologies in advance if you haven't had your breakfast yet, but it was still moist. Could have been chewed by one of the workmen, but we're checking the DNA. No match has been found yet, but we live in hope,' Cairns added, stroking the long chin which, thanks to his high forehead and wiry hair, led some of his work colleagues to make comparisons with Bruce Forsyth.

'If Osman had a motive to hire someone to do it,' Mangan pondered, 'the guy who owned the café they blew up had a stronger one.'

'Manny Jacobs,' said DS Din, pleased to have an opportunity to retrieve the situation following his earlier faux pas. 'Shall I check out the people he's been seeing? We've got someone monitoring the comings and goings at his house for his own protection, and we're monitoring his calls because he may still be at risk. We could see if anyone who's called or visited him might be of interest.'

'Excellent idea,' said Mangan. 'You get on with that. We'll see what the gun ownership records throw up and what intelligence we can pick up on the ground.'

The woman from the security service interrupted. 'The sixty-four-thousand-dollar question for you, Ma'am, is whether to allow the Bayram meeting to go ahead, given the tension in the area.'

'We could use sections twelve and fourteen of the Public Order Act to at least impose conditions,' Cairns said.

'And you could adopt much wider measures under anti-terrorism legislation,' the spook added.

'Woah, let's just hold our horses here,' Mangan responded. 'This is an important public meeting that many people in the local community have been looking forward to. My job is to facilitate it, not ban it. If Bayram's Boys exist, which seems unlikely, they'll hardly pose a threat to the man they're named after. If they don't exist, the shooting was revenge for a bit of gang activity unrelated to Bayram's visit. Banning public meetings as a first resort may be common in President Erdogan's Turkey, but it's not what we do here. The default position must be that the September meeting goes ahead.'

'You may need to speak to your commissioner about that,' the woman from MI5 said cryptically.

When the gathering dispersed, Detective Inspector Cairns pulled Mangan to one side.

'Just to remind you, Louise, I'm dealing with this shooting; you're the assistant commissioner overseeing the security arrangements for the visit of that Turkish writer.'

Louise smiled sweetly. 'And we both have the same objectives, don't we, Jack?'

But she knew her colleague had made a valid point. He was the detective; she was the administrator.

Early that same evening, Mangan was called in to see Commissioner George Irvine for the discussion she'd asked to have in that phone call from Crete. They met in his office and, unusually, the commissioner offered her a drink, striding across to his drinks cabinet to dispense it himself. The only part of the uniform that he'd divested himself of was the cap. On warm summer evenings such as this, most senior officers would have been in shirtsleeves.

Louise was sipping a vodka and tonic as, whisky in hand, Commissioner Irvine told her how much he was looking forward to his usual holiday, walking in the Lake District with his wife, Susan.

'We've done ten Wainwright routes so far, and we're looking forward to number eleven. Only twenty-five to go after that,' he said.

Louise knew that Mr Wainwright was famous for the Lake District walks he'd mapped, and that the commissioner was a Cumbrian, but taking vigorous exercise in the rain wasn't her idea of a summer holiday.

'I hope it's safer than walking in the White Mountains appears to be,' she said, signifying a desire to get down to business.

'Before we get on to that, let me tell you about the intelligence we picked up about a possible assassination.'

Irvine told his assistant commissioner that GCHQ in Cheltenham had been trawling the dark web to uncover information that could prove useful in counterterrorism. They'd picked up part of an exchange that appeared to relate to a gangland killing.

'Nothing much, just a scrap of intel that says . . .' The commissioner put his glasses on to read from a note taken from a file that rested on his knee. "'Re: Condor. Kill arranged. Top man engaged.'"

'What's "Condor"?'

'A condor is a South American vulture, as I'm sure you know, Louise, but God knows what it means in this context. The lads and lasses in Cheltenham are on the case. They need to break through encrypted codes and goodness knows what – but you know GCHQ, they're like a dog with a bone. The spooks are worried that it may relate to an assassination attempt on your man, that Turkish writer chappie.'

'Burak Bayram? Why do they think that?'

'Because a near-identical formulation of words had been used in a message discovered after an attempt to murder a Turkish dissident in Hamburg a couple of years ago. The perpetrators used a code word to disguise the actual target. Condor could well be such a word. Like Bayram, it has six letters. Our intelligence people think there will be a coup attempt in Turkey before the end of the year. Obviously, if we suspect that such a plot is being hatched, the Turks will know as well. The fear is that they'll try to get their retaliation in first, and Mr Bayram has been a thorn in their sides for many years.'

'You'd better know that I had a meeting this morning about Stoke Newington and refused to countenance a ban on Bayram's meeting.'

'Quite right too,' the commissioner responded. 'We can't deprive London's citizens of the opportunity to hear from someone they want to listen to. In any case, until GCHQ can give us more information, we have no context for what they've picked up. It could just as feasibly be about that shooting a few days ago; there's a whole range of possibilities. No, I don't want you to stop the meeting, and I think the Home Secretary will be okay with it going ahead. But I do think this means you now need to concentrate fully on Stoke Newington, which is why I've lined up somebody else to liaise in Crete.'

This was Mangan's opportunity to properly inform her boss about what had happened since he and his opposite number in Athens had authorised her and Captain Diamantapoulis to pursue their strong suspicion that Lord Bellingham had vanished deliberately and was still alive. She told him about Lady Bellingham knowing precisely where the phone had been found, their suspicion that she'd placed it there herself, and the deletions from Lord Bellingham's phone.

When she'd finished, the commissioner sat deep in thought, slowly swirling the alcohol round his glass. 'They may not have found a body in that lake, but they did find the jacket he'd been wearing,' he said eventually.

'But Lady Bellingham could have planted that jacket in the lake, just as she planted the phone on the mountainside. Don't you see? If she's complicit in his attempt to fake his own death, she'll want to do whatever she can to suggest that his body is in Lake

Kournas. The discovery of that jacket does nothing to destroy our theory.'

Her boss didn't respond, instead gazing down at his glass as if the whisky would suggest a way forward.

'All I'm asking is that you let me continue in both of the roles you gave me. I can multitask, you know I can.'

'Our?' said the commissioner eventually.

'Pardon?'

'You said "our theory" – is this you and your Captain Whatsisname?'

'Diamantapoulis, he's Captain Diamantapoulis.'

'It seems to me,' continued Irvine, ignoring the implied admonishment, 'that you haven't got the Greek police on board – just one Greek policeman.'

There was another silence as Louise reflected on her rather too aggressive defence of the captain.

'I hear what you say, Louise,' the commissioner said, after a moment, 'and you deserve great credit for finding that missing journalist, but the political pressure has declined considerably since those revelations in the Sunday papers the other week. As far as Her Majesty's government is concerned, Bellingham being at the bottom of that lake is the perfect outcome. Our ambassador is telling the Foreign Office that there's no further need for liaison with the Metropolitan Police, and that he's perfectly capable of doing any liaising that may be necessary.'

'That's a bit rich. It was him who wanted me to visit Lady Bellingham following those revelations, precisely because the situation had become more sensitive. It needed to be a "woman to woman" meeting according to him. Please let me go back, at least for Tuesday's meeting. Then we can see how things pan out. I promise my work in Stoke Newington won't suffer.'

'Well, it does make sense for you to meet Lady Bellingham rather than the male replacement I've lined up. You can return for that meeting, but after Tuesday, there are no promises – understood?'

'Understood,' Louise confirmed.

31

NATI COMES UP TRUMPS

DS Din was waiting for Mangan when she came into work on Friday morning.

'Bloody hell, Rushil, at least let me get a cup of tea in my hands,' Mangan said with fake indignation. The slim, handsome detective sergeant was the closest thing she had to a son. Rushil had come to England from India with his family at the age of two and the Met had recruited him straight from university. Mangan loved his enthusiasm and admired his energy, and she had invested a lot of emotional collateral in his progression through the force. 'You give Din a job,' she'd once observed to the commissioner, 'and off he bounds, like a golden retriever. Although sometimes he'll come back with the wrong stick.'

'Sorry, boss, you might want to follow up on the job you gave me yesterday before you go off to Crete. I've looked through all the phone calls and visits that Manny Jacobs has had over the past few weeks. The only one that might be of interest was a Mr Brady, who went to Mr Jacobs' house with a gift on Thursday 17th August.'

'And why might he be of interest?' Mangan asked.

'You were looking for people who are close to Manny Jacobs. This guy was with him at the scene of the burned-down café when you and DI Cairns first visited the area. It's in the file notes.'

'Gosh, you have been meticulous,' Mangan said, reaching for the mug of tea that had been placed in front of her.

'You'll recall that he didn't initially report to Stoke Newington nick as requested,' Din continued. 'DI Cairns had to track him down via the school where his wife teaches. It was pretty strange behaviour, and you did ask me to find anyone who may have wanted to avenge what happened to Mr Jacobs.'

'It's stretching a very long bow, but you may as well check whether Mr Brady has a gun licence, and . . .'

'Already done that, Ma'am. He doesn't.'

'Well, best leave it there, then.'

'But we already discussed that the weapon was probably illegal. Couldn't we get the spooks to search his house while he's out, find out if there's any hidden weapons?'

'Rushil, are you out of your mind? That kind of search would require authorisation from the Home Secretary.'

'It's just that I've got a feeling about this Brady character,' Din said defensively.

'Have you, indeed? So, our request for authorisation would say that a) this man has a vague association with a victim of crime, and b) DS Din has a *feeling* about him. There is as much chance of the Home Secretary signing off a raid on that basis as there is of you succeeding him in the post after he's been sacked for improper authorisation. Tell you what,' Mangan added quickly, noticing the crestfallen look on Din's face, 'go and have a chat with Mr Brady; find out what he was up to on the night of the shooting. I doubt if even that will be a productive use of your time, and you can only do it if Jack Cairns agrees. He's in charge of the investigation into the shooting, not me.'

'Yes, Ma'am.' Din brightened up, but remained standing in Mangan's office.

'Well?' she said. 'Away you go.'

'I was just wondering if you could tell me about what happened to DI Cairns. From what I've heard, when he was about my age, he acted with great bravery and got penalised for it. I wanted to know if you think he's been victimised by the system.'

Mangan, knowing how much importance her young DS attached to the ethical dimension of policing, felt he was entitled to a proper answer rather than a cursory response. 'Jack certainly helped to put Billy Danvers away and destroy one of the most vicious gangs we've ever known in London,' she said. 'In normal circumstances, it would have given a huge boost to his career, but the incident with Danvers' son put paid to that. I forget the son's name, but he was the apple of his dad's eye, and it was said that Jack encouraged him to jump to his death. It must have been over twenty years ago now, but Jack certainly feels he's been victimised, and I tend to agree with him. Others would say he was fortunate not to have been sacked. You should look up the story and tell me what you think. I know that you're really interested in this kind of historic stuff. I still remember you spending your summer holiday reading all about the Great Train Robbery.'

'Will do. Thanks for that, Ma'am.'

A catch-up call with Captain Diamantapoulis had been arranged for later that afternoon. Mangan took the call in her office, delighted to be in contact with Crete once again. The captain had good news to convey.

'Despina has found something,' he announced, referring to Lieutenant Nati's trawl through the footage from the cameras on the main road to Chania on Wednesday 2 August – the day Lord Bellingham had disappeared. 'It is Lady Bellingham's car, heading west along the E75.'

'But couldn't she have been heading towards the town where she was due to meet her husband?'

'No. Georgioupoli is on the E75, but she's driving beside Souda Bay. Georgioupoli is further east, in the opposite direction. In any case, her husband is beside her in the car. The photo was taken at midday; he was supposed to be in the White Mountains at that time. They're heading to Chania, towards that ferry crossing we found deleted from his phone. I was right – she dropped him at the ferry and then drives back to where she's supposed to meet him. She makes those calls she knows won't be answered to the phone they've planted on the mountainside, pretending she's waiting for him . . .'

'Because they know the phone will be checked,' Mangan added.

'Yes, precisely. They fake his disappearance, and he goes off to make a new identity somewhere.'

Louise gave a little cheer, sitting alone in her office. 'Yes!' she exclaimed. 'Is it definitely Lord Bellingham beside her?'

'The image could be clearer because the sun visor is down, but who else can it be? Of course it's his lordship. You will see for yourself when you come over. We have some very difficult questions for Lady Bellingham next week.'

'It looks as if Despina has come up trumps,' Louise observed. 'Lord Bellingham can't be in the lake if he was in that car. He didn't vanish in the mountains; he faked his own death to avoid the scandal he knew was coming. Have you told your commander in Athens?'

'Not yet. Despina is trying to improve the quality of the image.'

'The lovely Miranda can't say it wasn't her at the wheel, but I suppose she could claim to be driving someone other than her husband. You'll remember that Sharron, the British girl who was their nanny, was convinced that Lady B had a lover on the island.'

'Despina says the technicians will have a better image by the time you come over, so I will say nothing to my commander until then.'

The captain went on to ask Louise what she was up to, and she gave a thumbnail sketch of the Stoke Newington situation, ending by admitting it would probably be of little interest to Diamantapoulis, given how busy he was over there.

'I am interested in everything you do, Louise,' the captain replied, his deep voice giving the words added profundity.

Louise was surprised to feel herself blushing, in a way she hadn't done since she was a teenager. She moved the conversation swiftly on to what the captain would be doing that evening. He told her that the narcotics squad, of which he was now nominally in charge, was tracking down those who had fled the compound. The raid had boosted morale and cemented the captain's relationship with this elite force. The fact that the thugs they were chasing had left a man chained up to face a slow death had reminded them of just how ruthlessly inhuman this mob could be.

The gang appeared to have made their escape from the compound in a convoy of people carriers that had then dispersed. One had been captured at a roadblock north of Spili, with five gang members detained. One of those, in the captain's words, 'was singing like a bird'. The captured man had told the police that the gang was to regroup that evening in a remote location on the south-east tip of the island. This was the principal spot they used for bringing people and drugs from Libya ashore.

'I am on my way there now. I will lead my men on the coast to catch the smugglers in the act.'

'Sounds exciting. Has our friend Pelkas approved what you're doing?'

'We won't trouble Inspector General Pelkas with this. He is only in charge of the search for someone who isn't there. Thanks to you, my commander has put me in charge of breaking this gang as well as looking for Hassan. I still don't believe he went back to Libya like that girl says, incidentally. People smuggle their way out of that country, not back in. No, I will not disturb the important work Pelkas is doing at the lake. Are you talking to your commissioner to convince him to look for Lord Bellingham elsewhere, in his new identity?'

'I only just managed to convince him to let me come back out next Tuesday. The theory here is that Edward Bellingham did know he was about to be disgraced, but whereas you think it led him to fake his own death, over here they think he killed himself by jumping in Lake Kournas with a rock or something weighing him down.'

'I can appreciate he may want to kill himself,' the captain said, 'but why should he try to ensure his body isn't discovered?'

'I agree. Sounds like a convenient explanation for not finding a body. Nobody is much bothered about him anymore.'

'He's your citizen, so your problem, not a Greek one. If Brits want to fool themselves, that's fine. I'm just concerned to provide good evidence that he left this island – that's my job done then. Now I must go. See you on Tuesday, and don't work too hard in the meantime.'

'It's my birthday tomorrow, and I definitely won't be working hard at all. My girls are taking me out for dinner,' Mangan said, immediately worrying that it may seem unprofessional to mention domestic arrangements, particularly as the captain never referred to his own.

'That's nice,' he replied. 'Happy Birthday, Louise.' Captain Petros Diamantapoulis said this softly, as if to a close friend rather than an associate; as if to someone he cared about, rather than just a woman he worked with.

32

COMING ASHORE

There was a strong north-east wind blowing off the Libyan Sea as the armoured police unit gathered in the dark about five kilometres from the village of Xerokambos. There were twenty men under the captain's command mainly from the narcotics unit based in Heraklion, but with some from the customs office further east at Sitia. All carried semi-automatic assault rifles, except the officer in charge; Captain Diamantapoulis was armed only with his police-issue Glock 22 handgun. While the best assumption was that they'd outnumber their quarry, it was impossible to be sure.

The unit had gathered above the small inlet that the captain's 'singing bird' had told them was used to import and export the gang's illegal cargo. They watched and waited, their police uniforms as dark as the night. A waxing crescent moon provided little light, but every officer was equipped with a thermal night vision device attached to their helmets. All, including the captain, wore body armour.

By necessity, the unit moved down towards the beach on foot. There was no road to the inlet, only a couple of tracks through undulating scrubland. Diamantapoulis led ten of his men towards the cove, leaving the other ten close to the roadside clearing where the 'singing bird' had said the gang would assemble. The plan was that the ten left here would detain the vehicles and anyone left in them, but not before they'd watched the other gang members go down to the inlet so they could be captured there. A customs surveillance officer based at Kavali was monitoring the Libyan Sea, and had already reported a ship without lights travelling across. It was by now just a few kilometres from the coast.

It was after dark when the officers waiting by the roadside reported the arrival of three SUVs and a people carrier, out of which emerged eleven men. Four of these remained with the vehicles, while the rest made their way down towards the coast. To avoid the gang members above alerting the ones below, the captain had insisted that his two ten-man units act together when he gave the order. He now knew that the gang would be outnumbered in both locations.

The blacked-out ship from Libya arrived, anchoring about a kilometre from the shore. Two rowing boats were lowered from its deck. Diamantapoulis knew he couldn't capture the ship. It would return to Libya – but hopefully without the two boats, those gang members crewing them and their passengers, the bedraggled souls who'd paid a small fortune to be transported to Europe. It was the Crete end of this trade in human misery that the captain was determined to break, hopefully picking up Hassan in the process.

The gang members making their way down from the road wore heavy boots that made a crunching sound as they navigated the steep slopes on their way to receive their latest consignment. The captain had positioned his men so as to pose as little danger as possible to the passengers in the two rowing boats heading into the cove, which he knew would include women and children – entire families fleeing the ungoverned hell of their homeland. He needed to ensure his men captured both sets of gang members – those in the cove and those waiting above on the roadside – before the rowing boats beached. Precision was vital.

He waited until the two crew members in each rowing boat had leapt into the shallows, clutching the ropes with which they would pull their vessels to shore. Only then did the captain give the signal, releasing a flare that lit up the scene for a few moments as one of his men used a megaphone to order the gang members to drop their weapons. The temporary illumination was enough for these men to see the force they were up against.

At that precise moment, the same instruction was being given to the men who'd been left behind with the vehicles. They surrendered immediately, recognising that they were outnumbered by more than two to one.

The gang members weren't outnumbered as heavily on the beach, which was why there was some resistance. A few gang members began firing indiscriminately, and the men pulling the rowing boats towards the shore tried to scramble back into them. The captain and a few of his men waded into the water to apprehend them. The smugglers fought back, punching and kicking as best they could in the waist-high water. Diamantapoulis, who'd yet to draw his gun, had one man in a headlock, but was being pummelled from behind by the man's gangmate. The captain felt a ligature go round his throat. He tried to attract the attention of his colleagues, but none of them were close enough, and he could feel himself slowly losing consciousness. Just then, three of the refugees, a woman and two men, leapt from one of the rowing boats to come to his aid. Within twenty seconds, they had taken the captain's assailant captive, with one of the refugees forcing the man's arm expertly up his back while the woman placed a strong hand against his windpipe.

'We are ex-Libyan police,' the woman told the captain later. 'These people are criminals, but how else could we escape our country? Only by paying these scum. Please don't send us back.'

The captain offered some reassurance, aware that the decision wouldn't be for him to make, but determined to intervene on their behalf. He doubted there were any safe deportation channels back to Libya anyway.

The shooting hadn't lasted long. The gang members had no night vision, and were literally fighting in the dark. When two were hit, one fatally, the others dropped their weapons and surrendered. The captives on the beach were herded together to join those at the arrival point, where Diamantapoulis lined them all up.

'Which one of you is Mohammed Tatanaki?' he asked. There was silence. 'Where is he? Where is Hassan?'

'Hassan is not with us,' one of the men called out.

The captain shone a torch into the face of each handcuffed prisoner, comparing their features to a photograph of Hassan. None matched.

'What's happened to Hassan?' he asked again.

None of the men answered, and Diamantapoulis sensed a collective horror that went far beyond their fear of being labelled an informer.

33

A HOSPITAL VISIT

When Tam Mackay arrived at the hospital in Athens on Saturday morning, the first thing that impressed him was the way the Greek police had protected his star reporter. The editor of the *Daily Candour* had felt obliged to visit as soon as he heard that Chris Finch was conscious, albeit still in intensive care. A few strings had to be pulled to get here. While the police were guarding him, neither they nor Embassy staff had been given permission by the clinicians to question Finch, despite their eagerness to discover what had happened at the compound where he'd been found. To suggest that the editor was more concerned with the paper's circulation figures than his journalist's health would be unfair. Mackay's reputation as the hardest man on Fleet Street belied the sensitive nature he was said to harbour beneath the surface. Somebody said they'd seen a tear in his eye when the Queen Mother died, and an editorial team had once witnessed him leave a meeting, apparently overwhelmed by emotion, when Scotland were eliminated from the 1978 World Cup.

However, there was a commercial as well as a compassionate reason for his presence in Athens. The *Daily*

Candour's sales had rocketed as its readers followed the progress of Finch ('The *Candour* Reporter They Tried to Silence') and Mackay was determined that when the journalist first spoke, it would be to them. In any case, he'd decided that for him to be there in person would demonstrate the importance the newspaper attached to Finch's welfare. The *Candour* was paying the considerable medical costs, and when Mackay arrived, four days after the journalist had been found, and saw the significant policing operation underway, he made a mental note to check that they weren't paying the security costs as well.

Finch was under twenty-four-hour armed guard. Mackay counted six officers in full body armour, visors down, guns at the ready, and that was just in the hospital corridor. The editor and his secretary, along with a man from the embassy, passed several more on their journey into the facility where Finch was being cared for.

'Remember, Mr Mackay, your colleague is hardly conscious and still extremely weak,' the young man from the embassy was telling him. 'The medics won't allow the police to interview him yet, and the only way we managed to get them to agree to your short visit was by stressing that Mr Finch has no known relatives and has specifically asked to talk to you. Sir Ralph had to argue that your visit was pastoral.'

'Aye, that's right, son; it also seemed to help that my proprietor was at school with the ambassador. It's a shame we couldn't persuade them to let my pastoral photographer accompany me on to the ward. I suppose our readers will have to make do with a couple of snaps of me walking through the hospital entrance.'

They were entering the inner sanctum, at the heart of which Chris Finch lay completely still amidst an array of tubes, wires and gently bleeping machinery. A doctor was present to supervise the visit. Masked and gowned, she introduced herself to Mackay in faultless English, insisting that the two people accompanying him wait in the outer observation room.

'The boy has lost a lot of weight,' the editor observed, shocked at the diminished figure that lay before him as he approached the bedside.

'It's a miracle he's still alive,' the doctor said, her hand reaching out to adjust a piece of machinery by the bed. 'He'd been without food, was severely beaten, and stabbed in the groin. He's far from out of danger, and will need to be kept under close observation for some time. He may never be back to normal.'

'Believe me, the last thing this great lump of horsemeat will want is to be back to normal,' Mackay said, standing with the clinician a few steps back from the bed. 'He leads a lonely life, does our Chris. I've probably given him more love than anyone he knows, and I fucking hate him. Has he said anything yet?'

'Not much. Only that whatever it is he wants to say, it must be to you. That was yesterday, and his condition has deteriorated overnight. He's delirious, and may not recognise you. I'm not sure this was a good idea, but your people' – the doctor glanced towards the embassy official who was watching through the observation window – 'said that you were a father figure to him.'

'Aye, that'll be right,' Mackay said, moving closer to the bed to ensure his face was in the patient's line of vision.

After a few minutes, the reporter's eyelids fluttered open. 'Tam, listen,' Finch croaked in a barely audible voice. Mackay moved closer, tilting his head so that his ear was next to the patient's mouth. Finch's eyes widened, and he repeated four words repeatedly like a mantra, becoming more and more agitated until the doctor intervened, and two nurses began pulling Mackay away.

'That's enough now, Mr Mackay. Please leave.'

When the great newspaper editor was reunited with the junior embassy official, the fresh-faced young man was sitting, notebook in hand, fountain pen at the ready, asking him to recite exactly what had been said.

'You civil servants are all the fucking same. Obsessed with your *minuta scriptura*. He told me a lot of private stuff that's between him and the paper,' Mackay growled, lying through his teeth but already formulating ideas for Monday's 'exclusive'. 'Apart from that, he said four words that are probably as much a mystery to you as they are to me. They were "Hassan win crypt photograph". You said he'd been delirious; it was probably some dream he'd been having.'

As Mackay walked back down the corridor, mentally composing the piece he would write, he hardly noticed the clinicians rushing past to administer to the patient he'd just left. Before the editor of the *Daily Candour* caught the plane back to London, he was made aware that the four words he'd heard were the last that Chris Finch would ever speak.

34

CHANGES

Brady read the note three times, as if repeating the process would change the words.

> *I've gone. I couldn't take any more of your cold indifference. You'll be happier without me. I'm not going off with anyone – just to a bedsit where I can't be any lonelier than I am with you. I thought it best to write you a note, knowing how much you hate to talk. I'll be in touch about collecting my things – once you've had a chance to come to terms with this.*
>
> *I don't know if you ever loved me, but I loved you – past tense.*
> — *Cathleen*

It was Saturday morning. He'd taken a cup of tea into his wife's bedroom, the room they'd once shared – until he'd decided they should sleep apart. The bed hadn't been slept in. The note was on the pillow. She must have placed it there before going out last night, to her Friday night book club, where, as he understood it, ten women read a book and then spent hours discussing it over bottles of Pinot Grigio. Cathleen was always late home from these literary gatherings, so he'd gone to bed without waiting up.

Now, reading her note, he stood rooted to the spot. Cathleen, whom he relied upon; quiet, dependable Cathleen, had left him. Did she think he was going to accept this? Forget the wedding vows she'd made? Fifteen years of marriage gone, finished, wiped away like chalk from a blackboard.

'Ch-ch-ch-ch-changes.' The Bowie song came unwittingly into his head. Everything was changing, becoming destabilised. His work, and now his life. He'd become known to the police – she'd done that, Cathleen. She'd told the police where he lived. And just yesterday, they'd paid him a visit; the second time he'd been interviewed by the police in a month. This time, it was a young Asian copper, asking where Brady had been on the evening of 22 August, the night of the shooting. He told the policeman he'd been working – and no, his wife wouldn't be able to corroborate his whereabouts, as she'd been out that night.

'And what is your work?' the copper had asked, and a chill had crept down his spine and into his bowels. *What was his work?* A police officer was asking what he did for a living. Brady knew he'd made a mistake saying he was working. He should have said he was watching telly, doing some carpentry, making a scale model of the fucking Taj Mahal – anything but say he'd been working – because the next and obvious question was to ask what his work was. This Asian copper was no fool, but even if he was, he'd be bound to ask that question.

What if the police followed it up? What if they asked for evidence of the trading in bonds and gilts that was supposed to have been his occupation for the best part of twenty years? Brady had never traded a bond in his life – but he had been working on Tuesday evening. Working when he shouldn't have been. Working for nothing. Pro bono.

Apparently, the policeman had come to see him because he'd visited Manny. They were checking on all the people who'd left their image behind, as well as their names and addresses, in the old man's visitors' book: those close to Manny who could have been motivated by revenge. That's exactly what the copper had said, and he'd got it in one. It was exactly why Brady had done it – for revenge against people who were nothing to do with him.

'But I read that a group who called themselves "Bayram's Boys" had admitted responsibility,' he'd told the police officer.

'Yes, but we think that was a rather amateurish attempt to divert attention from the real motivation.'

Amateurish! A fresh-faced, know-nothing copper telling him he'd been amateurish. That was something he could never have been accused of in the past. And the reason for his current discomfort was that he'd become emotionally involved in something that was none of his business.

Yesterday, he'd received a letter from Manny thanking him for the prayer lectern. One visit to the old man, one entry in his visitors' book, and suddenly there were police at the door and letters arriving at an address that was once unknown to anyone.

It was a lovely letter, though, full of warmth and appreciation. At the end, Manny expressed his delight that 'those thugs have had their comeuppance'. 'Osman can't stop crowing about it,' he wrote. 'He says he feels safe to walk the streets again thanks to Bayram's Boys.'

Manny would never know that he was thanking his friend for more than just the prayer lectern.

It wasn't as if intervening had made Brady feel good about himself. Even Manny's letter didn't do that. All he could think of was that he had one more job to do before retirement, and yet he was risking everything by being 'amateurish'. Brady told himself he had to get a grip. That officer – what was his name? Din, that was it; Detective Sergeant Din – had made it clear that he didn't expect to get anything out of interviewing those close to Manny. He'd said himself that he was just going through the motions. The police were bound to think that if anyone in the 'friends of Manny' category had ambushed those thugs it would be Osman, who'd lost his job because of the fire and been badly beaten up by the Bombacilar gang. No, the visit to Brady's house had been routine. There was nothing linking him, the quiet, law-abiding bond trader, with that shooting; nothing at all. In a few weeks' time, he'd have done the job that was pending, and that would be it. There'd be more holidays with—

Cathleen. He'd been thinking about that copper's visit so much, he'd almost forgotten the note that was still in his hand.

He'd talk to her. Plead with Cathleen to come back. Tell her he'd ch-ch-ch-ch-change his ways – be a different man. He thought about calling her mobile, but he knew talking on the phone wouldn't work. They needed to meet face to face. The new school year would begin soon. If he could find no other way to see her, he'd go to Dalston Academy and ask, – no, demand – to see his wife.

The tears came without warning. He'd not cried since his mother's death, but now, note in hand, Brady sat on Cathleen's bed and sobbed.

35

A BIRTHDAY DINNER

The restaurant was packed when Louise and her daughters arrived. Chloe, the youngest, and Michelle had come home that afternoon in a whirlwind of energy and noise. The flat they used to share with their mother hadn't experienced such commotion since they'd left for university. Louise had been suffering empty-nest syndrome ever since. In the two years since Chloe had left, she'd only been reunited with them both on one occasion, and that hadn't been at home.

They'd spent a rather awkward Christmas with Louise's eighty-five-year-old father in 2015, at a hotel close to his care home in Guildford. She'd found it impossible to find any enjoyment in that family get-together. Louise's father had always been such a meticulous man in dress, speech and character, and to see him rumpled by infirmity and the onset of dementia was upsetting. But there was also a realisation that it would probably be his last Christmas, and that had made it worthwhile.

The girls had been due to come home for Christmas 2016, but Louise had had to cancel their arrangements when something came up at work. This had been a regular feature of Michelle and Chloe's childhood – arrangements made and then unmade when 'something came up at work'. The birthday meal this evening had been touch and go, only confirmed when Louise was able to reassure her daughters that she would be back from Crete in time. And so Michelle's idea for a birthday dinner with just the three of them, followed by a night back in the girls' childhood home, had gone ahead. The restaurant in Brixton was within walking distance, and already brimming with ambience when they arrived.

Louise could tell that her daughters were on a mission to rescue their mother from what they perceived to be a lonely life of dedication to duty. As soon as they'd conversationally disposed of their father, his second wife and their new boyfriends, they focused remorselessly on their mother. Louise could only admire their interrogational skills, which she felt were equal to anything available to her in New Scotland Yard. Having established that there was still no man in their mother's life, and convinced that there needed to be, they moved on to what she could tell was a rehearsed finale.

'My friend Keeley's mother is getting married again at fifty, to a wonderful guy,' Michelle said to Chloe.

'Oh, really?' said Chloe to Michelle. 'I remember Keeley – isn't her mum a doctor?'

'Yes, a heart surgeon, actually. Very senior, always at work.'

'And yet she managed to meet the gorgeous guy she's about to marry? How come?'

'Excuse me,' Louise interrupted. 'How do you know he's gorgeous if you've never met him?'

'Because Chelle said he was wonderful, and to me that means gorgeous,' her youngest daughter replied.

'I've met him,' Michelle added, 'and believe me, he's really gorgeous, as well as being wonderful.'

'Where did she meet him?' Chloe asked Michelle.

'On an internet dating site,' replied the older sister.

'Okay, you two amateur agony aunts, you've recited your lines. I will *not* be visiting any dating sites, and I do not require your help and advice, thank you very much.'

'Oh, you do, Mummy dear, you so do,' Chloe said. 'There is no shame in using a dating site – everyone does it now.'

'Neither of you met your new boyfriends on a dating site,' Louise observed.

'Correct,' said Michelle. 'But we're young, and we met them at uni, which basically exists as a physical dating site.'

'Anyway, for all you two know I might already be signed up to Tinder,' Louise suggested.

'Mmm, you're a bit too old for Tinder. I'd switch to Silver Singles if I were you,' Michelle said, immediately covering her head against her mother's pretend blows.

They were still laughing when Louise's phone, which was lying on the restaurant table next to her, pinged with a text message. She was forced to read it with a daughter leaning over each shoulder. The message read: 'I need to talk with you. Happy Birthday, Petros x.'

'Who the hell is Petros?' the girls chanted, almost in unison.

'He's the senior Greek police officer I'm liaising with in Crete.'

'You're *liaising* with him! Oh my, I'm breaking into a sweat,' Michelle said, fanning her face with the dessert menu.

'You're probably suffering early-onset menopause,' her mother responded frostily. 'Now sit yourselves back down and behave. This is police work.'

'Since when did senior police officers end their text messages with a kiss?' Chloe asked.

'Since everybody in the world started to put an "x" as the obligatory sign-off to every text message sent, even to those they only vaguely know,' Louise said, without conviction. She'd been amazed to see an 'x' from Captain Diamantapoulis – amazed and delighted.

She went outside to make the call, away from the noise of the restaurant and the prying ears of her daughters. The late-August weather had turned colder, and Louise was pleased she'd worn a cardigan over her thin cotton dress. She was growing her hair, and it was long enough to be piled on to the crown of her head. A few strands had come loose during the evening. They framed the even features of her slim face like pencil marks on a sketch pad.

It was nine o'clock and the pavements of London SW3 were crowded with Saturday-night revellers.

'It sounds as if you're in a football crowd,' Diamantapoulis said when he answered.

Mangan was a little abrupt in response, saying that it was probably much quieter than downtown Athens, as if his observation had been a criticism of her country. The kiss at the end of his text had had a strange effect. She felt duty-bound to be more business-like than she'd have normally been in an out-of-hours call.

But the captain didn't appear to notice. 'I will send you all details, but we captured most of the gang last night,' he said.

Louise congratulated him, before asking if he knew who'd masterminded the operation.

'No, not yet. But we're almost certain that the land where we found the journalist is owned by Dimitri Limnios.'

'Our Dimitri? The one who owns the restaurant?'

'Yes, our Dimitri. Ownership is registered under a false name, but we knew his restaurant got its produce from there, and now we have documents being examined by handwriting experts, who we expect to confirm it is "our Dimitri", as you call him.'

'What about Hassan? Was he with the gang?'

'No. We have almost the entire gang, but not Hassan. He is still on the run and not seen by anyone since you saw him at the restaurant. Maybe your English girl is right, perhaps he has gone back to Libya, strange though that would be.'

They talked about the arrangements for next week. Louise would fly out on Monday for the meeting with Lady Bellingham on Tuesday. She told Petros that she didn't think she'd be staying for long, and they discussed how to make best use of the time available. After ten minutes, Louise ended the call and went back to her daughters, who were keen for her to give a verbatim account of the conversation.

'It was about work,' was all Louise would say.

'And on that very subject, I was just telling Chelle that we saw that Lord Bellingham guy in Dimitri's when we were over in May,' Chloe said.

'You must be pleased he's been found in that lake,' Michelle added.

'*He* hasn't been found in the lake – a piece of his clothing has been found in the lake,' Louise said, keen to move off the subject.

'Okay, Mum, we understand. You've never wanted to talk about your work. Let's discuss something else,' Michelle suggested.

'Yeah,' said her sister. 'Tell us more about Petros.'

In bed later that night, Louise pondered whether to reply to the captain's text. She'd already spoken to him, so there had been a response of sorts. Courtesy demanded nothing further. This was her forty-seventh birthday; she shouldn't be acting as if it was her seventeenth. But she felt she'd been brusque and over-formal with Petros. In contrast, his text had wished her 'Happy Birthday' and ended with a kiss. The lovely meal, the wine she'd drunk and having her girls back in the house, albeit just for one night, had provoked a distinctly mellow mood. She knew it was probably a mistake to text a man she'd grown increasingly fond of while she was feeling like this, but she went ahead anyway – and put the kiss in capitals.

'It was lovely to talk to you tonight – on my birthday. Thanks for your message and sorry if I was a bit rushed when we spoke. Louise X.'

36

THE AMBASSADOR IS EMBARRASSED

It was Monday morning before news of Chris Finch's death was reported in the *Daily Candour*. Tam Mackay had managed to suppress the information until his newspaper could carry it as an exclusive. He'd convinced the Greek authorities, via the embassy, that he needed to inform Finch's family, although he knew his reporter didn't have one – just an ex-wife who was now remarried. Saturday's paper would have needed to go to press too early to do the story justice, and Mackay was damned if he'd let the *Sunday Candour* steal his thunder again. Besides, he needed time to try to make sense of his star reporter's last words.

If Finch had been offering him a headline, it was admirably succinct but completely unintelligible. 'Hassan win crypt photograph'. Having concluded that this was indeed the ramblings of a delirious mind, and realising that only he had heard the words, Mackay had taken poetic licence. According to his 'on the spot' exclusive, which spread over three pages of that Monday morning edition, Finch, with his final breath, had asked his editor to 'Look after our readers.' By replacing four words that no one understood with four that conveyed what he was probably thinking, Mackay told himself, he was only doing what Chris Finch would have wanted.

Louise Mangan picked up a copy of the paper in the departure lounge at Gatwick on Monday afternoon. From the front cover photograph of the paper's editor entering an Athens hospital to the centre-page spread headlined 'The Message He Wanted You to Hear', there was 'coverage to die for' (as Tam Mackay had tastelessly put it to his editorial team). Mangan was horrified to read about Mackay being given access to the seriously ill reporter. If anyone had been allowed to see him, it should have been the police. She resolved to raise this with embassy officials when she landed.

Her morning had been spent handling lots of mundane office stuff, save for half an hour talking to DI Jack Cairns about Stoke Newington. Cairns had told her that there had been no further incidents since the shooting a week ago. The fear that vigilante groups such as 'Bayram's Boys' would emerge on the streets hadn't materialised. There had been no progress in the search for the gunman, and the DNA from the chewing gum hadn't yielded a match. The young man who'd been shot in the thigh was about to be discharged from hospital, and Cairns was now busy interviewing anyone who might have had a grudge against the hooligans who'd been attacked. It was a long list. Bombacilar had upset an awful lot of people. Nobody had seen anything of them since the shooting. Cairns felt that, perversely, the incident had calmed the atmosphere, and that the

Burak Bayram meeting in a little over three weeks' time would be a peaceful event that should undoubtedly go ahead. It was important for Mangan that she stay closely in touch with the situation. While the commissioner had given her dispensation to return to Crete, he'd made it plain that he expected her back later that week, and that the Bayram visit was to be her absolute priority.

Lieutenant Despina Nati met Louise at Heraklion airport, but without the familiar jeep. This time she was at the wheel of a marked police Volkswagen.

'Petros asked me to meet you,' Nati said, greeting Louise with a peck on the cheek. 'He has to speak to our commander about your visit to Lady Bellingham tomorrow. She has complained to people high up that she's being persecuted, that Captain Diamantapoulis doesn't like Inspector General Pelkas being in charge of search and is refusing to accept that he has succeeded where the captain failed. She says that now that her husband has been found in Lake Kournas, she should be left alone to grieve.'

'Well, I trust she'll get short shrift. It was only his jacket that was found and we now have CCTV evidence that she was driving the man she wants to grieve over towards Chania when he was supposed to be lost in the White Mountains. And she knew where the phone was found without being informed.'

'Yes, but you remember Petros only confided in us about that. He wants to surprise her with it tomorrow, and is also restricting information about CCTV –

basically because he trusts no one while Pelkas is around. Hopefully, he will tell the commander, otherwise he's fighting a battle without any weapons.'

Louise asked if they'd managed to improve the CCTV image to more clearly identify Lord Bellingham as the man in the passenger seat, and Despina felt they had. 'It's not perfect,' she said. 'Our technicians could do nothing about the sun visor being down – but it looks more like him than it did before. It's enough for Petros to show the commander. The problem we have had in Athens is maintaining interest in the case. Pelkas is now a hero because he found your minister in lake.'

'A hero for finding a jacket?'

'Yes, but he still says he will find the body.' Nati went on to explain how the navy submersible had been ineffective in the underwater jungle of Lake Kournas, and that a crack team of divers had been brought in to try to cut through the undergrowth in the deepest parts. 'These divers are the final attempt to find a body, and Pelkas seems confident that they will.'

As they approached the Crystal Beach Hotel, where Mangan would again be staying, she asked whether Dimitri was being questioned now that his ownership of the compound had been established.

'No, not yet. Inspector General Pelkas is admired because he finds Lord Bellingham (so they say), but now Captain Diamantapoulis is also a hero for capturing people-traffickers. Part of Petros's problem is that the commander thinks his time would be better spent concentrating on that rather than questioning Lady Bellingham.'

'Sounds as if we've got similar problems with our superiors,' Louise muttered.

'Petros has the respect and loyalty of the narcotics team and border force,' Nati continued, 'and he tells me he has found a perfect way to shadow Dimitri, listen to his conversations and map where he goes and what he does. That way, we can find out much more about who is running this operation than by arresting him. It wasn't easy to discover who owns the land; Dimitri will assume we still don't know.'

By the time Louise had wheeled her case into the hotel lobby and checked in, Nati had received an update on the meeting between the captain and his commander in Athens. Mangan was to visit Lady Bellingham accompanied only by embassy staff. It had been decided that this was a matter for the Brits alone.

'My advice to the Greek government was that there was no necessity for anything other than a British presence at the meeting.' Sir Ralph Evans, Her Britannic Majesty's Ambassador to the Hellenic Republic, was speaking slowly so that those who were less intellectually gifted could keep up. Accompanied by the vice-consul for Crete and a couple of junior officials, he was with Louise Mangan in a conference room of the Crystal Beach Hotel that had been hired specifically for this meeting. It was 7pm on Monday evening, and the sun was setting spectacularly into the tranquil sea below the window.

'In giving that advice, you interfered with a police investigation,' Mangan said frostily.

'Assistant Commissioner, I was asked for my view by a Greek government minister; all I did was comply with that reasonable request.'

Mangan suspected that it had taken a supreme effort of willpower for Sir Ralph not to have begun that sentence with 'my dear'.

'We were cognisant of the fact,' he continued, 'that a "woman to woman" conversation had been your original intention, in recognition of the trauma that Lady Bellingham would have been forced to endure vis-à-vis the article that appeared in a certain British newspaper.' Having completed his explanation, the ambassador sat back, legs crossed, exuding grandeur.

'But why didn't you speak to me first? You know a lot has happened since that article was published, including the death of the man who wrote it,' Mangan responded.

'I apologise if my explanation lacked clarity – I was asked for *my* advice, not *our* advice. Had the singular been a plural, I would, of course, have done my best to comply. As it was, I expected that the Metropolitan Police would be separately consulted in a similar fashion.'

'I want you to alter that advice.'

Sir Ralph allowed the slightest trace of a smile to flit across his distinguished features. After a pause to look out on the ravishing sunset, he turned his dark eyes back towards Mangan, as if trying to understand some strange and unfamiliar dialect. 'But I cannot accede to your request – if a request it be. My advice cannot change because the circumstances pertaining to that advice have not changed.'

Mangan, remaining still and calm, looked unblinkingly into Sir Ralph's eyes and said: 'But they have. You now know that the Commissioner of the Metropolitan Police, upon whose behalf I speak, believes it important to have a certain representative of the Hellenic Police present at that interview.'

'But what new evidence is there?' the ambassador asked, a sense of discomfiture creeping into his demeanour.

'I am under no obligation to present police evidence to you. All you need to know is that the Greek police have acquired evidence that Lady Bellingham may not have been entirely truthful in her statements concerning her husband's disappearance. You now know that if you had sought my opinion, it would have been contrary to yours.' Mangan maintained eye contact for a few seconds more before going on to say, 'Would you prefer it if my boss, the commissioner, went directly to the Foreign Secretary with this request?'

'I see no need to disturb anyone at the Foreign and Commonwealth Office with this issue,' Sir Ralph said. 'If you wish me to advise the Greek government that Captain Diamantapoulis should be in attendance with you tomorrow, I'm happy to consider conveying that through the usual channels.'

'Good,' said Mangan. 'While you're thinking about it, can you explain why a newspaper editor was allowed in to see Finch when the police were being denied access?'

'Please, Assistant Commissioner Mangan, I would appreciate you moderating your rather interrogational tone. I was contacted by the proprietor of the Candour group of newspapers, who explained that Mr Christopher Finch had expressed a desire to speak to the editor of one of his publications, a Mr Thomas Mackay, who was apparently a paternal figure in the journalist's life. I merely passed on that request to the health minister here in Greece.'

'And as a result of your favour to a fellow Old Etonian, the press is reporting a conversation that may well be crucial to police enquiries.'

'As far as I know, it is legal for Old Etonians to speak to one another,' Sir Ralph responded. 'And what Mr Finch said seems innocuous to me.'

'And how do you know his words were accurately reported in your friend's newspaper?'

'Assistant Commissioner, may I just point out that nobody actually knows for certain what Mr Mackay heard Mr Finch say.'

The awkward silence that followed was broken by the bespectacled embassy clerk clearing his throat. He'd been bent over the table, studiously taking notes, but now said quietly, 'I was at the hospital and took a note of what Mr Mackay told me was said by Mr Finch.'

'Well, why haven't I bloody well seen it?' Evans responded, furious at the intervention.

'You have. I sent it in to you on Friday,' the clerk said, 'with your weekend documents.'

Sir Ralph Evans spluttered and coughed before leaving the room, mumbling something about getting in touch with a Greek minister to retract his previous advice.

Having made her case that Captain Diamantapoulis should be at the meeting with Lady Bellingham the next day, Mangan's immediate preoccupation was now with those final four words of Christopher Finch as recited by the junior embassy official from his notebook.

'Hassan win crypt photograph.'

She didn't yet know what they meant, but had an instinctive feeling that they held a deep significance in the search for Lord Bellingham.

37

A SECOND VISIT TO LADY BELLINGHAM

When they arrived at the Bellingham's villa outside Agia Galini, the noon sky was blazing but there were dark clouds in the distance. A storm was approaching. Nati, having driven them here in the familiar jeep, had agreed to wait outside. A young British girl, Sharron's replacement, opened the door. Mangan and Diamantapoulis followed her out on to the wide expanse of the terrace, where Miranda Bellingham sat beneath an enormous parasol as she had on their first visit. Next to her, in a pinstripe suit, making no concessions to the weather, was her lawyer, Quentin Kane.

There were no pleasantries. Kane instead asked Mangan to state the purpose of the meeting and what her status was under Greek law.

'I am liaising with the Hellenic Police on behalf of the Met concerning the disappearance of Lord Edward Bellingham. Captain Petros Diamantapoulis has been leading the investigation.'

'We understood that Inspector General Pelkas was in charge,' Kane responded, forcing Mangan to give a convoluted explanation of the responsibilities shared between the two Greek police officers.

'And precisely why do you want to interview my client, who has already told you all she can about her husband's disappearance?' Kane asked, as if questioning a witness in the dock.

'We appreciate how difficult this is for Lady Bellingham, particularly after the newspaper revelations about her husband's past, but we would be obliged if she would continue to help us to understand the events of 2 August, when Lord Bellingham was last seen.'

Throughout these preliminary exchanges, Miranda Bellingham gazed out across the hills, as if searching for a landmark. She wore a pink cotton dress, her bare legs elegantly crossed, auburn hair pulled back tightly into a bun. Kane announced that the two visitors had half an hour to interview his client, but that he would terminate the conversation should there be any breach of Greek procedural rules.

'Anyway,' he concluded, 'my understanding is that the police here know where poor Edward is – what is there to investigate?'

'If he's in Lake Kournas – and currently, that's still an "if" – we need to know how he got there,' Mangan explained.

'How did you know where the phone was found?' Captain Diamantapoulis had been sitting quietly on a canvas chair, a little away from the others. His abrupt question, directed at Lady Bellingham, surprised everyone, including Mangan. They had rehearsed their roles, and agreed that she would do a bit of preliminary softening up. She didn't think that phase had ended yet.

She also thought there were gentler ways to pose the question. However, as the captain was to explain later, he felt that Lady Bellingham needed to be shocked out of her pomposity.

'This is not a court of law,' Kane said, 'and, unless I'm informed otherwise, this conversation is not taking place under the Greek Code of Criminal Procedure. That's because my client is not a criminal and should not be questioned as if she is one.'

'Oh, shut up, Quentin; I'm perfectly prepared to answer the captain's questions. Now, please clarify what you're asking me. I presume you're referring to my husband's phone.'

Mangan could tell she was playing for time.

'Yes, I mean Lord Bellingham's phone. Last time we spoke to you, you knew it was found near the gorge – but how did you know?' the captain persevered.

'You must have told me.'

'I didn't, and neither did anyone from my office.'

Miranda Bellingham removed her sunglasses to look directly at her inquisitor. 'You are mistaken, Captain,' she said. 'Either you or one of your officers must have told me. How else would I know?'

The captain continued to hold her gaze, leaving the obvious answer hanging in the air.

'This is the first time we've spoken since the newspaper revelations about your husband were published. Did he know the story was about to break?' Louise asked gently.

'I think he did,' Miranda responded. 'He was quiet and withdrawn and, oh, I don't know – just not himself. When I saw that story, it all suddenly made sense. He must have known he was about to be disgraced.' Lady Bellingham removed her sunglasses again, this time to dab her eyes with a tissue.

'I'm sorry to have to ask these questions, but it's important that we understand his state of mind. Did you know he'd made that schoolgirl pregnant?' Mangan asked.

'No, I did not. It all happened years before I met him.'

'Why were you driving to Chania at 11am on Wednesday 2 August, the day your husband went missing?' The captain resumed his role of interrogator, and the question exploded on to the Bellinghams' terrace like a firework in a basement.

Miranda sat bolt upright, spilling the lemonade she'd been lifting to her lips, while Kane got to his feet, standing between her and the captain as if separating contestants in a boxing ring at the end of a round.

Diamantapoulis didn't move a muscle. 'It is a simple question,' he said.

'This interview is terminated,' Kane was saying. 'My client didn't drive to Chania, and these questions are outrageous.'

'But I did drive to Chania.' Lady Bellingham's quiet admission silenced her lawyer, who sat back down, looking quizzically at his client and running a hand through his thick hair in a gesture of frustration. 'I presume you've been checking your cameras on the highway,' Miranda said. 'I have no idea why you should go to such trouble, but yes, I did drive to Chania that morning. So what?'

'Were you alone?' asked the captain.

'If you've got the CCTV footage, you'll know that I wasn't.'

'Who was with you?' Mangan asked.

'A friend. A man who is a friend – a lover, if you must know. Is it illegal to have a lover in Greece?'

'We think the man in the car with you was your husband,' Diamantapoulis stated baldly.

'Really? I'm not interested in what you think. My husband is dead, as I think your Inspector General Pelkas will confirm.'

'But even if you're right, and he is found in Lake Kournas, he could still have been with you in that car on 2 August,' Mangan observed. 'If it wasn't your husband, who was it?'

'My client is not obliged to answer that question,' Quentin Kane intervened. 'And your time is almost up.'

'Where were you driving to in Chania?' the captain asked.

'None of your business,' Miranda responded calmly. 'I have no intention of revealing who my lover is, and to tell you where I was going would obviously compromise his privacy – and mine.'

The solicitor called time on the meeting before any more questions could be asked.

As they walked back towards the police jeep, Louise

reflected on the interview. 'She is one hell of a cool customer. Miranda knows we can't pursue those questions any further unless we arrest her – and we can't arrest her without pursuing those questions further.'

The captain nodded in agreement. 'I was watching her lawyer,' he said, 'and thinking how his reaction was not as cool as his client's. He was seriously disturbed, particularly about the trip to Chania.'

'And so he should be. Perhaps he now thinks this is not as clear-cut as everyone seems to think it is.'

'I am thinking he's a friend of his lordship, and knows where he is.'

Louise had already given the captain a full readout of her meeting with the ambassador, including the final words of Chris Finch. 'Do you think "Hassan – win – crypt – photograph" has any connection to all this?' she asked now.

'Of course,' Diamantapoulis said. 'We know Hassan is central to this. Without his name being there, I would have doubted, but now I'm sure that the journalist was saying something important.'

'So am I,' Mangan confirmed.

They were waiting by the jeep while Nati finished a conversation she'd been having on her mobile, having moved away to get a better reception.

'Looks as if the case is ended,' she said upon her return. 'I've just had a report that the body of Lord Bellingham has been found in Lake Kournas.'

38

TIME TO MOVE ON

Louise Mangan returned to London on an evening flight, determined to put Lord Bellingham and Crete and Petros Diamantapoulis out of her mind. It was over. Time to move on.

The captain had come with her to the airport, Despina Nati still at the wheel. The journey had passed in almost total silence as the passengers read the full story about the discovery in Lake Kournas on their iPhones. The divers had seen a body entangled in the thick weeds at the bottom of the lake, too deep for them to reach. What was easily discernible was that distinctive red safety helmet, and, albeit less clear, the clothes that Lady Bellingham had said he'd been wearing when he vanished.

The current view was that there was no feasible way of freeing the corpse without endangering the lives of those involved, and that Lake Kournas would therefore be its final resting place. The formulation used in the police press release was that the body was 'almost certainly that of Lord Bellingham'.

Arriving at Heraklion airport, the captain wheeled Louise's case to the departure gate. Their mutual sense of defeat was palpable, but they said nothing about the discovery of the body or their continuing suspicions. Instead, they stood silently for a few seconds before embracing and mouthing platitudes about staying in touch, as people do when they know that nothing will ever be arranged. They were of a similar height, and as Louise put her face forward to kiss his cheek, Petros chose the same moment to attempt to kiss her lips, with the result that she kissed his shirt collar, and he kissed her ear.

Louise smiled at the recollection of this as she flew back to Gatwick. In general, she felt as if she'd suffered a bereavement. At home that night, she listened to Joni Mitchell, drank wine and wished she was back in Agia Galini.

At New Scotland Yard the next day, the commissioner dropped by to thank her.

'A job well done, Louise, even if it did take a little longer and end more tragically than I would have wanted.'

'Are you sure it's finished now?' Mangan asked.

'Yes, of course. What more is there to do? We know what happened to Bellingham – couldn't have happened to a nicer chap, by all accounts. The government has a new minister, we have other priorities, and the world moves on.'

'What about Chris Finch?'

'What about him?'

'Well, he's a Brit killed in Crete.'

'Yes, and the Greeks say they have the gang that murdered him. Finch had no family, and whatever needs doing by way of liaison can be safely left to the embassy. If it was anyone but you Louise, I'd think you were looking for an excuse to be back in the Mediterranean.' Irvine's stern features broke into a gentle smile. He knew how much his assistant commissioner had enjoyed being out of uniform.

Alone again in her office, Louise found plenty to keep her occupied, but nothing that particularly attracted her interest. The exception was a situation report from Jack Cairns regarding Stoke Newington. Reflecting the conversation they'd had, the report confirmed that the security arrangements already in place for Burak Bayram's event were sufficient, and that the shooting was probably an outbreak of gang warfare, with a rival mob such as the Hoxton Boys or the Stokey Gang upping the ante against Bombacilar. Even on this, the most fascinating aspect of her current workload, a dull predictability had descended.

She'd hoped that GCHQ might by now have deciphered more of that message about an impending assassination attempt, perhaps at least identifying where the message had been sent from and who was due to receive it. Unfortunately, the code word 'Condor' hadn't thrown up anything useful. It wasn't the name of any known person, gang or political movement, and GCHQ no longer believed the message had anything to do with Burak Bayram's visit. It was more likely to be one of the many messages intercepted on the dark web that owed more to fantasy than fact.

The leaves had begun to fall from the sturdy plane trees spaced out along the Embankment beneath Mangan's office window. For her, they signified the end of a golden summer – an unsatisfactory end that left much unresolved, and even more unsaid.

The first day of term at Dalston Academy was always chaotic. There were new pupils: trepidatious eleven-year-olds ripped away from the comfort and security of a small local primary and mixed in with children big enough to be adults in a school large enough to be an army camp. There were revised lessons and often a change in the curriculum, either to accommodate the whims of interfering politicians or to meet the demands of a constantly changing exam regime. There were also some new teachers, although the turnover had slowed since the school had received its first 'outstanding' Ofsted rating.

Cathleen and Benjamin arrived together. No longer lovers, they remained friends, and Benjamin had been a source of comfort and support in the weeks since she'd walked out on Brady. That morning, he'd picked up Cathleen from her digs – two rooms at the top of a once-grand four-storey house in Hackney. She planned to find a better place when things had settled down a bit, and she also intended to buy a small car, having left the Peugeot Estate with Brady. She wanted nothing from her old life except her books; she'd go back to get those, in time.

Benjamin was the only person she worked with who knew what had happened. She'd need to inform the school of her new address and that would be the first indication of any change in her circumstances. But she wouldn't do that today. Today, she'd be too busy with work to even think about anything else.

In the past, Cathleen had always been pleased to be back at school after the long summer break. She wondered how much of that had been relief at getting away from her unhappiness at home. Now, she was disappointed that the holidays were over. She could have done with a few more weeks to settle into her new home and prepare lessons for the coming term.

The day was going well. She'd done her bit to welcome the new intake, and was in the staff room alone doing some last-minute preparation when Vanessa, the school receptionist, popped her head round the door.

'Ah, Cathleen. I guessed you might be in here. Your husband wants to talk to you about something you forgot to do this morning.'

'Can you tell him I'm busy now and I'll ring him back?' Cathleen said, her heart sinking at the thought of a confrontation with Brady.

'He's not on the phone, he's here in person. It's quiet in here – why don't I send him in?' Vanessa disappeared before Cathleen had a chance to respond.

A few minutes later, Brady was ushered in, and the receptionist was asking if they'd like tea or coffee. They stood in silence for a minute or two after Vanessa had gone. Cathleen looked at the tall man in front of her and wondered at how quickly the affection she'd once had for him had turned into cold indifference.

'Is there another man?' he asked eventually.

'No,' Cathleen replied, mentally congratulating herself for having had the wisdom to break with her lover at the same time as breaking with her husband. It was part of the process of changing her unsatisfactory existence, and also allowed her to give the answer truthfully.

'Why leave me, then?' Brady said, in a tone that was meant to elicit sympathy, but which Cathleen found pathetic.

'Because you are a selfish, uncaring, self-absorbed man who puts no effort into our marriage.'

Cathleen surprised herself by how combative she was being. She knew this was probably a time for soothing words; a time to say something designed to get Brady out of the school, reserving the showdown for a different time and place. But she had no appetite for appeasement. The fact that this man, whom she had once loved, hadn't noticed how wretched her life had become infuriated her.

'But I worked hard to give youse what you wanted, so I did,' Brady pleaded, slipping into Belfast vernacular as he always did when he was flustered. 'And I just made you that lovely jewellery box.'

'The jewellery box! The sodding jewellery box! You made that for your own satisfaction. You have always done exactly what you wanted to do. Time spent with me was time wasted – go on, admit it, even if only to yourself. You took no interest in my life, my work, or me . . .'

At that moment, the door was pushed open, and Vanessa, who'd heard nothing of the altercation, came in with their coffees on a tray.

'Why don't you two sit down?' she said, placing the drinks on a small round table in the corner. The couple obeyed, even going so far as to begin sipping their drinks so that they could get the receptionist out of the way and return to their argument.

'I was trying to change,' Brady said, when Vanessa finally left the room.

'In what way?' Cathleen was genuinely incredulous.

'I borrowed that book by the Turkish fella.'

'The Burak Bayram book?'

'Yes. I figured it was time I started to see if we could like the same things, have something in common – things we could talk about.'

For the first time, Cathleen felt a pang of pity. She'd been puzzled as to why her husband had borrowed that book, and had thought it was because Bayram would be a celebrity visitor to the area. Her demeanour softened as she said, 'Look, I know I wasn't perfect. I wasn't exactly keen to discuss bond trading. I'm not saying all the fault lies with you – just that we've run our race together, and it's time to accept that and move on.'

'Move on?' Brady raised his voice for the first time. 'Move fucking on? What the fuck does that mean? Where was "moving on" in our marriage vows?'

Three teachers had walked into the staff room for their mid-morning break. They stood in embarrassed silence near the door. One of them was Benjamin, who now felt obliged to step in.

'Look, man,' he said, placing his substantial frame between the rowing couple. 'This ain't going to solve anything.' He made the mistake of placing a hand on Brady's shoulder, a gesture that seemed to infuriate the spurned husband.

'Fuck off, you interfering bastard,' Brady shouted, pushing Benjamin in the chest with such force that he toppled back into the chairs and tables set up for the staff break. Benjamin struggled to his feet, and other teachers were intervening to keep the men apart – but by then, Vanessa had already phoned the police.

39

THE IMPORTANCE OF AN EMPTY CUP

Detective Inspector Jack Cairns was in a pensive mood as he walked into the police station on Stoke Newington High Street. His beloved Arsenal had beaten Bournemouth three-nil on Saturday, but he remained pessimistic about the season given heavy defeats in August. On the home front, his wife Eileen, who'd been for some scans after discovering a lump in her breast, had been told it was probably benign, but that more tests were needed. And at work, while there was a consensus that the recent shooting was not a terrorist incident, nobody was sure what it was or who'd carried it out. As for the explosion at Manny's a few weeks before that, he knew who was responsible, but couldn't assemble the evidence to bring them to justice. He was convinced that the explosion and the shooting were linked, but as yet they remained unsolved crimes – and he was responsible for solving them.

It took a lot to disturb Jack Cairns' natural equanimity. He loved his family, liked his job, supported his team. The flame of ambition no longer burned within him. There was now an easy contentment where there'd once been an exacting zeal. Jack had long ago realised that the mistake he'd made as a young copper would stunt his advancement within the force, but he'd come to terms with it. He had shouted those fateful words when Sam Danvers was threatening to jump. Yes, it was in the heat of the moment, and Danvers was a murderous thug, but that didn't excuse his outburst. Police officers had to be able to deal professionally with whatever they were facing, and act with restraint and decency. At the time, he had felt that the Met could have been more supportive, but they could also have been more draconian. It had all happened over twenty years ago. There were colleagues who were convinced he could have risen higher in the Met or perhaps made it to chief constable in some provincial force. But Jack had come to realise that detective inspector would probably have been his career pinnacle regardless of the Danvers incident, because it was as high as he'd want to rise anyway.

He'd come to the nick in Stoke Newington this lunchtime to use the room he'd been given to conduct interviews in connection with his investigations. He was leading them on behalf of what was now called a Basic Command Unit, but which Jack and his colleagues continued to refer to as Borough Command. As he entered, the desk sergeant, a big, jovial fellow who had the serious character defect (as far as Jack was concerned) of being a Spurs supporter, called him across. After a bit of obligatory football banter, he told Cairns about a disturbance at Dalston Academy.

'Given that you had to go out there a few weeks ago, I thought you ought to know.'

'Who have you sent?' Jack asked.

'A couple of PCs who happened to be in the area. We got the call about an hour ago – sounds like it was an assault on one of the teachers.'

'By a pupil?'

'No, by the husband of one of the other teachers, according to the lady who rang.'

'Not the one we had to track down through his wife – the teacher there?' Jack exclaimed.

'Haven't a clue,' the sergeant responded. 'Do you want me to get the lads to come and see you when they're back?'

'No, it's okay – I think I'll nip over there myself now.'

By the time Jack Cairns arrived, the assailant had fled and the two young coppers had finished, having taken statements from Benjamin Abiola, the teacher who'd been assaulted, Cathleen Brady, the newly estranged wife of the attacker, and the other teachers who'd witnessed the altercation.

'Seems to have been a racially aggravated assault,' one of the PCs told DI Cairns. 'Guy called Brady was having a ruck with his wife, Mr Abiola intervenes to try to calm things down, and gets a mouthful of abuse and a shove in the chest for his trouble. He doesn't want to press charges, but I've told him that it may not be his choice.'

They were standing in the staff room where the incident had happened, and a couple of the teachers had begun the task of putting the furniture back in place, having previously been prevented from 'disturbing the crime scene' when the PCs had arrived. Vanessa, the school receptionist, now joined the conversation. Having let Cairns in when he'd arrived, she was keen to explain why she'd inadvertently facilitated the confrontation.

'I had no idea he'd split up with Cathleen. I'd have never let him in if she'd told me. How was I to know? I even made them a cup of coffee, thinking they needed to talk about some domestic stuff – how was I to know?' she pleaded for a second time.

'You weren't to know at all,' Jack agreed. 'Where are the coffee cups?'

'On the floor over there. I was just on my way to collect them. It's a wonder they weren't smashed in all that commotion.'

'Leave them to me, I'll take them,' Jack announced.

'What on earth for?' Vanessa was incredulous. 'Don't you have enough cups of your own down at the police station?'

Jack laughed, making a joke about cuts to police funding. It wasn't something he could explain to Vanessa, but he knew it was important to take the cup that Brady had drunk from into custody.

40

OUT AT WORK

The sighting of the red-helmeted body at the bottom of Lake Kournas was widely reported, albeit on the inside pages of most newspapers. That the minister was in the lake had been received opinion for weeks now: confirmation of that was hardly front-page news. Only the *Daily Candour* gave it the headline treatment, describing Bellingham as the 'Lake-mess Monster'. As for the broadsheets, they were carrying obituaries of Bellingham, such was the certitude concerning the noble lord's fate.

Since returning from Crete, Louise Mangan's thoughts had been concentrated on the Burak Bayram event, which was now only ten days away. At least, that was where her professional thoughts were focused; her private ones remained with Captain Petros Diamantapoulis. She hadn't heard from him since their inauspicious parting at the airport. He hadn't contacted her; she hadn't contacted him. She would respond, and with enthusiastic immediacy, if only he'd call or text or email or WhatsApp or FaceTime or . . . write. She hoped he'd be feeling the same, but doubted he would. Petros would go back to leading the life he'd led before in Athens, just as she must concentrate on her job in

London and the half-life she felt she'd been leading before her latest visit to Crete.

It was eleven o'clock in the morning, and Louise was about to go to one of the routine meetings she was obliged to attend as the assistant commissioner for professionalism when Detective Sergeant Din poked his head round her door. 'Sorry to disturb, Ma'am, but there's someone downstairs who wants to see you.'

'There often is, Rushil, and it's the job of my staff to deal with them,' Mangan replied, gathering her papers.

'Bit different this time. It's a bloke by the name of Keith Brewer, and he won't be fobbed off.'

'Since when has persistence been the key that opens my door? If there's a single characteristic those with a bee in their bonnet share it's being boringly persistent. What's it about?'

'Lord Bellingham,' Din responded. 'He read in this morning's *Candour* that you're back to London now that Bellingham has been found.'

'And?'

'He says that Bellingham is not in that lake.'

Mangan sat back down at her desk and waited a few seconds before asking, 'And how does he know that?'

'He won't tell me. Says he'll only talk to you.'

'Why would I waste my time with some random nutter who's been watching too many police dramas on telly?'

'Because he does seem to have had an association with Lord Bellingham. I wouldn't have troubled you if I thought he was just a "random nutter".'

The detective sergeant's response forced Mangan to spend a few more moments reflecting on her options before saying: 'I'm sorry, Rushil, you'll need to get rid of him. I no longer have anything to do with the Bellingham case. If Mr Persistent continues to play up, take his contact details and suggest he emails us with his thoughts. As far as I'm concerned, the Bellingham case is closed.'

In Athens, Petros Diamantapoulis was deep in thought.
Hassan win crypt photograph.
He was speculating that Finch had discovered something about Hassan, and that was why the journalist had been tortured and beaten. The file on Hassan that the captain had been re-reading mentioned that he'd been a photographer in Libya, and his girlfriend Sharron had told Louise that he always carried a small camera with him. The last words of Christopher Finch must relate to a photograph Hassan had taken – but of what? A crypt? And what would he win?

None of the gang members now in custody would talk. Even the 'singing bird' said nothing about Hassan. Whether or not the four words Petros was contemplating related to Lord Bellingham's disappearance, as he and Louise suspected, they were certainly relevant to the two operations he remained in charge of: bringing to justice all those involved in the murder of the British journalist and destroying the organised criminal network responsible for smuggling refugees and drugs between Africa and Europe.

He wanted to share his deliberations with Louise, but worried that his intrusion into whatever she was doing now would be unwelcome. If she'd only contact him. He was surprised by how much he missed her.

Hassan win crypt photograph.

Something came back to him then – something he remembered Louise saying. He was due to go back to Crete the following week. He needed to establish if his theory had any substance.

When Jack Cairns returned to Borough Command, he brought with him two coffee cups that had been carefully placed in transparent polythene sandwich bags. He didn't know which one Brady had drunk from, but he was pretty sure that Cathleen wouldn't have disposed of that piece of chewing gum found on the scaffolding from where the gun had been fired. If the DNA on one of those cups matched that on the chewing gum, it would be Brady's cup. He'd given Brady's address to the PCs at the school, but told them there should be no arrest. They just needed to check if he was there.

He wasn't – there'd been no reply. They'd waited outside for an hour with no sign of him.

'He must be out at work,' one of the PCs had suggested when he radioed in from outside the house. They would pay another visit later.

The PC didn't know how right he was; Brady was, indeed, 'out at work'.

*

After he'd pushed the interfering teacher to the floor, Brady had stood defiant, fists clenched, eyes blazing. A couple of the other teachers had quickly intervened, diffidently placing nervous hands on Brady's chest as if controlling a queue on the underground.

His anger had dissolved as quickly as it had erupted. Brady wished he could turn back time. Benjamin had lain amongst the wreck of overturned tables and chairs, but the image that stayed burned on to Brady's memory was of Cathleen tenderly attending to the stricken man, then turning her face towards her husband with a look of utter disdain. Brady hadn't thought Cathleen capable of feeling the hatred her eyes portrayed – towards him. It shocked him more than the incident itself.

No serious attempt to restrain him had been made, so Brady had simply walked away. He'd parked his Peugeot in one of the teachers' bays outside the main doors. Within two minutes, he was through the security gates and out on the main road. He'd passed a police car, sirens blaring, half a mile further on, and guessed where it was going. Brady had to get home quickly, but knew he couldn't stay long – only as long as it took to get what was necessary to carry out the last job he'd ever do. His life with Cathleen was over; he knew that. When he'd gathered all the things he needed and closed the door of his house behind him, he realised he'd never come back. He'd lie low until 21 September, complete his final contract, and then shed this identity, as a snake sheds a skin. When he killed his final victim, his time as Brady would be over.

41

KILLER ON THE RUN

'We don't know where he is, but we're certain he's armed.'

Louise Mangan was briefing Commissioner George Irvine on the current situation. Jack Cairns had been perceptive enough to have the coffee cup that Brady had been drinking from checked against the chewing gum found on the scaffolding in Stoke Newington. The DNA matched, but Brady had vanished, his car abandoned in a central London side street.

When the security service had broken into his house (having received the appropriate authorisation from the Home Secretary), they had found no trace of the bonds and gilts trading that was supposed to be Brady's profession, but they had eventually uncovered 'a stock of weapons that would adequately arm a small emerging nation' (as the spooks had described it in their report).

Amongst this cache was the Remington semi-automatic used in the Stoke Newington shooting, making it doubly certain that Brady had been the gunman. He would have had plenty of time to pack before the police arrived, and it was inconceivable that he would have left unarmed. The stash of weapons they'd uncovered had simply been the ones he'd left behind.

It was now Friday, and the Burak Bayram event was due to take place at Stoke Newington Town Hall the following Thursday. The commissioner was about to go on holiday, and was meeting Mangan for a final update, but he had his own important contribution to make to the discussion.

'GCHQ has uncovered one more crucial piece of information about Condor,' he told Mangan. 'If I can remind you, the intercepted message said: "Re: Condor. Kill arranged. Top man engaged." They still don't know who sent or received it, but there's little doubt now that it relates to the Bayram meeting.'

'Why? If they don't know who it's from or who it's to . . .'

'Because the message went on to say: "Will happen on 21 September. Sweet." The final word may be a code name or just an expression, but there's no ambiguity about the date – it's next Thursday, and the "top man engaged" is, in all probability, this Brady fellow. Some of the weapons found in his house have already been linked to several unsolved murders going back years. You and Jack seem to have stumbled across a contract killer.'

'But why would a professional like Brady draw attention to himself by shooting at a few hoodlums and claiming it was "Bayram's Boys"? It doesn't make sense.'

'I agree, but there's lots of things that don't make

sense in our world, Louise, and posting that message does at least link Brady with Bayram. The question for us now is if we still think the event next Thursday should go ahead.'

'I'm not sure we have the authority to cancel it,' Mangan said, 'but we could try to convince Mr Bayram not to go ahead. Given all we know about him, though, he'll refuse. He's somebody who believes in passive resistance, and that every attempt to silence him is a badge of honour.'

'We have the authority to cancel it, Louise; don't worry about that. This is a counterterrorism issue, and under that legislation, we can do things that would be more difficult if it was a normal domestic policing issue.'

'What do the spooks say?'

'Don't worry about them – they love banning things. They'd ban their own birthday celebrations, given half a chance. We're the "citizens in uniform", not them.'

'Well, I'm instinctively inclined to stick with our original decision to let it go ahead. If we've caught Brady by then, the panic's over. If we haven't, he may well not be a top "man" anymore. If he's on the run, he surely won't want to break cover. But the key argument for me is this: to ensure Bayram's safety, we've made arrangements to protect him from assassination, as we always do in these circumstances. Because we now know where the threat emanates from, and who the potential assassin is, we must surely be better placed to protect Bayram than we have been up to now.'

'And if he's still on the loose, the best chance of catching Brady will be at Stoke Newington Town Hall next Thursday,' the commissioner added. 'I was hoping you'd stick to your guns – if that's the appropriate expression, given the circumstances.'

Mangan smiled and Irvine placed an affectionate hand on her shoulder. 'I'll have a much better holiday for having had this conversation. You know you can disturb me at any time,' he said.

Mangan remembered a few previous occasions when she'd tried to contact her boss when he was on one of his 'Wainwright walks' in the Lake District, where telephone reception was sporadic at best. She was pretty sure she'd have to deal with next Thursday's challenges without the help of the Commissioner of Police of the Metropolis.

42

CONVERSATION IN A CAR

Midnight in Agia Galini. It was mid-September, and the season was almost over. The darkness that had descended so quickly at sunset seemed to thicken as the activity receded. The evening trade at the shops around the harbour had been brisk at eight o'clock, light at nine and all over by ten. Those selling trinkets and souvenirs were always the last to close, but in Agia Galini, even at the height of the season, they'd have been closed by midnight. Now, they'd been shut and shuttered for two hours. In the densely populated cities and more garish holiday resorts up on the north coast of Crete, the night would have hardly begun. But Agia Galini is neither a city nor a resort, garish or otherwise. Those who live and holiday here value their sleep.

At Dimitri's, the finest restaurant in the Rethymnon region, there was still a steady stream of diners every evening, but there was no longer a need for extra tables outside, and the interior was never more than half-full. The restaurant would close as usual at the end of the month, leaving its owner free to dedicate himself to his other interests, which were many and varied – petrol stations on the mainland, a travel company he'd founded, and, most lucrative of all, the drugs trade he'd been building for fifteen years. He'd been reluctant to add people-trafficking, but demand was irresistible after Gaddafi's overthrow in Libya. The boats that brought the drugs might just as well add refugees to the cargo. It made good business sense.

Dimitri Limnios knew there was a tough winter ahead. The men he'd recruited and paid to run his criminal operation in Crete were almost all in captivity. But Dimitri had not been implicated. There was a clear connection to him through the estate he owned, the one that the police had raided, but its ownership would be difficult to establish, and he felt sure that if his secret had been discovered, he'd have known by now. The Libyan end of the operation remained intact, with demand as high as it had ever been. All he needed to do was find a different place to store goods in transit, as well as recruit some new 'staff'. He felt sure that those who'd been captured would be keen to work for him again as soon as they became available; not that they realised they were working for Dimitri. His involvement was well disguised, and the latest little difficulty had at least been a useful test of how robust the subterfuge was. It had proved to be impenetrable.

Tonight, Dimitri had an appointment to keep; someone to meet out on the lonely coast road heading west, where only wild goats and falcons roamed at this time of night. After locking up the restaurant, he took a twenty-minute drive to a clearing half a kilometre off the narrow track running parallel to the coast. The restaurateur parked, turned off his headlights and waited. Another car drove up from the opposite direction ten minutes later, parking a few metres away. A short man got out and walked gingerly across, as if stepping on broken glass. He got quietly into the car and sat in the front passenger seat beside Dimitri. They sat in silence for a moment, looking out at the moonlit sea: Dimitri Limnios and Inspector General Kostar Pelkas.

As he handed over a canvas bag stuffed with cash, Dimitri said softly, 'I pay you to avoid the kind of police interference we've had recently.'

'That bastard Diamantapoulis has been put in charge. I can't control him. But don't worry – soon I will resume total command. The question I need to ask you, my friend, is what the hell happened with that journalist? Hassan was problem enough, but an English journalist? Were your people out of their minds on drugs?'

'That's always an occupational hazard, I'm afraid, but let me explain. Hassan decided to pursue a little extracurricular activity. He had this crazy idea of blackmailing Lady Bellingham,' Dimitri said. 'He'd taken a photograph at her place, and demanded a thousand euros or he'd go to the police with it.'

'It would have come to me, and I would have dealt with it.'

'It probably wouldn't have come to you, actually. Our friend Diamantapoulis seems to be dealing with the Bellinghams. Anyway, that's all irrelevant now. We knew nothing about what Hassan was up to until Lady Bellingham drove into the compound with the money, shouting and screaming that we'd regret the day we ever tangled with her. My guys hadn't a clue what she was talking about. Hassan had called Lady Bellingham to make his demands, thinking he'd be alone at the huts. He was supposed to be preparing for the next consignment. Unfortunately for him, three of the toughest and most psychotic of my recruits turned up unannounced just before the good lady arrived.'

'Hassan was even stupider than we thought,' Pelkas proffered.

'He's no Aristotle, that's for sure. Not only did he get the wife of a British government minister to come to our hideaway, but he was also only blackmailing her for a thousand euros.'

'Blackmailing her for what, though? What was it a photograph of?' Pelkas asked.

'I don't know. Maybe it was pornographic, given what we now know about Lord Bellingham, but she certainly wanted that photo back. She must have thought the guys who came out to greet her with guns were in on the blackmail, but they didn't have a clue what was happening. She handed over the money, and they had the good sense to refuse it. She drove away shouting about wanting that photo or there'd be trouble.'

'And Hassan?'

'He tried to drive away in that old Renault of his, but it wouldn't start. Just as my loyal psychopaths were getting to work on him to find out what the fuck was happening, this big Englishman rolls up, asking questions. My guys naturally thought he was either police or secret service trailing Lady Bellingham. The guy said he was a journalist, which didn't help, and that he'd witnessed what had just happened.'

'So, you detained them both – Hassan and the journalist.'

'That's one way of putting it,' Dimitri said. 'My men beat the shit out of them trying to find out more, then they chained them up in that lovely underground detention centre we'd created. When we got wind of the police raid – not from you, Kostar, I'm disappointed to say . . .'

Pelkas shifted uncomfortably in his seat, but didn't respond.

'. . . the men took Hassan with them and left the journalist behind,' Dimitri continued. 'The journalist hadn't revealed anything and that's probably because he had nothing to reveal, but he knew too much, so they tried to finish him off with a stab wound before leaving him there to die.'

'The only positive thing to come out of this is that we found a good use for Hassan,' Pelkas observed.

'Indeed. So you guessed the body my men gave you for the lake was him?'

'His face wasn't as pretty as in the "wanted" photograph we were circulating, but yes, I figured it was him.'

'You did well to get the red safety helmet from Lady Bellingham,' Dimitri said.

'Fortunately, she didn't associate me with the guys at the compound, and was happy to oblige, as she had been with the jacket she'd given us. She seemed to want to prove that her husband was where I thought he was.'

'She won't know that it's Hassan down there in Lake Kournas wearing her husband's helmet.'

'She'd be even happier if she did, given he was the one who was blackmailing her. It helps that she hates Captain Diamantapoulis, too. He always rubs her up the wrong way,' the inspector general said, making a rubbing gesture with his small hands.

'So given that it's Hassan at the bottom of that lake, where *is* Lord Bellingham?' Dimitri asked.

'Somewhere in that lake or in the White Mountains. What does it matter? The Greek police has done its job and Lady Bellingham can more easily get access to his money.'

'A perfect solution for her. She probably hated him even before those press reports about the child he seduced. I suspect her only worry now is that photograph. It's still out there somewhere. Hassan refused to tell us what he'd done with that damn camera he always carried around with him, despite our best efforts. Your police guys believe Hassan's gone back to Libya. We told him that would be the extent of his punishment if he wrote a note to his girlfriend that we could put through her door, together with the passport he stole.

The poor fool thought he was going home right to the end. My only real complaint is that you couldn't stop that bloody captain from capturing almost all our men,' Dimitri said.

'I knew nothing about that operation. Diamantapoulis kept it from me. But worry not, my friend; nobody knows about your involvement, let alone mine. Having seen what happened to Hassan, the men will be reluctant to reveal anything they do know, anyway. You can use the winter to recruit some new troops and restore your links with Libya. Diamantapoulis will be moved on to other things, and we'll be back to normal by next summer. Your only worry should be that I may be promoted to an even higher and more important position now that I am credited with finding the missing English minister.' Pelkas verbally preened himself in his drab attire as unashamedly as he had in his resplendent uniform.

'Time you were off,' Dimitri said, looking down at the huge Rolex on his wrist.

Suddenly, the glare of a searchlight forced both men to shield their eyes. Somebody shouted instructions through a megaphone.

'Get out of the car, put your hands on your head and stand apart.'

Kostar Pelkas cut a shrivelled figure, small and inconsequential, his face betraying the alarm he felt. Dimitri Limnios, usually so suave and relaxed, looked around in panic. Police officers, guns primed, surrounded the car.

After a moment or two, Captain Petros Diamantapoulis stepped through their ranks.

'Thank you for giving such a full testimony,' he said. 'It's amazing how useful an expensive watch can be, with only a few adjustments.'

43

21 SEPTEMBER

Stoke Newington Town Hall in Church Street reflects the municipal pride of the decade in which it was built. Its decadent 1930s glamour is preserved most demonstrably in the council chamber, with its curved mahogany speaker's table and walnut panelling, but for most visitors, it's the art deco glory of the Assembly Hall that is the building's most attractive feature. On this day, 21 September 2017, almost 400 chairs would be arranged on its original Canadian maple sprung dancefloor in preparation for a speech by Burak Bayram, the internationally acclaimed Turkish novelist and polemicist. Security concerns had forced the timing to be altered from the evening to the morning so that the event would take place entirely in daylight. The balcony at the far end of the hall would be closed to the public, reducing capacity by fifty, but enabling armed police officers to occupy that vantage point. Given the rigorous searches that those attending would be subjected to, this seemed unnecessarily heavy-handed, but Mangan and her team were leaving nothing to chance. The stage at one end of the Assembly Hall had been set up for two speakers: Burak Bayram and the woman who chaired the Britain Turkey Literary Alliance (BTLA), the organisation hosting the author's visit. The pair would sit behind a bulletproof transparent construction that resembled a Perspex bus shelter.

At 9am, two hours before the event was due to begin, Louise Mangan arrived outside with DS Din and checked that the various teams were in place via an encrypted two-way radio system. There were three armed details on the surrounding rooftops, four armed officers located at local transport hubs, a team accompanying Bayram to and from the venue, and another in the Rose and Crown pub opposite the Town Hall. Its strategic location had led to the pub being requisitioned for the occasion; agreement having been reached with the landlord for suitable compensation.

The weather was overcast; a sporadic drizzle was expected to become heavy rain later. Having checked that everything was in place, Mangan and Din were walking up the Town Hall steps when a squad car pulled up, out of which stepped Detective Inspector Jack Cairns.

'Morning, Louise. Everything okay?' Cairns called out. 'Shouldn't Rushil have an umbrella up for you?'

'He knows that if I saw him with a brolly, I'd break it over his head,' Mangan responded. 'Yes, everything's okay here. How are things with you?'

By now, Cairns had fallen in step with his two colleagues. 'All good,' he said. 'We've found reasons to haul Taylan Ayhan and his Bombacilar pals in for questioning, just in case. Told them we had some information to discuss about the shooting and timed their interviews for 11am – not that we think they're any threat to Bayram. Better to be safe and all that.'

'We're just going to grab a coffee,' Mangan said as they reached the reception area. 'Why don't you join us?'

'No thanks, Louise. I wanted to take a quick look and make sure everything's okay, and check you don't need anything else from Borough Command. I have to take Eileen to hospital for her appointment later, otherwise I'd stay to see the fun.'

Mangan knew that Jack's wife had been ill and that he insisted on being free to accompany her to every hospital visit. She admired him for ensuring that, in this respect at least, the job came second.

They parted, and Mangan and Din had their coffee break before becoming immersed in all the things that needed to be checked, coordinated and confirmed. The arrangements flowed smoothly, the only glitch coming when Bayram insisted on meeting a tranche of his supporters, who'd come early to vociferously lobby for the privilege of meeting their hero. When he was advised not to meet them, Bayram pointed out that many were close friends whom he hadn't seen since beginning his exile in Germany. In the end, Mangan relented, but the backstage meeting was the only time the author wasn't with people who had been individually vetted. Fortunately, it passed without incident.

Afterwards, as Mangan stood in the gallery, surveying the ticket-holders as they arrived, a local PC who'd been called to the school incident pointed out Brady's wife and the teacher who'd been assaulted, Benjamin Abiola. They'd arrived with a small group of colleagues from Dalston Academy. Mangan had vetoed the idea of any approaches being made to Cathleen Brady to discuss their suspicions that her husband was about to make an unwelcome appearance at this event. She feared that the couple may still be in touch, and therefore felt it was too big a risk to take – although at some stage, Brady's estranged wife would need to face some vigorous questions about what she knew and what she'd seen during their lives together. That would be for others to pursue. Mangan's involvement in Stoke Newington would end when Burak Bayram was safely on his way back to Germany.

The security arrangements were working so well that Mangan doubted a fly could have entered the Assembly Hall without her being aware. There had been no sightings of Brady or anybody acting suspiciously. At 11am precisely, the event began. Having been introduced, Bayram made a rapturously received speech and then took questions. The whole thing was over by 1pm, but Bayram would be kept under armed guard until his evening flight to Berlin. If 21 September was the designated day for an assassination attempt, as the message intercepted by GCHQ had suggested, there was still plenty of it left for an attack to be mounted. While this public meeting had been the obvious opportunity for the assassin to strike, given that at all other times the writer would be under close protection with his precise whereabouts unknown, the 'no-risk' strategy that Mangan had insisted upon had to continue. However, she was satisfied that the moment of maximum danger had passed.

As the audience trooped out of the Town Hall and the various armed units placed around it were decommissioned, Mangan asked Din to call Jack Cairns to let him know that the meeting had passed uneventfully.

'Happy to do that,' DS Din responded. 'By the way, I've been reading up on what happened with him and Sam Danvers, as you suggested. Fascinating stuff.'

'You have a great talent for taking an issue you once knew nothing about and turning it into your specialist subject on *Mastermind*.'

'Thanks, boss,' Din said, dubiously. There was a pause before he said, 'Actually, today is the twenty-fifth anniversary of when it all happened.'

'Really? How riveting,' Mangan said, teasing her companion.

However, she began to find Din's observation more interesting as what he'd said gradually sunk in. She knew that Din didn't have a high enough security clearance to have seen the actual intelligence picked up by GCHQ, and so asked: 'If I was to say "Condor", what would it mean to you?'

'It would mean a bird of prey and, I think, a pipe tobacco.'

Louise turned away, impressed by Din's general knowledge, but unmoved. He'd only told her what she knew already.

'Coincidentally,' Din continued, taking out his phone to make the call to Cairns, 'given that we were talking about Jack and the Danvers gang, that was also the name of the car park that Sam Danvers jumped from when he killed himself.'

Mangan, who'd been walking towards the exit, stopped so abruptly that Din almost bumped into her.

'Sorry if that came as a shock,' the DS said, nervously. 'The car park was in a little turnoff in the City called Condor Walk, next to the Condor pub. I tried looking it up in the *A to Z*, but it doesn't exist anymore. It was all pulled down about fifteen years ago.'

'Oh my God,' Louise exclaimed. 'It's not Bayram who's the target today. It's Jack.'

Jack Cairns had read somewhere that phones could affect sensitive medical equipment and, noticing that nobody else in the oncology unit of University College London on the Euston Road was using their mobile, switched his off. This not only enabled him to concentrate on the well-being of his wife without distractions, but it also gave him a surprising sense of tranquillity. He'd done the same thing on their previous visits, and Jack reckoned these appointments had been the only occasions on which he'd managed to escape the tyranny of the phone since mobiles had become ubiquitous, whenever that was.

Eileen's appointment was for 12.30pm, but everything was running late. At 1.30pm, they were still sitting side by side in the waiting area when the armed officers burst through the heavy plastic flaps that served as doors.

'I'm sure they'll see Eileen soon,' Jack Cairns said, moving nothing beyond a raised eyebrow. 'It's nice of you guys to try to move things along, but we're happy to wait our turn.'

Later, back at New Scotland Yard, Louise Mangan was pacing the conference room. There was a detective superintendent present, together with Din and several detective inspectors, including Jack Cairns. The deputy commissioner, Karen Dale, was on her way. She was in temporary charge while the commissioner was on holiday, and she and Mangan had never got on. Many of those who knew the two women best would describe their relationship as being one of mutual detestation.

'So, Billy Danvers decides to avenge his son on the twenty-fifth anniversary of Sam's death. I presume he's out of prison?' Mangan asked.

'Yes, he was released after serving fifteen years,' one of the senior detectives attending this hastily convened conference confirmed. 'He's lived quietly since. We've got him and his two other sons under surveillance.'

'Presumably he's living comfortably on the proceeds of his crimes,' Mangan mused.

'He's in a council flat in Stepney, but he'll have a cash pile somewhere to draw upon.'

'Enough to hire a hitman?'

'Enough to hire an army of them, I'd imagine.'

'It's no good keeping the Danvers under observation

for this if they've contracted the job out,' Jack Cairns pointed out.

He'd insisted on remaining at the hospital with his wife until she'd seen the doctor. The news about the tumour was that it was definitely benign, and the danger that Jack was being told he was in hadn't diminished the sense of euphoria that this news had inspired. As he'd told Louise on their way here, 'That tumour was a bigger threat to life than Billy bloody Danvers.'

'Something's not right,' Mangan was saying now. 'If he was planning to assassinate Jack, what was all the "Bayram's Boys" stuff about?'

'Perhaps Brady was trying to make sure that Jack was at the Bayram event? The shooting and the text that Brady put out afterwards would heighten the tension and make Jack's attendance more likely. He wouldn't have known about the hospital appointment.'

'But it would have been easier to kill Jack away from the Town Hall,' Mangan responded. 'I think it's much more likely that Brady was genuinely upset at the attack on Manny's restaurant and the subsequent beating of Osman. They were his friends. Brady's attack on the Bombacilar gang had nothing to do with the contract he'd taken on to kill Jack.'

'You mean he's a hitman with a heart,' said Deputy Commissioner Karen Dale sarcastically, having entered the room as Louise was in full flow.

'We're in the course of checking Brady's background; perhaps we'll find something that helps establish a link,' one of the other detectives said, keen to diffuse the sudden tension in the room. 'Now that the Bayram event is over, we can also question Brady's wife.'

'In the meantime, we need to keep you safe,' Mangan said to Cairns.

'I'm sure that's right, Assistant Commissioner,' Karen Dale responded. 'But now that your role in coordinating security for the Bayram event has concluded, I think you should get back to your duties and leave this to the officers responsible. I think you'll find that Mr Brady is too preoccupied with self-preservation to be a threat to Jack at this moment. I've just been informed by the ops room that they have a CCTV image of Brady, and he's nowhere near here.'

The gathering reassembled five minutes later in the operations centre. Mangan, ignoring the deputy commissioner's pointed remarks, had arrived with everyone else, and a young technician was talking them through the moving images they were looking at.

'This is Preston station,' the technician was saying, 'at mid-afternoon, just over a week ago – the day after Brady disappeared. Watch the newsagent's at the centre of the image.' The screen showed a bustling crowd in slow motion. 'Look, there – the man with the beanie hat.'

A man in a green waxed jacket walked into view. He had a rucksack on his back, and was carrying a long canvas bag. He was looking down, apparently aware of the camera and keen to avoid it.

'Watch carefully,' the technician demanded.

A woman coming out of the newsagent's collided with the man, who stepped backwards, his face suddenly revealed to the camera. Something buzzed, and the photo of Brady that had been taken when he visited Manny with the prayer lectern popped on to the screen with the word 'MATCH' flashing on and off beside the frozen photo.

'That's your Mr Brady,' the officer working the console announced. 'The technology doesn't lie.'

'Do we know where he came from or where he went?' Cairns asked.

'Afraid not. As you can see, he recovers himself, apologises to the woman he collided with and slips out of view. He doesn't appear again at the station, but this is a man who knows how to evade CCTV. If it wasn't for the mishap with the woman leaving the newsagent's, we wouldn't have known he'd been through Preston.'

'Wait a minute,' Mangan said. 'Isn't Preston on the route to Carlisle?'

'Are you still here, Louise?' the deputy commissioner said, noticing her for the first time since they'd left the conference room. 'I've already said you can now return to your normal duties.'

Receiving affirmation that Preston was indeed where many trains changed for Carlisle, Louise ignored the interruption and turned to Jack Cairns. 'I've just remembered. The commissioner told me *he* worked on the Danvers ambush all those years ago.'

'That's right,' said Jack. 'George Irvine was on the Flying Squad planning team that devised the operation.

But if you're thinking what I think you're thinking, his was a backroom role; he wasn't with us on the actual hit. Nobody would know about his involvement.'

'Yes they would.' DS Din spoke from the periphery of the gathering. The others turned towards him. 'I've been reading up on it. Danvers' legal team called him as a witness when they were trying to pin responsibility for Sam Danvers' death on the Met. They were arguing that it was the nature of the entrapment that gave Sam Danvers no opportunity to surrender and forced him to kill himself. They named the commissioner, who was a detective inspector at the time, as the man who had engineered the whole thing. In the end he didn't have to appear in court, but his name was out there.'

The shocked silence gave way to a flurry of activity as they all realised that a contract killer had travelled to the Lake District a week ago, with the aim of avenging Sam Danvers on the twenty-fifth anniversary of his death – 21 September. It was Commissioner Irvine who was the target, and the day was already half over.

44

THE VALEDICTORY MISSION

Brady was pleased with how well he'd blended in. The police would be looking for him, but had no reason to look here. They were after someone who'd been involved in a fracas in Stoke Newington; there was nothing to connect him with faraway Cumbria. He couldn't have risked hanging around in London while his false identity was gradually peeled away, layer by layer; neither could he take with him all the incriminating evidence they were bound to find in a full search of his house.

He'd brought with him all he'd need to complete this, his final contract: the Barrett M82 rifle, the Glock 19 pistol, the long-bladed dagger. Realising he'd eventually have to abandon the car, it would have been foolish to load it with weaponry he wouldn't be able to carry, so the rest of his armoury had been left behind. When they found it, they'd know what he did for a living – but they wouldn't know where he was.

Even without the disruption of the last few weeks, which had ended the inconsequentiality of his life in London and for which he blamed Cathleen, he would have needed to set off for the Lake District at this stage anyway to make his final preparations. In all probability, he'd have driven rather than travelling by train, but in all other respects it would have been as it was now. He'd be dressed in the same rugged attire: woollen hat, waxed jacket, T-shirt, jeans and good strong boots, the uniform of the Lake District fell-walker. And he'd have booked into a small B&B, exactly as he had done – as Brady. Eventually, the police would trace his movements, but that would be after the event, and by that time, he wouldn't be Brady anymore.

He knew exactly where the commissioner would be, because Brady's usual meticulous research had uncovered an interview he'd given for the Christmas edition of *The Job*, the in-house magazine of the Metropolitan Police. The commissioner had talked about his hobbies, his love of fell-walking in the Lake District, and how he and his wife were 'walking the Wainwrights' in numerical order. They were determined to do all thirty-six circular walks covering all the peaks described in *A. Wainwright's Pictorial Guides to the Lakeland Fells*. The commissioner had said in the interview that they were currently up to number ten. That was at Christmas last year, which must mean that when they next went on holiday, in September 2017, they would walk route eleven, the Troutbeck Medley, which was helpfully mapped out in several printed guides.

Brady had arrived here in sufficient time to walk every inch of it, covering pine woods, ridges, becks and several fells, the highest of which was 1,691 feet. He'd been indiscernible from the other walkers, the only difference being that he was carrying thirty-two pounds of dismantled weaponry on his back, baggage that he couldn't risk leaving in his room, and which he'd need to have with him anyway, as he tried setting up the rifle in several locations until he found one ideal for his purpose.

When the commissioner had arrived with his wife on the afternoon of 19 September, Brady was observing, through binoculars, from the birdwatching hide he'd found. The hide gave him a good view of the A592, down which he knew Mr and Mrs Irvine must travel. He'd seen them check in to the Mortal Man Inn along with two protection officers. Brady had known there would be close protection, and was pleased to see it limited to two officers. He was watching again when they came out into the village of Troutbeck the next morning, setting off to walk the first eight miles on a circular route. Brady noticed that the protection wasn't all that close. While the tall, slim man being protected strode away purposely with his wife, guidebooks in hand, the two officers, a man and a woman, chugged along gently, some distance behind.

There had been a perfect opportunity to carry out his task on that first day, just as the commissioner ascended the precipitous eastern flank of Troutbeck Tongue. Brady had watched through his binoculars from some high ground to the west, the Barrett rifle ready for action, his escape route planned – but it was 20 September, and the terms of his contract stipulated that the commissioner must be eliminated the following day.

Brady's accommodation was a farm B&B near Kentmere, which he left at dawn on Thursday 21 September. He'd paid cash for an ancient Land Rover that the farmer had been pleased to dispose of. It was taxed, had four good wheels and a reliable engine. This was all Brady needed. When the job was done, he'd only use it to drive up to Scotland. From there, he'd cross to Northern Ireland and quietly reappear as his old self. He might eventually travel south to the Republic, and perhaps, once things had quietened down, he could go to Canada to see his sister. So much would be possible once he'd retired – after this, his valedictory mission.

He'd been concerned that the commissioner might decide to rest before tackling a second day of route eleven. There were contingency plans to cover any eventuality. If necessary, he'd dispose of the commissioner at the Mortal Man Inn, thus proving the wisdom of its name – but that would have been a last resort, and he soon knew it wouldn't be necessary.

At around 11am, no doubt after a good night's sleep and a hearty breakfast, the Irvines emerged in full walking mode, each carrying a stick. The two protection officers had separated today – one (the woman) walked forty metres ahead of the couple, and the other forty metres behind. The sky was leaden, with heavy rain forecast for the afternoon. Brady was confident he could stick to his plan of firing the fatal shot when the commissioner reached the top of Wansfell.

Once he'd seen the party set off, he drove the Land Rover to the hide and proceeded to assemble the

Barrett. He calculated that he was around 800 metres from the pinnacle of Wansfell: half a mile, well within the Barrett's range. The hide was off the beaten track, away from the smattering of other walkers out on the fells that day, who all seemed to be following the Wainwright route. He worked out that the commissioner would reach the top of Wansfell in two and a half hours, at around 2pm. All Brady could do now was wait.

The commissioner hadn't bothered to bring his mobile. There was no point. It was impossible to get a consistent signal in this terrain. His two protection officers carried satellite phones, so any messages that needed to be conveyed to him could come through them. He hoped to have a peaceful morning doing what he and Susan liked to do best – rambling across Wainwright (and Wordsworth) country.

It was 1.45pm, and his little entourage had passed through a broken section of dry-stone walling to pick up the path that led to the summit of Wansfell. He and Susan had stopped to admire the view south towards Windermere. A shaft of sunlight had broken through the thin dark clouds that hung like wisps of smoke in the sky above them. The rain had held off. It was a perfect day for walking.

The protection officers were struggling. They weren't part of the commissioner's regular team, and he'd specified that they should be officers who were not only able to cover the topography, but also capable of enjoying the experience. George Irvine couldn't help feeling a stab of satisfaction that he and Susan, at least twenty years older than their protectors, were maintaining a steady pace, while the girl in front was constantly having to stop to catch her breath and the man at the rear was falling further and further behind. These two were no fell-walkers, that was for sure.

Having paused to take stock of the picturesque surroundings and give the officer at the back a chance to catch up, they moved on and were at the top of Wansfell when the officer in front lifted the satellite phone to her ear. The commissioner, twenty metres away, noticed her reach for the gun in her shoulder holster before he heard her shout, 'GET DOWN, LIE FLAT!' at exactly the moment a gunshot echoed across the landscape.

Had he hit his target? Brady couldn't tell. The commissioner was in his sights, rather than the protection officer ahead of him. He hadn't seen her lift the phone to her ear; hadn't heard her shout. He'd seen his target fall when he'd squeezed the trigger. Brady looked through his binoculars and saw that nobody was standing on the summit of Wansfell. If he'd hit his target, there would be activity. Mrs Irvine would be tending to her husband; the protection officers would by now be surveying the landscape to try and discern where the shot had been fired from. Brady desperately wanted the satisfaction of seeing the bullet strike its target; then he'd be able to dismantle the gun, jump into the Land Rover and head off to his new life. He put down the binoculars to squint through the even more powerful lens of the Barrett's telescopic sights. The commissioner and his wife were lying just below the ridge.

He'd only just discerned this when the second protection officer suddenly appeared on the scene, gesturing down, presumably towards them. The idiot was standing, gun in hand, looking around, and, Brady assumed, ignoring the exhortations of the others to lie flat. Calculating that he'd need to move in to finish the job, Brady decided that both protection officers would need to be disposed of, starting with this one. He hadn't calculated on killing anyone other than his contracted prey. He had no desire to kill for the sake of killing. He did what he was paid to do. A third of the fee for this job had gone into his Swiss bank account in advance. The rest would be paid upon completion, irrespective of how many others he needed to exterminate in order to get it done. The task had to be completed. He squeezed the trigger and the protection officer fell – disposed of efficiently, cleanly, effectively.

Brady hoped the second shot might cause the commissioner to break cover, but nothing moved. He knew that three people were still alive up there on Wansfell: the commissioner, his wife and the remaining protection officer. He put the rifle on to the back seat of the Land Rover without dismantling it, primed the Glock pistol, then jumped in and drove across to Wansfell to finish the job.

*

The commissioner was holding his wife down, determined to prevent her going to the aid of the officer who'd just been shot.

'He's dead, Susan. There's nothing you can do. We have to lie flat, or we'll be shot as well.'

The second protection officer, the woman who'd been ahead of them, was repeating this advice loudly from further to their right. She was holding a phone to her ear.

'There's an armed unit coming by helicopter from Manchester,' she called across. 'I've given them the coordinates; they'll be here in ten minutes. We need to stay below the level of the ridge.'

There followed a period of silence; a short respite in which the three hunted fugitives could imagine they were safe; that their attacker had fled. Then they heard the sound of a vehicle driving off-road, heading their way. It stopped and there was silence again. The remaining protection officer scrambled down the fell to greet whoever it was who'd come to assist them. When she got near the bottom, she stood up, gun in hand. She saw the empty Land Rover before she saw Brady, who raised the Glock and fired. The protection officer fell.

Brady walked up Wansfell until he could see the commissioner lying prostrate close to the summit, his wife kneeling over him as if stupefied with grief. It looked as if he may have succeeded with his first shot after all, and there'd been no need for him to take the risk of driving over. But he had to be sure. Unable to get a clear view because of the woman kneeling over her husband, he needed to move closer, push the wife aside and finish the job. There was a noise in the distance: the sound of a helicopter approaching. He may have to deploy the Barrett again, this time in anti-material mode, to bring the chopper down. But first things first. The huddled figure of the commissioner's wife represented a devotion that Brady found touching. It reminded him of his mother. But it was a devotion that needed to be interrupted if he was to assure himself that this task had been completed.

As he walked closer, Susan Irvine suddenly threw herself sideways. Brady barely had time to register that the commissioner was holding a gun that he'd taken from the fallen protection officer. It was fired once, the bullet hitting Brady's forehead, right between the eyes.

45

A LIAISON RESUMES

'The commissioner is old school. He doesn't even recognise the concept of trauma, let alone any condition with the phrase "post-traumatic" in it.' Louise Mangan was on the phone to Captain Diamantapoulis. 'He and his wife were unharmed physically, and so he thinks he'd be shirking if he wasn't back at work after his holidays.'

Louise had told the captain about the events of 21 September: how both of the commissioner's protection officers had been killed; about the Danvers gang and the events of twenty-five years ago; about Billy Danvers, who had now been arrested; and about Brady, the contract killer whose real name was Patrick Grace, a Belfast man suspected of having been involved in paramilitary activity. Grace had left Belfast eighteen years ago, but nobody knew where he'd gone. That Grace was Brady and Brady was Grace seemed to be as much of a surprise to Cathleen, his wife, as to anyone else. Mangan told the captain that the police were trawling the files for unsolved murders which may now be solvable, at least in terms of who the murderer was. Who had commissioned the killings was another matter.

It was the week after the shootings in the Lake District, and Captain Diamantapoulis had made the call that Louise had been hoping he'd make ever since she'd returned from Crete a month ago. She'd been determined not to be the one to break the silence. It may have been caused by indifference on his part, or, as she hoped, by his natural diffidence, but she knew she had feelings for Petros that she hadn't felt about any man in a long while. She wasn't sure he felt the same way about her, so he would need to be the one to make contact.

She knew he now had a reason. Mangan had been copied into one of Ambassador Sir Ralph Evans' elegant missives (quaintly still described by the Foreign Office as 'telegrams') reporting that the body found in Lake Kournas was actually that of Mohammed Tatanaki, aka Hassan, and not Lord Edward Bellingham. The 'telegram' went on to report the arrest of Inspector General Kostar Pelkas and the restaurant owner, Dimitri Limnios, revealing that the latter had been running the drug-smuggling and people-trafficking operation while the former ensured as little police interference as possible. Limnios had been charged with the murder of the journalist Christopher Finch, as had Limnios's three associates, who'd been the ones to actually inflict the wounds. Pelkas had been charged with corruption and conspiracy to pervert the course of justice. The 'telegram' had gone on to report that Lady Bellingham still refused to identify the man who had been in her car, but insisted it wasn't her husband and that the search for him should therefore be resumed. The ambassador made no mention of Captain Diamantapoulis, let alone giving any indication of his role in capturing Dimitri and Pelkas.

When the captain had arranged to contact Louise, it was via official channels in a call patched through from Athens to Scotland Yard, with officials listening in at both ends. It had been a terse conversation, in which the captain had reiterated his view that Lord Bellingham had faked his death and left Crete under an assumed identity. He said that the Hellenic Police had called off the search and had no intention of resuming it. The call was to formally record these developments with the UK officer with whom he'd been liaising.

Now, though, they were talking informally, the captain having rung Mangan's mobile, as she had guessed he would, that same evening. Petros had asked her to tell him what she'd been up to, and so she had relayed the story of the attempted assassination. She was in her flat and had not long stepped out of the bath when he'd rung. Now she was on her settee, a white towelling robe around her, bare feet resting on a cushion laid across the coffee table, a glass of cold Sauvignon Blanc in her hand.

'Anyway, enough about me. Tell me how on earth you managed to knobble Pelkas and Dimitri?' she asked.

There followed a request to explain what 'knobble' meant before the captain went on to tell her how he'd put the monitoring device into Dimitri's Rolex.

'You remember Dimitri making a fuss when you were there at the restaurant?'

'You mean when Hassan came?'

'Yes, when you dined there alone. You told me how Dimitri was worried because he couldn't find his watch. It gave me an idea. We know that Dimitri insists on getting involved in washing-up, mainly because he doesn't want to pay for more staff to do it. Every evening he rolls up his sleeves, takes off that expensive Rolex watch and spends half an hour, forty-five minutes washing dishes. It's all we need. We gave a financial incentive to one of the waitresses, told her to take the watch, hand it to our man who is outside. We take the back off to insert a tiny chip, put the watch back together, and it's ready then to go back on Dimitri's wrist. This allows us to hear everything Dimitri says, and almost everything that is said to him, as well as always pinpointing his exact location. We heard him arrange to meet Pelkas, and we tracked him all the way. Every incriminating word those bastards say is on record. Thank goodness for new technology.'

'And big watches,' Louise added. 'So, you're now free of the Bellingham case and back in Athens?'

'Back in Athens, but not free of Bellingham. Think back to the evening we were just talking about, when Hassan drove up to Dimitri's. If he wasn't there to steal a watch, what was he there for? It was on a Friday, yes?'

Louise agreed.

'It must have been the day before Lady Bellingham went to the compound to pay Hassan the money he'd demanded for the photograph,' the captain continued.

'On that Saturday, Hassan's fellow gang members find out he is trying to blackmail Lady Bellingham for himself, not for the gang. They want the photograph. They beat the shit out of Hassan, but he doesn't reveal where the camera is – not to them. He knows having the photograph is the only thing keeping him alive. But he tells Finch, the journalist who Hassan is chained up next to. He thinks Finch will be released and will pay him for the photograph.'

'And what is this a photograph of?' Louise asked.

'I don't know. We'll only know when we find it, and I think we will find it at Dimitri's restaurant; that was what he came there for the evening you saw him, to hide the photograph. Remember those four words that Finch repeated over and over – "Hassan win crypt photograph". Finch said it how Hassan said it to him: "win" in Arabic is wine; "crypt" is the word he knows for cellar.'

Louise took her feet off the coffee table and leaned forward, carefully putting down her glass of wine before saying, 'The photograph that Lady Bellingham is willing to part with loads of dosh to get her hands on, is hidden somewhere in Dimitri's wine cellar?'

46

A HOLIDAY IS ARRANGED

Captain Diamantapoulis wanted Louise to come to
Crete so that she'd have the satisfaction of going with
him to question Lady Bellingham about the incriminating evidence he was convinced they'd find in the wine
cellar. Louise explained why that would not be possible.

Her assignment had ended. A detective sergeant had
been detailed to pick up whatever collaborative work
might still need to be done in Greece. Such was the
public disinterest in Lord Edward Bellingham's whereabouts that even the *Daily Candour* had ceased its daily
coverage, which had culminated with the capture of
Chris Finch's murderers.

While Tam Mackay was convinced that Bellingham
had 'done a Stonehouse', he couldn't raise any enthusiasm amongst the editorial board. Most people, if they
thought about Bellingham at all, believed the official
line that he was missing, presumed dead, somewhere
in the White Mountains. The words 'good riddance'
usually concluded any conversation about him.

It was DS Din who reminded Mangan about Keith
Brewer, the man who'd been asking to see her a couple
of weeks back, claiming that he knew it wasn't Lord

Bellingham's body in Lake Kournas, contrary to what the media was saying at the time.

'Given that he was right, and he happens to be one of the last people – in this country at least – to have seen Lord Bellingham alive, bringing him in for a half-hour chat might be useful,' Din had suggested one dreary September morning as they were going through the diary.

'You are nothing if not persistent, Rushil, but I suggest you ask the assigned DS to meet him.'

'Keith says he'll only say what he has to say to you.'

'Oh, for Christ's sake – okay, find a slot in my diary. But make it in a few weeks' time. By then he may have lost interest, or an asteroid may have destroyed the planet. I have to get back to my endless round of bloody meetings.'

Despite the dull prospect of returning to her duties as assistant commissioner for professionalism, made all the more tedious because Deputy Commissioner Karen Dale was taking a close interest in her deployment, there was something to look forward to: the exciting prospect of being with Captain Diamantapoulis in Crete once again.

The Lord Bellingham liaison role may have finished, but Louise was due a holiday, and October in Crete really wasn't that bad. Many of the hotels were closed out of season, but Petros had already said that he could get her a room at the guest house in Matala where he stayed, the one that was run by a retired police officer. But the captain's plans for them to confront Lady

Bellingham together would require the commissioner's permission and that was only likely to be given if the search of Dimitri's wine cellar yielded the photograph.

It took a couple of days for the captain to assemble the team he needed. He told Louise he had enough men and machinery to take the cellar apart brick by brick if necessary. She made him promise to ring her as soon as the search had been completed

On Wednesday evening, after two days in the wine cellar, the captain rang. The search was complete. Nothing had been found.

'I think you should still come for a holiday,' Petros said when he called the next day. They'd fallen into a habit of daily phone calls, whether or not they had anything particular to convey. 'I could book some time off and show you the island properly. For we Cretans, out of season is the best time. We know the tourists are vital to the economy and we welcome them, but in October we get our island back again.'

'Says the man who hasn't lived in Crete for thirty years.'

Petros laughed. 'Better a sinner who repents,' he said. 'But seriously, a holiday would do us both good.'

So Louise booked the flight. She had some important meetings to attend the following week and booked her leave for the week after. She felt like a giddy schoolgirl as she contemplated the prospect of a holiday with Petros Diamantapoulis.

On Monday morning, as Mangan began to prepare for the cluster of bureaucratic gatherings in the diary for that week, DS Din brought in a letter. 'I fished this out of the correspondence file that you're due to receive tonight, because I thought it might cheer you up.'

It was a letter from Sharron Fuller, the Bellinghams' former nanny, who wanted Louise to know she was in London and would love to meet up to talk about their time in Crete.

'You're right, Rushil, this has lifted my spirits – and I intend to lift a few more, with added ice and tonic, as soon as I can fix something up with Sharron.'

By the time they met on Friday night, Louise was demob happy. Her week of meetings was over, and she'd be flying to Heraklion on Monday. She'd been thinking a lot about Petros Diamantapoulis; how impractical a romance would be with him in Athens and her in London; how long it had been since she'd experienced any kind of relationship with a man. There had been no deep and meaningful discussions in their nightly phone calls, but in truth, she wasn't keen on such conversations anyway. All she was sure of was that the prospect of this holiday with Petros made her happier than she could remember being in a long while. Fortunately, she only had to endure interrogation by her daughters separately and by phone. If they could have ambushed her together and in person, she'd have known what it was like to be cross-examined by the Stasi.

Louise met Sharron at a bar on Greek Street. Sharron told her that she'd left Crete to take up a nanny position offered by a family who'd been holidaying in Chania.

'I served them at the restaurant most nights and we'd get chatting, like. She's a fashion designer and he's a businessman, and they're lovely people with smashing bairns living in a gorgeous house in Wimbledon. You should see my room. It's the size of this bar.'

Louise asked what had happened to her boyfriend, and Sharron said she had a confession to make. 'Christos was a bastard,' she said. 'A real shit who thought he could get away with battering me like he'd done with all the girls he'd been with, so I dumped him and got some pals in Chania to have a little word with him, like, making sure he understood it was over. But I'm sure he was mixed up in all that people-trafficking malarky.'

Sharron said that when he'd brought her over from Chania to meet Louise in the Crystal Beach Hotel and pay back the fifty euros, she'd had no idea that he was untrustworthy, and had told him what Louise had said about the police having located the gang's hideout.

So that was how they were tipped off, thought Louise. 'It was my fault,' she told Sharron. 'I should have kept my mouth shut. Why wouldn't you have told him? You weren't to know what a snake he was. Sometimes it feels like women spend their whole lives apologising for the dickheads they're in relationships with.'

By the third vodka and tonic, Sharron was crying over Hassan. She'd heard about his body being found in Lake Kournas.

'For all his faults, I loved him,' she said, tears streaming down her face. 'He was a rogue, but he never hit me. The worst thing he ever did was take pictures of me in the nude; not pornographic, like – nice ones, just for him to look at. He loved those bloody cameras more than he loved me, I think. And the photos he took were proper ones with film and everything.'"

'So, he carried the digital camera to take snaps when he was out and about but used the old-fashioned one on you,' Mangan observed.

'Yeah, he had to develop the photographs. He'd spend hours in that bloody crypt.'

'Crypt? What crypt?' Despite the vodkas, Louise was suddenly alert, mentally recording everything Sharron said next.

'It's in those derelict buildings next to Dimitri's restaurant. A really spooky place, dark and awful. Hassan used to kip there when he first arrived from Libya. You walk down into it and it's full of things you wouldn't want crawling up your legs. It used to be the wine cellar for the restaurant, but it was abandoned yonks ago. Before that it was some kind of ancient place of worship. Hassan always called it the crypt.'

47

THE PHOTOGRAPH

Crete was out of season, but nobody had bothered to tell the weather. It was a gloriously sunny thirty degrees when Louise stepped off the plane. Diamantapoulis was waiting, just as he had been in August when she had mistaken him for a taxi driver. This time, they embraced like the friends they were, and kissed, but not like the lovers they were to become; a peck on the cheek was the only intimacy that passed between them in the arrivals area.

Louise thought Petros looked ruggedly handsome in his dark grey seersucker shirt and black chinos. Petros thought Louise looked alluring in her floral blouse and knee-length red skirt, her thick chestnut hair newly shaped and styled.

The derelict land at the back of Dimitri's restaurant in Agia Galini was already being cleared under Lieutenant Nati's supervision, as the captain explained on the journey from Heraklion.

'After you rang me to tell me what Sharron had said, I insisted we have a team in place. Despina was keen to see you again, so I've brought her along.'

'I guess it must have been difficult to get the authority

to do this, given that the search of Dimitri's wine cellar proved futile.'

'After my recent successes, I am in the good books.'

'Perhaps they'll promote you to inspector general,' Louise teased, not entirely in jest.

'I doubt they'll do that,' Petros said with a smile, 'or even pay me more. But I'm happy to be captain.'

He drove them to the site, where around a dozen officers in protective equipment were cutting through thick undergrowth around a cluster of abandoned buildings. A small advance guard had already entered the crypt to lay electricity cables, position lighting equipment and prepare drilling tools.

Despina gave Louise a hug and the two women chatted while Petros went to fetch some safety wear.

'He is very excited that you are here,' Nati told Mangan.

'I'm not sure your captain is capable of any emotion beyond mild earnestness,' Mangan responded.

'Oh, believe me, he has been worried that he'd never see you again. I've known him a long time, and never thought I'd see him acting like a boy going on his first date.'

'Well, he has managed to get me to spend the first day of my holiday in a derelict tomb, so there must be something about him.'

From the outside, with all the vegetation cleared away, the crypt looked like a small storehouse. There was no outer indication of its depth. Once through the portal, a winding stone staircase opened out into a chamber. Two powerful lamps lit up the space, which was obviously the area Hassan had used to develop his photographs. There was a ceramic basin, into which a piece of rubber hose brought water from a tank situated further along. Bottles of the various chemicals he'd have needed were lined up on a low shelf cut into the stone.

Despite the stout door, some animal life had found its way in, and the floor was strewn with what looked like scattered fragments of bone and fur. Anyone above about five-foot-eight wouldn't be able to stand fully upright other than in the photo-developing area, where the sloping ceiling gave the most room. Louise was five-foot-nine, and was pleased she only needed to be in the crypt to get the lie of the land and observe the search in action. She could see how thorough it was from the sight of officers edging their way into the far reaches, where there was barely enough room to crawl.

At 3pm, three hours after the captain and Louise had arrived, and just as it seemed as if the exercise would again be abortive, one of the team let out a yell so loud it could be heard above ground, where Louise was drinking coffee in the afternoon sun. In a narrow gap, at the furthest perimeter of the chamber, behind a heavy slab of slate, was a small Nikon camera. It was brought out by the jubilant officer who'd found it, and within a few minutes the captain, Nati and Louise were looking at a photograph taken on 1 August 2017, the day that Hassan had driven Sharron over from Chania to pick up the rest of her belongings from Lord and Lady Bellingham. Sharron had told them that she'd left

Hassan in the car, but he must have decided to revisit the hiding place in the cypress grove that he'd once used to survey the territory before going through the kitchen window for his erotic encounters with Sharron. It was from that hiding place, with its perfect view of the terrace, that he had taken a photograph with his digital camera, of the terrace's only occupant – not Lord Bellingham, but another man, one who Petros and Louise both recognised from their last meeting with Lady Bellingham. It was Quentin Kane.

Things moved quickly after that. Louise broke off her holiday to fly back to London. Given that he'd met Lord Bellingham and Quentin Kane together the last time that Bellingham had been seen alive, she knew she now had good reason to speak to Keith Brewer and to speak to him quickly. There were some internal process and personnel issues to sort out, but the commissioner had used his influence to ensure that Assistant Commissioner Mangan wasn't obstructed in her work.

Keith proved to be a difficult man to interview; edgy, distrustful and suspicious of anyone in authority who wasn't, as he termed it, 'officer class'. It was an approach he'd learned from his grandfather, who, he told Mangan, had recently passed away.

'Grandad always said that you could trust the ones at the top, 'cos they was educated. It was the ones what come from where we come from that was the worst.'

He'd read in the *Candour* that Assistant Commissioner Mangan was in charge of liaising with the Greek police about Lord Bellingham's disappearance, hence his insistence that, if he reported this at all, it must be to her.

'But why not come to us as soon as Lord Bellingham went missing?' Mangan asked.

'Because I was worried that it might be bad for Grandad. We needed that solicitor to make sure we got the money we was promised, and I never wanted Grandad to be dragged to court. Now he can't be dragged anywhere, bless his soul.'

They were in her office at New Scotland Yard, with DS Din taking notes. Keith explained how Lord Bellingham and his solicitor had come to his grandad's house in a final attempt to get the old man to move so that Bellingham Developments could pull the place down. The two men had left before ten o'clock so that his grandad could watch the news in peace. About an hour later, old Mr Brewer, who'd gone up to bed, had shouted down to Keith that he'd run out of one type of the many pills he had to take for his various ailments, and asked his grandson to go to the all-night chemist in Shoreditch to get a fresh supply. As Keith drove back at about midnight, he passed the place where he knew Bellingham had parked his car.

'My headlights picked up a man going back to the car, but it was at least two hours after they left our gaff. And it wasn't Lord Bellingham; it was his solicitor.'

'But perhaps he'd dropped Lord Bellingham off somewhere and was borrowing the car,' Mangan suggested.

'Dropped 'im off in what?' asked Keith. 'They'd come in Bellingham's car – they told us, straight from the House of Lords, they said. Where did they go after they left here? It's a bloody long walk to get anywhere, and why wouldn't 'e have gone in the car? What had they been doing in all that time, between leaving our house and the solicitor gettin' in the car? Stands to reason, don't it? The solicitor left the building site, but Lord Bellingham didn't. That's why you can't find 'im in Crete – 'e never went there.'

48

BENEATH THE MATALA MOON

While Lady Bellingham remained defiant under questioning, Kane admitted everything. He'd spent years planning revenge on Edward Bellingham for the persecution of Bobby Cheong, and had purposely befriended him in order to get close enough to do him harm. Kane had been Miranda's lover before she'd met Bellingham, and had tried to warn her against him, but to no avail. Miranda wanted things that Kane couldn't offer. However, their relationship had resumed four years ago, by which time Miranda's contempt for her husband almost matched Kane's own. All she'd wanted from life were children and status. Now that she had both, she no longer needed the man who'd generated them.

Quentin and Miranda had developed a plan. They'd pay big money for a professional hitman, money that would be recouped and multiplied after the event when Miranda would inherit her husband's wealth. The idea that they should report Bellingham as being lost in the White Mountains had been Miranda's. She'd convinced her lover that with his hair brushed differently and a good-quality false moustache, Kane could pass as Bellingham. It would get him through Gatwick, where real stringency was understandably confined to incoming passengers, and there was only elementary passport control. He'd also be able to get through Heraklion airport, where there was no facial recognition technology in use. Quentin was taller than Edward, but height was indistinguishable in a passport photograph.

Once this deception had left a trail suggesting Bellingham had travelled to Crete, Kane could have flown back to the UK using his own passport, but then there'd have been a record of him departing the island. So, for the return trip, Miranda drove Kane to Chania before reporting her husband missing. Kane had been the one to take that express ferry, before making his way back to the UK overland and ensuring he wouldn't have to show his own passport until he was far from Crete. It was important there was no trace of Kane either arriving on the island or leaving if the plan was to work.

Louise had been explaining all this to Petros Diamantapoulis, having resumed her holiday in Crete. Thankfully, the good weather was holding well into October. Louise and Petros were dining al fresco at Matala, in a restaurant so close to the sea their table was practically on the beach.

'I'm still not entirely sure why they used Bellingham's phone to download those ferry times. I doubt Kane had even brought his with him given that it may have revealed his presence in Crete, but Miranda could have surely used hers,' Louise reflected.

'I doubt they'd have given it much thought. They were savvy enough to delete it before leaving the phone for us to find but they wouldn't have expected anyone to be interested in such mundane stuff,' Petros observed.

'Yes, I suppose so. It's so often the inconsequential that catches a criminal out.'

'But what fascinates me is why do they go to such trouble to pretend Bellingham comes here?' Petros asked.

'That was a stroke of genius. They knew that the murder of a government minister and peer of the realm would unleash the full force of the law to find his killers. They also knew that if they could shift that effort to a different country, one where Bellingham often went walking in dangerous terrain, it wouldn't just switch the focus by over two thousand miles, it would also remove the suspicion of murder all together.'

'Thank goodness for Hassan and his camera.'

'Yes. Miranda had encouraged Sharron to travel across on that Tuesday so that she'd be able to give the impression of Edward being at home, without Sharron actually seeing him. The children had been sent back to England to get them out of the way; everything was hunky dory. But they hadn't reckoned with Hassan's curiosity. Sharron had been convinced Lady Bellingham had a lover, and we know she shared this suspicion with Hassan. When he saw that the man on the terrace wasn't Lord Bellingham, he thought he'd spotted her lover. He was right, of course; Kane was her lover. So he decided to take a photo with the aim of blackmailing Miranda. Bellingham's disappearance hadn't yet been reported. Hassan couldn't have known he'd stumbled into the middle of a murder plot.'

'Otherwise, he'd have demanded much more than a thousand euros from Lady Bellingham,' Petros said, gathering another forkful of the delicious prawn dish they were eating.

'I wish I could have been with you when you arrested Miranda. How did she react?' Louise asked.

'She said she knew nothing about a plot to murder her husband, and that Kane must have done it out of jealousy.'

'I suppose we should be grateful to her for making that mistake about where the mobile phone was found. If you hadn't latched on to that, they might have got away with it.'

'Perhaps they still might in court – with no murderer and no corpse,' Petros suggested.

'No way! We've got Kane's confession, for a start. And as for her involvement, we've got the photograph. In addition, we have the CCTV footage from Bellingham's home security app that shows a man looking very much like Quentin Kane driving up to the Bellingham house in London on the Friday night and not appearing again until Monday morning.'

'Ah yes, the footage they deleted from the phone.'

'Yes, no wonder they did. It clearly shows Kane going into the house and only reappearing a few days later to drive to the airport in full Bellingham guise, moustache and all. The footage shows he's too tall to be Bellingham but it wasn't relevant – all that mattered was getting through passport control. Miranda would have told him where her husband's passport would be. All he had to do was be a recluse over that weekend.'

Louise leaned back to breathe in the warm breeze coming in from the sea. Looming over them were the caves cut into the limestone cliffs.

'I was reading that this was where Joni Mitchell came on the hippy trail in the late sixties and met Carey – the subject of one of my favourite songs from my very favourite album.'

'You mean *Blue*,' the captain said, much to Louise's surprise. 'That guy Carey was actually Cary Raditz, an American chef at the Delphini Taverna here in Matala. He really did have a cane, like it says in the song.'

'But I thought you didn't like Joni Mitchell's music.'

'I never heard her until you told me you liked her – then I listened, and I like her too.'

Louise felt there was no better place to be in the world than here, with this man, entranced by the soft night air and the view across the bay.

'This isn't the place to talk about murder and death,' she observed.

'No, but it is the time, and I come back to central question – no murderer, no corpse. Where are they?'

'Kane had no idea who he'd contracted with but we're almost certain the gunman was a killer called Brady, now deceased. He was the one who tried to murder the commissioner, and we're busy unravelling his finances and linking him with a host of unsolved killings. Kane seized the chance to put his plan into action after getting Bellingham to agree to go with him to persuade the last resident on a huge London regeneration site to leave. All the CCTV cameras on that site were disabled between 10pm and midnight on 28 July. The last time Bellingham was seen alive was when he left the resident's house with Kane, at around ten that evening. Kane suggested they go to look at where the foundations were being sunk for a huge hotel/casino complex. Brady was waiting. He used a handgun with a silencer to kill Bellingham and tip his body into the pit, ironically to form part of the foundations for a twenty-storey hotel built by Bellingham Developments.'

'Okay, no more questions, no more work. If the Mermaid Café still existed, I'd take you there.'

Louise laughed and said she was impressed by his knowledge of Joni's lyrics. 'The café may not be there, but you can still buy me a bottle of wine,' she insisted.

'Maybe a glass.'

'Oh, you're a mean old Daddy – but I like you fine.'

And so they walked off towards the town, and when Louise awoke the next morning, bound tightly to a sleeping Petros by the single sheet that covered their nakedness, the sun shining into the room like a shaft of honeycomb, she felt as if it wasn't just a new day that had begun, but a new life.

ACKNOWLEDGEMENTS

My thanks to Alex Clarke, Serena Arthur, Caitlin Raynor and all at Wildfire for their enthusiasm and encouragement.

To Martin Fletcher, Tara O'Sullivan and Nikki Sinclair for their editorial expertise.

To my literary agent, Claire Alexander, for being consistently brilliant.

And to the Australian backpacker in Crete who told me so much about Lake Kournas. Whether it is true or not doesn't matter – this is a work of fiction.

Alan Johnson's childhood memoir *This Boy* was published in 2013. It won the Royal Society of Literature Ondaatje Prize, and the Orwell Prize, Britain's top political writing award. His second volume of memoirs, *Please Mr Postman* (2014) won the National Book Club award for Best Biography. The final book in his memoir trilogy, *The Long And Winding Road* (2016), won the Parliamentary Book Award for Best Memoir. *In My Life – A Music Memoir* was published in 2018 and his highly acclaimed first novel, *The Late Train to Gipsy Hill*, was published in 2021.

Alan was a Labour MP for 20 years before retiring ahead of the 2017 general election. He served in five cabinet positions in the governments of Tony Blair and Gordon Brown, including Education Secretary, Health Secretary and Home Secretary.

He and his wife Carolyn live in East Yorkshire.

Sign up to the brand-new Alan Johnson newsletter for book updates, extracts, and exclusive year-round content from Alan Johnson himself:

https://www.headline.co.uk/landing-page/
alan-johnson-newsletter/